JORDAN SUMMERS

Fall FROM Grace

ATLANTEAN'S QUEST

ELLORA'S CAVE
ROMANTICA PUBLISHING

What the critics are saying...

ℰ℺

Redemption

"Jordan Summers is one of the most talented writers in this genre. The story is sensuous, building up to a beautiful love story." ~ *Reader Views*

"Ms. Summers is an author to watch in the future as she captures the brilliance of a planet that is the most imaginative, sensual place in the universes. The passionate sex scenes alone will have the reader on fire as the story races along at top speed taking the reader for a wild, edge of the seat ride from beginning to end." ~ *Love Romances*

Atlantean Heat

"This is one book as well as series to take the reader to the heavens and experience the heat that is Atlantean's Quest!! Ms. Summers writes with passionate flair that is her trademark for t his series. The emotional story that she tells here will draw the reader in, deliver the readers to another place and soar through the heavens." ~ *Love Romances*

"Jordan Summers' writing style is fresh and sassy and even though limited to the length of a quickie, makes our heroes seem alive and real.

All in all an enjoyable read!" ~ *Mon Boudoir*

"Jordan Summers is a talented author. I always look forward to her latest offering. Personally I hope she keeps writing the Atlantean Series. The plots are fascinating." ~ *Reader Views*

Return

"Jordan Summers is one of my favorite erotic romance authors. Her talent is immense." ~*Reader Views*

"The relationship between the two main characters was incendiary and very well written. As I said before, I really enjoyed returning to this series and truly hope that Ms. Summers revisits it again. I think that there are still many characters hiding in the curtains that we'd love to read about." ~ *Fallen Angel Reviews*

"Oozing sex appeal and mesmerizing pleasure, Return is a wonderful addition to the Atlantean's Quest series." ~ *Ecataromance reviews*

"The love scenes scorch the pages, and Orion's "enhanced" attributes are simply drool worthy. Return can be read fully as a stand-alone; however, be forewarned, as once you are done with this title, you can rest assured that if you haven't read the first 3 books (plus the quickie) yet" ~ *Just Erotic Romance Reviews*

An Ellora's Cave Romantica Publication

www.ellorascave.com

Fall From Grace

ISBN 9781419955419
ALL RIGHTS RESERVED.
Redemption Copyright © 2003 Jordan Summers
Atlantean Heat Copyright © 2003 Jordan Summers
Return Copyright © 2006 Jordan Summers
Cover art by Syneca

Trade paperback Publication May 2007

Excerpt from *Cheer Givers & Mischief Makers* Copyright © K.Z. Snow, 2007

Content Advisory:

S – ENSUOUS
E – ROTIC
X – TREME

Ellora's Cave Publishing offers three levels of Romantica™ reading entertainment: S (S-ensuous), E (E-rotic), and X (X-treme).

The following material contains graphic sexual content meant for mature readers. This story has been rated E–rotic.

S-*ensuous* love scenes are explicit and leave nothing to the imagination.

E-*rotic* love scenes are explicit, leave nothing to the imagination, and are high in volume per the overall word count. E-rated titles might contain material that some readers find objectionable — in other words, almost anything goes, sexually. E-rated titles are the most graphic titles we carry in terms of both sexual language and descriptiveness in these works of literature.

X-*treme* titles differ from E-rated titles only in plot premise and storyline execution. Stories designated with the letter X tend to contain difficult or controversial subject matter not for the faint of heart.

Also by Jordan Summers

About the Author

I'd like to say I'm the life of the party, a laugh-a-minute kind of gal, and outrageously cool, BUT that would be a slight fabrication.

I'm actually a thirty-something, ex-flight attendant with a penchant for huge bookstores and big dumb action movies. I prefer quiet dinners with friends over maddening crowds. Happily married to my very own Highlander, we split our time between two continents.

In my spare time...LOL...I'm kidding, I don't have any spare time. The hours of my day are spent writing, and when I'm not doing that I'm thinking about writing. I guess you could say I have a one track mind.

Jordan welcomes comments from readers. You can find her website and email address on her author bio page at www.ellorascave.com.

Tell Us What You Think

We appreciate hearing reader opinions about our books. You can email us at Comments@EllorasCave.com.

FALL FROM GRACE

ঙ্

Redemption

~13~

Atlantean Heat

~133~

Return

~175~

REDEMPTION

Dedication

ಬ

This book is dedicated to the readers. Thank you for all your support, encouragement, and enthusiasm. You've made working on the Atlantean's story a pleasure.

Trademarks Acknowledgement

ಬ

The author acknowledges the trademarked status and trademark owners of the following wordmarks mentioned in this work of fiction:

M & M's: Mars, Inc. Delaware
Tarzan: Edgar Rice Burroughs, Inc. California

Chapter One

℘

Ariel blew out a ragged breath. Relief curled in her belly like a satisfied cat wraps around your legs. Her people were now safely on Zaron—well almost all of her people. She'd find Coridan and get back here as soon as possible then her duties to her people would be complete. Ariel paused, imagining what her new life would be like on the planet she'd never seen. Would Zaron be as beautiful as Earth? Would it possess the wonder this lush blue planet held for her? There was only one way to find out.

She closed her eyes for a moment as emotion overwhelmed her. The vision she'd had the night before of a warrior streamed through her consciousness like the currents of the wind rustling the branches of a tree. Her stomach clenched. Surely she had been mistaken. Her fate lay with her people, didn't it?

Yet she knew better than most her visions could not be ignored. Psychic from birth, she trusted them with her life.

A white-throated toucan squawked with distress nearby as if something approached its nest. Ariel looked in the direction of the cry but saw nothing out of the norm. She brushed away the feeling of uneasiness that accompanied the loud caterwauling.

Ariel shifted one of the marked stones effectively shutting down the device. She stared at the transport longingly for a few more moments before reluctantly turning back to the village. She picked her way down the narrow trail, brushing past aromatic ginger flowers and purple orchids, soaking in their comforting fragrance, all the while cataloging the odor in her memory as things she would miss about this planet.

After a few moments she reached the abandoned clearing. A light breeze caught at her blonde tresses brushing the locks gently from her face and across her bare breasts.

It was quiet—too quiet.

The birds' songs no longer filled her ears with music and not being able to hear the chatter of her people caused excruciating mental pain. In that moment she realized that being left alone on this planet, no longer able to use her telepathic abilities to communicate, would drive her and any other Atlantean insane. Abandonment was tantamount to death.

She and her people had unknowingly sentenced Coridan to death. The thought had Ariel's lungs seizing, crushing inward with a pain rivaling the icy fear she felt but refused to examine too closely.

Her skin prickled as a rustling noise came from inside her dwelling, drawing her thoughts back to present. At first it had sounded like a breeze moving the flap yet the air was not powerful enough to move the heavy hide. Tension filled her lungs making it difficult to breathe. A cry from a primate shattered the silence. Ariel relaxed.

Monkeys may have already taken up residence in her hut, goodness knows she'd had a difficult time keeping the curious creatures out when she had lived there. The noise grew louder and something crashed to the ground in her hut. Ariel inched nearer. Perhaps Coridan had sensed the shift in energy that had taken place with the Atlantean exodus and had returned.

She decided not to call out to him as some things were best done in person. Her heart swelled with anticipation—and fear. It was time to meet her destiny. She stepped forward and threw back the hide flap, a tentative smile painted on her face.

"How nice of you to join us, my dear," the red-haired man's voice purred menacingly.

Ariel felt the blood drain from her face, the normal warmth replaced with cold. She raised her hands to defend herself but before she could fire off a single energy burst, two men stepped from the shadows shackling her with their hands. Ariel struggled to no avail, the men easily keeping her subdued.

Her full breasts bobbed as she put all her strength into escape. The brown hands holding her arms tightened, threatening without words to snap bones if necessary. Sweat beaded her brow and dripped lazily down her chest. Her gaze narrowed on the devil sitting behind her small table.

As if in a trance his gaze followed the movement of the perspiration droplets as they caressed her pink nipples and rolled down her abdomen. Ariel ceased her struggles. She didn't want his eyes roaming any lower.

The professor's ruddy face split into a cold snake-like smile. She could see no teeth but knew without a doubt he could and would bite if provoked. "You're not exactly who I was hoping for but you'll do." His voice coiled around her.

"You must be Professor Donald Rumsinger." It wasn't a question. She knew from Queen Rachel's thoughts that this man could be no other. Ariel watched the man stand and come around the table. He looked at her as if she was a mere insect under glass. "What can I do for you?" she asked, willing her voice to remain calm.

He reached out with fat groping fingers and ran the rough pad of this thumb over her nipple. Her sensitive skin puckered and beaded under the abrasion. "There are many things you can do for me." He licked his cracked lips. "But most will have to wait until I get more equipment." He flicked her nipple as if he were tossing a coin in the air and then returned to his seat. The wood creaked under his weight as he sat down.

"I am a lowly tribal member. I'm of no use to you. My people may not even miss me." Ariel tried to act as humble as she could given the circumstances. It wouldn't do for the red-devil to realize who she really was to her tribe.

"You'd better hope they do miss you." The threat in his voice was apparent. "I'm counting on them to come looking for you." His bushy eyebrows arched, challenge sparking in his expression along with anticipation. A native entered the hut and walked straight to the professor. He leaned down and whispered something in the red-devil's ear then turned and left without paying her any notice at all. Rumsinger stood abruptly.

"Speaking of your people… Where are they?"

Ariel shrugged.

His gaze narrowed, pinning her in place with the hatred she saw swimming in the brown depths of his eyes. "Don't lie to me. I've grown tired and impatient tramping around in this godforsaken place," he all but growled. "If you don't tell me where your people have gone I'll let my men take turns plumbing that tight ripe cunt of yours." He leaned across the table, nearing her face. "Do you understand me?"

Ariel swallowed her immediate response. He dare threaten her? Did he not know she was the seer, holy woman and guide to the beyond? Of course he didn't, she'd just told him she was an unimportant tribal member.

If she had access to her potions Ariel would have him believing he was a frog within minutes. She paused. Maybe a frog was too good for this wart of a man. Perhaps a slug… Ariel smiled to herself. Unfortunately, for now she'd have to go with another plan since he wasn't buying her lowly position.

"If you or any of your men fuck me then I'll be unable to aid you. I am the seer. My power is great but cannot be tainted by a male cock." Her statement was the truth, for the most part. Now that her people were no longer on the planet she wasn't exactly needed in the same capacity but he didn't know that. Ariel watched as her words sank into the slug's twisted mind. His thoughts were instantaneous.

What if she's telling the truth?

She smiled, this time showing him. "Rest assured little man, I am telling the truth."

The professor's face grew as red as an overripe berry before he finally released an anger-filled breath. "Take this blonde whore to the hut located on the furthest branch. Bind her and then post yourselves on guard duty. If she tries to escape you have my permission to sample any part of her flesh you like but save her ass for me." His brown eyes narrowed and he grinned, anticipation plainly written on his vile face. "You'll learn not to lie to me, bitch."

Ariel's blood seemed to thicken in her veins. The man's mind raged with torturous thoughts. For a few seconds she saw herself bound by vines and suspended up in the air, her long legs pulled apart to the point of pain exposing her pussy and back orifice to his turgid cock. He'd like nothing more than to plant his deranged seed inside her, not because he found her attractive but because it would be one more successful experiment. This man truly enjoyed hurting people.

Too bad the mere act of fucking her wouldn't do it. Only a true-mate could impregnate her and then only after they'd built up enough power to perform an energy bind.

The professor held no care for others, only himself, like a parasite growing from its host's body. He devoured souls instead of blood. His sole focus was on locating the famous lost tribe and he had. They were simply no longer here. He'd planned on plundering their wealth and bringing back a male specimen for experimentation and breeding purposes.

The male would have made the professor famous amongst his peers. He'd worked the whole thing out. Rumsinger would start by parading the poor caged specimen around showing him off to all the famous scientific minds of the world until the male was no longer of use to him. Then he'd run a barrage of tests on the male to determine his origins. Death would follow and it would not be swift.

Panic slammed into her chest. She desperately tried to drag air into her lungs. A slow chill came over her body and Ariel shivered, unable to draw warmth. She could not let this human demon near the transport or Coridan…if he was still alive. She would die before she allowed her people to fall victim to his deranged mind. Escape was the only answer.

The men jerked Ariel's arms behind her back and quickly bound her. The vines bit into her tender flesh and she winced. They led her out of the hut, over to the lift and then placed her into the basket. She didn't miss the hungry looks the two natives gave her as the basket lifted into the air. Ariel smiled to herself. She might be able to use their lust to her advantage. She considered no woman her sexual equal. In fact, she'd yet to meet a man who she thought could stand up to the demands her body would place on him.

Well perhaps one man…

* * * * *

Coridan wandered through the jungle aimlessly. His scratched body bled but he refused to heal himself. What was the point? He'd be dead within days. The endless silence was like the slice of a razor across his mind cutting out pieces of his sanity. Soon there would be none left.

They were gone—all gone.

He'd sensed the energy shift a couple of hours ago signaling his people's departure leaving nothing but gaping emptiness behind. In that moment blind panic the likes of which he'd never experienced lanced through him. A scream had torn from his throat, a primal wounded cry emanating from the depths of his bowels. Coridan had clawed at his flesh like a frenzied beast allowing insanity to embrace him for a moment before reining himself back from the edge of the abyss to clear thought once again.

He was alone.

Damn his selfish behavior. What had started out as admiration turned into jealousy until he was no longer able to tell right from wrong. Now he paid the price. Exile. He pushed a fern out of the way wending his way deeper into the jungle. He'd continue to trample through the vegetation not caring whether he destroyed the plant life until madness overtook him. It would not be long now.

Coridan prayed to the goddess that his death would not be drawn out. He didn't bother asking for her mercy for he deserved it not. He'd acted out of frustration. The frustration that comes when a man realizes there is no chance of finding his true-mate.

Now Jac was gone.

Gone with Ares—her true-mate.

Coridan hadn't wanted to admit it to himself at the time but today the truth was as clear as the azure color of Jac's fiery eyes. The moment she'd taken to the river risking life and limb to save Ares he'd known that beyond a doubt she'd never been his true-mate. He'd been wrong about her. Coridan snorted. He'd been wrong about many things. There was no point dwelling on his past mistakes. He'd find no redemption here in the middle of the jungle without his people.

He pushed on, ignoring the pain surging through his muscles. He'd been walking ever since he'd voluntarily left the Atlanteans, refusing to allow his body to seek nourishment or rest. Soon his limbs would collapse and he'd have no choice but to allow exhaustion to claim him. Until then he'd journey on getting far away from the reminders of his shame as far as his legs would carry him. Maybe then he'd find a small modicum of peace.

* * * * *

The men shoved Ariel into Eros' old hut and followed closely behind. They stroked her ample breasts and plucked at her nipples until they engorged, bolstered by the fact they were concealed from the professor's prying eyes. She sensed their pent-up frustrations. It wasn't difficult to amplify them in the men's minds.

Ariel made herself stand still and even lean into their clumsy caresses. Her tongue darted out in mock appreciation leading the two men to believe she wanted their attention. She could easily convince them to please her and once she was free she'd blast the cocks right off of these two.

The thought almost made her giggle. A bit of Jac must have rubbed off onto her. The men began to argue in their native language. From what she could see of their thoughts they were trying to decide just how far they could take their fondling before the professor's wrath came down upon their heads.

Ariel became even more docile shifting her legs slightly so that the musky odor of her sex reached their nostrils. She shimmied until her skirt dropped to the floor. The men's lustful gazes locked onto her shaven pussy, an Atlantean tradition that affected human males and warriors alike.

Soon she'd have these men eating from her hands and out of her cunt. Until then she needed to give them a false sense of security, convince them she was harmless, all the while making them believe beyond a doubt she'd bed them both. And she would if necessary.

Ariel had never invited anyone to lie amongst her bed furs due to her vows to her people but she had to admit she found the thought of having sex with a man intriguing.

Just not with these men.

Ariel rolled her hips and one of the men groaned. Her actions seemed to be working, their voices rose even higher and they turned their attention from her but refused to release her delicate flesh.

Apparently the slug had his men quite intimidated. The professor had convinced the men he would share the riches he planned to acquire once they accomplished their objectives.

Ariel snorted. He didn't fool her for a moment. The professor would sooner kill every one of his men than share his find and probably intended to do so. He was extremely dangerous. No doubt his men knew that. Then again, so was she. Humans, particularly men, assumed just because she was a woman they held the advantage over her. They could brutalize and bully her any way they saw fit. She chuckled.

They would be surprised just like the people of Greece had been when they made the mistake of trying to invade Atlantis. Humans had no idea she could melt their hearts inside of their chests with little effort. Even Atlantean warriors with their superior strength knew the female of a species was often the most deadly. Right now, the red-devil wasn't aware of exactly how dangerous she could be but soon he'd learn…like all the others who had tried to hurt her people.

Ariel grew tired of the men's arguing. She'd finish her seduction some other time. She whispered thoughts in their minds sending terrifying pictures of exactly what the professor would do to them if they continued any further. The men released her and rushed out of the hut leaving her alone for the first time in over an hour.

She expelled the breath she hadn't known she'd been holding and walked to the bed of furs. Four stakes surrounded the sleep area creating a crude frame. Taking care not to harm her bound hands, she lay down on the bed, closed her eyes and began to concentrate. Her mind reached out, searching.

Coridan, where are you? Silence answered back.

Ariel refused to accept the silence. She scattered her consciousness far and wide seeking any sign, any flicker, any tenuous string of hope that Coridan still lived. Something flared inside her for a second then evaporated into mist before she could ascertain what it was. She groaned in frustration deciding to conserve her energy for the time being. She'd try again this evening.

* * * * *

Many miles away Coridan was so wrapped up in his misery that he almost missed the mental brush across his mind. It was as gentle as a lash as it flutters against a cheek yet it was there. Or was it? Had he simply wanted a connection so badly that he'd wished it so? He wouldn't allow the luxury of hope to fill his chest. He couldn't. The reality was far too devastating. He was alone, 'twas time he accepted his fate.

Chapter Two

Several light years away, under a pale green sky, in the royal palace on the planet Zaron...

ഔ

"We won't let you leave her there." Jac's and Rachel's voices said in chorus.

Why is it you both insist on speaking aloud when the Atlantean way of communication is more civilized?

"Because we aren't Atlantean and we want to make sure you're both listening."

"How could we not?" Eros groaned in frustration.

"It doesn't matter how we express ourselves. You both have to do something." They stared at the stubborn men otherwise known as their husbands standing before them.

'Tis not safe to send anyone until the seer arrives. It hasn't been that long. Eros crossed his massive arms over his chest, his impatience showing in the set of his handsome jaw.

"She's been gone a month according to Zaron time. What if she doesn't ever return?" Rachel's voice quivered.

"Yeah, then what happens?" Jac added with barely concealed anger. "I can't believe that stupid transport only works in one direction." She snorted and rolled her eyes. "Advanced civilization, my ass."

Ares shifted, his gaze zeroing in on his mate. *My fierceness, we will retrieve your friend.*

"When?" Her hands fisted at her hips. "What are you waiting for, the moons over Zaron to align?"

Ares shot Eros a quick glance then cleared his throat. The King shrugged.

"I don't friggin' believe this...you were waiting for the moons to align." Jac's voice rose unchecked.

I'll summon my half-brother Orion, my fierceness, and let him know he'll be leaving on his mission ahead of schedule instead of waiting another lunar cycle.

Don't bother. I heard you. A strong masculine voice called out from the other side of the terrace. *In fact, I'm sure the entire palace has heard you.* He gazed at Rachel and Jac unflinchingly as if waiting for them to contradict him.

Orion strode across the iridescent glass-like opaque plates that made up the floor, flanked by two fierce looking Phantom Warriors named Bacchus and Kegar. The warriors were dressed in red combat fatigues as if they'd been pulled straight off patrol to escort him. Their expressions were hard, wary.

Their red eyes flashed in the moonlight giving them the appearance of hungry wolves. Ebony hair, the color of night, hung past their broad shoulders covering much of the tattoos that zigzagged across their necks. The sight was unusual and a bit awe-inspiring considering the Atlantean people rarely saw Phantom Warriors in the flesh. Phantom Warriors kept to themselves preferring their own kind to the company of outsiders. Originally from Kantar—a distant planet—they'd settled on Zaron thousands of years ago.

As Orion stepped forward the men stepped back fading into the palace wall like ghosts making them invisible to the naked eye. One of the many strange abilities their kind exhibited.

I'll be fueled and ready to go on the morrow. The group stared at the wall a moment longer. Orion glanced over his shoulder, his gaze tracking the warriors' movements for a second before turning once more to face Jac and Queen Rachel. He dropped to his knee and gave each woman, now ripe with babes in their bellies, a traditional Atlantean greeting before standing once more.

Jac and Rachel glanced at each other with raised eyebrows. It took everything ounce of willpower they had to prevent a burst of giggles from erupting.

With Orion standing this close it was difficult to tear their gaze away from him. His unusual ebony and blond striped hair hung unrestrained to the middle of his back. His uniform, black with jade colored accents, appeared as if it had been painted on like a second skin lovingly gripping every ripple of muscle beneath. With a face that could only rival perfection, he'd built quite a reputation for sexual prowess amongst the women on Zaron.

In addition to the already devastating picture he presented was an artfully applied tribal tattoo covering his cheek. The permanent paint gave him an air of the forbidden, like Eve's apple but far more tempting. One eye was aqua like the majority of Atlantean people while the other flashed jade signaling his family bloodline. As arrogant as Ares yet with the spiritual continence of a seer, he was as irresistible to women as chocolate to a dieter.

Jac and Rachel had both heard the tales of his exploits. Some of the stories included vague details about what he was able to do with his silver-ringed cock. Rumor had it the silver could make a woman's body sing.

Curiosity alone made it difficult to keep their gazes on his face. Yet neither one had worked up the nerve to ask him about his gift especially not under their husbands' watchful eyes.

Remember us? We're your true-mates. Ares and Eros burst into laughter. After a moment's embarrassment, Rachel and Jac joined in.

"You know I'd never forget you." Jac ran to Ares' arms and kissed him.

You had better not.

"Thank you, honey." Jac gave Ares a devastating smile. "You won't regret your decision of moving up the timetable."

23

He arched a brow and looked down upon her face. *I might not but will Orion?* Ares set Jac upon her feet then turned to face his half-sibling. *You are to seek out the Queen's and Jac's friend in the state known as New York. You'll find her at something called a Sci-fi Convention. We'll send word if the seer arrives with Coridan. Make haste and may the goddess be with you on your journey.*

Thank you, my brother. Orion turned to leave but stopped short. *Cassandra has requested permission to join me on my task.*

Why would she do so when we've only just returned to our home? Confusion marred Ares' voice.

Orion coughed then glanced down before once again meeting his brother's gaze. *I believe she said something about finding her true-mate.*

What about the warriors on Zaron? the King asked, disbelief coloring his words.

Orion shifted uncomfortably. *Apparently she has found none to her liking.*

Eros snorted. *Surely she hasn't met them all.*

Color rose in Orion's cheeks. *I believe she's been quite busy since your return, my King.*

She'll find no warriors back on that primitive planet. What is she thinking?

I know not, my King.

Jac and Rachel cracked up. The Atlantean women were as outrageous as their men. They found it refreshing that Atlantean women were comfortable in their sexuality. And to say Cassandra was comfortable was the understatement of the century. She'd gone through the men on Zaron faster than Rachel could get through a bag of M & M's.

Jac turned to her friend and arched a brow. "Who's this Cassandra chick?"

"You should have seen her." Rachel mouthed 'Oh my God'. "After my mating ceremony she and Ariel were on the ground going at it like bunnies." She added in a whisper. "It was enough to make a sailor blush."

Orion cleared his throat. *Do I have permission to take her along?*

Ares looked to Eros once more. The King drew in a deep breath. *Permission granted.*

Orion turned to Ares. *If that is all, my brother.*

'Tis. He nodded. *Our women are finished torturing you.* Ares winked at his younger brother.

Orion stepped forward acknowledging Ares' and Eros' rank and position with a slight bow then pivoted and left, taking the two now visible Phantom Warriors with him.

Eros drew his very pregnant Queen into a loving embrace. Their child was due in a few months. All of Zaron was aflutter. He rested his hand protectively on her protruding abdomen. All was almost as it should be. Now he just had to ensure the safe return of their remaining people.

* * * * *

The next day Orion's ship launched on time, the thrust from the engines hurling him and Cassandra out of Zaron's atmosphere in a burst of orange flame. They stared out the tiny observation windows as the green planet disappeared into a sea of black. The engine droned on peppered by short gusts of air from the life support system. Earth's coordinates had been programmed into the ship earlier, the flight pattern predetermined.

Orion glanced at the gauges one last time to check fuel levels. Everything checked out as expected...everything but the weight of the aircraft itself. His gaze narrowed as he tapped the screen. The gauges held at two hundred and fifty cords over proper launch weight. His brows furrowed.

He turned to Cassandra who was staring excitedly out into deep space. *Did you bring anything I should know about onboard?*

Cassandra tore her gaze away from the view panel to look at him. *I brought only the bare essentials. You have seen my belongings. Why?*

Orion shook his head, tapping the gauge one last time. *According to the gauge, we're overweight by two hundred and fifty cords.*

I didn't lie about my weight. Cassandra glared at him, daring him to challenge her statement.

Orion was an expert when it came to Atlantean women. He knew better than to touch that statement. Besides even if she had fabricated her weight it still wouldn't account for the discrepancy the gauges were showing.

He glanced over his shoulder mentally going through their supply checklist. Everything was as it should be. He turned back to the systems panel in front of him and rolled his suddenly tense shoulders. He'd been a warrior for too many years to simply ignore his instincts. Whatever caused the override was in for the long haul because he wasn't about to turn the ship around now.

In his peripheral, Orion caught a gray shadowy movement near the bulkhead. *Did you see that?* His head whipped around to get a better look at the same time warning bells went off in the control panel. *Quarg!* It was time to switch fuel tanks.

See what? Cassandra looked around the room.

Orion turned back to the panel, flipping switches quickly before glancing over his shoulder at the storage crates and bulkhead beyond. *I thought I saw something moving by the bulkhead.*

I don't see anything. She shrugged and looked out the window once more.

Whatever he'd seen had vanished like a ghost.

* * * * *

Ariel's body writhed as the vision came upon her. He was there on the bed with her, his blond head buried between her thighs, lapping at her engorged clit. His long serpent-like tongue probed her cunt, drawing out her juices, milking her essence. Her back bowed, muscles tensing as he sent an energy burst into her core setting off shock waves inside of her channel.

Ariel moaned, coming hard from his enthusiastic ministrations.

Coridan looked up and smiled flashing white teeth, his aqua eyes sparkling with intensity. Ariel's bound fingers grasped the soft fur and her eyes flew open as shock ricocheted through her. The warrior in her vision was Coridan. Quivering, her body lay covered in a fine sheen of sweat, her nipples stabbing skyward. Her pussy lips were plump, swollen and flushed a deep red. The fire inside her burned on, only slightly dampened by her release and the knowledge of who had given her such a gift.

Coridan, where are you?

Before she could make sense of her vision, the flap to the hut was thrown back and her two guards stepped inside. Their gazes darted from side to side ensuring that she was still alone before dropping the flap to once again cover the entry door. Her legs were still spread wide in welcome as if the Atlantean warrior had actually been there. But she knew he hadn't.

This was the second such vision she'd had of the exiled man but until seconds ago, she had not realized his true identity. She began to wonder if there wasn't more to her visions than met the eye. Could he be? Surely not. Her people needed *her*. She wasn't meant to be with a warrior or any man for that matter. Was she? And what of her magic? What would become of her powers if she joined with another, experienced the energy bind? Would she still have visions?

All questions that for the first time in her existence Ariel was unsure of the answers. One thing was for certain, she couldn't take the chance no matter how much her pussy ached. Her people needed protection whether they realized it or not.

Ariel's attention returned to the two men eyeing her cunt hungrily. Her body needed release again and she knew neither of these men would actually penetrate her with their cocks. They'd face death at the hands of the professor if they did so.

One man stepped forward until he stood at the foot of the fur bed. He glanced over his shoulder giving the other man a quick nod. The second native followed suit. With speed that astonished her, they moved to the side of the bed, untying her hands and then re-tying them to the stakes that formed the frame.

After they'd finished, one man grabbed one of her legs while the other slipped a vine over her ankle securing the other half to the stake at the foot of the bed. Soon she was spread-eagle on the bed and at their mercy.

She laughed to herself. Actually they were at her mercy. Ariel sent a mental command to the first man. *Drop to your knees.* He did so instantly, surprise lighting up his face. He was now level with her aching pussy and so enthralled he hadn't noticed she'd sent the command telepathically.

"What is your name?" she purred out the question.

"I am Santo."

"Well Santo…" She bucked her hips suggestively urging him on. With each gentle rock the fur beneath her bottom licked across her cleft causing her skin to rise in gooseflesh. "I want you to eat me." That suggestion didn't require any compulsion. The man bent at the waist and buried his face in her cunt, his small tongue greedily seeking her clit.

Ariel moaned as sensation shot through her. His technique wasn't near on a par with her vision of Coridan but it would do. She had no intention of acting upon her visions with the real warrior.

Next Ariel focused on the man standing closer to her hands. "What is your name?"

The native swallowed hard, his cock pressed against the zipper of his pants, straining for release. "M…my name is Raoul."

Raoul, I want you to play with my breasts and suck my nipples – now. He took a couple of steps then dropped to his knees and latched onto her nipple with his lips. His free hand sought her other breast and began to knead. Ariel groaned as her body once again raced toward completion. Her clit felt as engorged as her nipples.

Harder, she demanded from the man between her legs. He grasped her thighs, spread them further and then pressed deeper, tonguing her cunt. She was close, so close.

Raoul bit down gently on her tight bud of a nipple. The pleasure-pain sent Ariel's body into spasms. She cried out as her orgasm surged through her like a charge to battle. Her fingers dug into the vines and she tilted her cunt willing Santo to keep going, her sexual need voracious.

Goddess help her, the vision of Coridan had left her with a raging case of Atlantean heat. Impossible!

All women from Atlantis experienced Atlantean heat at one time in their life when they discovered their true-mate. That is, all women but seers. The physical reaction triggered by a true-mate's pheromones was one hundred times more powerful than the natural aphrodisiac found in the *bama bama* plant. Of course, the true-mate was normally in close proximity not gone and quite possibly dead.

No! This cannot be. Her body flamed.

Until this moment Ariel had believed seers immune to Atlantean heat but there could be no other explanation. She burned from within like an eternal flame flickering in wait for the spark that would once again cause an eruption. The question was why was she experiencing it now?

Moreover, if she could experience the Atlantean heat then could she also experience the sacred energy bind that bonded the women of Atlantis to their true-mates? The thought terrified her.

Was Coridan powerful enough to have done this? She didn't think so, but...if he were would he sense her pheromones from her multiple orgasms and come for her? Ariel didn't know.

She'd have to come once more just in case.

Santo's chin dripped with her pussy's sweet juices. His lashes lowered to half-mast as if the mere act of pleasuring her intoxicated him. *Continue, little man.* He growled in appreciation. His tongue swirled and he nibbled on her clit with his white teeth. His mouth made little sucking noises as he gingerly explored her nether lips. Ariel could feel renewed pressure building. Raoul glanced down at the native between her thighs.

So you want a taste too. She licked her lower lip. His eyes filled with such longing that she almost felt sorry for the man — almost. *Do you think you can do better?* He nodded, her nipple slipped from his mouth. *Fine. You down there enjoying my pussy, our friend here would like a turn.*

Santo glanced up, aggravation coloring his mocha features. He reluctantly rose allowing Raoul to take his place. Raoul's technique wasn't quite as good as Santo's but he had a lot of enthusiasm.

Santo, you may lick and bite my nipples until I tell you to stop.

Santo dropped down beside her, then gave his partner one last scathing glance before grabbing her breasts with both hands. *If they were jealous of each other it would make them easier to control.* Ariel smiled. Santo's moist lips toyed with her nipples as he rasped his tongue over her beaded flesh.

For a human male, his sensual skills weren't bad although he was a little on the small side for her tastes. He had cropped dark hair, haunting black eyes and mocha colored skin. If the size of his diminutive body was any indication of the size of his cock he'd be unable to satisfy her no matter how many hours he put into the task.

Only a warrior's cock could fill her greedy cunt.

The thought sent shivers through Ariel. Once again she pulled herself up short. There would be no warrior's cock thrusting into her pussy. 'Twas the oath she'd vowed the day she became a seer.

The musky odor of sex filtered through the air as the men feasted upon her body. Ariel's pheromones surrounded them, enticing them, sending their need raging through their bodies. She was the match to their tinder, a banquet to their raging hunger. Any sign of control had been lost the moment they touched her. The scent was too much for Santo and Raoul to take, they became ravenous. Ariel shuddered in release one last time as the flap to the hut was pushed aside. She blinked, half expecting to see Coridan standing in the doorway.

The two guards lapping at her flesh jumped away their eyes rounding to the size of *camu camu* fruit. They quickly wiped their mouths with the back of their sleeves as if removing the moisture would erase all evidence of what had been occurring in the room only moments ago.

It was a pity that the professor chose this inopportune time to arrive, considering she was just getting started and beginning to enjoy their efforts.

The professor stood in the doorway, hatred gleaming in his bug-like eyes. "What are you two doing?"

Santo and Raoul backed away, fear replacing surprise on their faces. "We…I mean…she…uh…"

"Don't say another word. I want you both back at your posts immediately." He moved deeper into the room and the men scrambled past him. "As for you, I'm not sure what you're up to but I will find out." The professor turned to leave but stopped short. "I thought you said your powers would diminish if you had sex."

Ariel kept her gaze locked on his repulsive face. "What I said was I'd lose my powers if I joined with anyone."

The professor reached down and twisted her nipple to the point of pain. Ariel bit the inside of her cheek refusing to cry out. The sound would give the slug too much satisfaction.

"I suggest you make sure that you keep that cunt of yours unoccupied unless you want me to allow the men to truly show you a good time." He leered a second longer before releasing her. His hand trailed down her belly and over her shaven mons. He dipped one finger into the moisture of her weeping cunt, stroking her clit in the process. Ariel's muscles tensed. He brought the digit up to his nose and inhaled deeply. His face twisted in disgust and his expression hardened. "But then again from what I just witnessed you'd probably enjoy that." He took his moist finger and plunged it into her anus.

Ariel shrieked in surprise as her body was rocked by an unexpected orgasm.

Rumsinger slowly pulled his finger out of her ass and then leaned next to her ear. "I guess I'll have to think of something you wouldn't like."

Ariel panted, gasping for breath. Anger surged through her muddled mind. "I'm sure you will." Her voice came out on a hiss as she strained to move away from his mouth.

She was going to derive great pleasure in destroying this man.

Chapter Three

ဢ

Night was upon the jungle as Coridan's legs gave out. He crashed, falling to the vegetation-covered ground with a mighty thud. His lungs heaved in gulps of air as his body demanded rest. For a moment he closed his eyes and sought out a mental connection. Vast nothingness answered. Coridan ran his hand down his face in frustration. Weary, he almost succumbed to slumber, almost dismissing the strange scent that reached his nostrils.

His brows furrowed for a moment, tension filling his frame. In the next breath, his eyes flew open and his body came alive. Coridan's cock hardened, pressing outward, tenting his loincloth. He swallowed hard and pushed himself up, fighting the fatigue with an inner resilience he didn't know he possessed until he sat up on the ground. What had roused him he could not be sure. The scent was faint as if the wind had been carrying it for miles. Vaguely familiar in its essence — yet not. Something told him he'd scented whatever it was before.

As if seized by an invisible force, Coridan rose to his feet, pain from exhaustion pulling at his muscles every inch of the way. He turned to face the direction the scent hailed from tilting his head from side to side. The jungle air pressed in around him, its hot breath brushing his skin, moistening. Whatever wafted on the breeze had invigorated him in more ways than one. He reached down and clasped his erect cock a second before releasing it. Had his mind finally snapped?

The seductive fragrance lured him back from whence he came, leading him in the direction of the Atlantean encampment. Unfortunately it would take him two days to reach the place he'd once called home. His chest squeezed at the thought. Could he face returning to the empty dwellings?

Coridan didn't think he had a choice. The aroma wouldn't allow him to do otherwise. It dragged and pulled at his body with unseen arms, wrapping around his cock like invisible fingers in a rapturous embrace. He had to find its origins. It was as if the fate of his heart and soul hung in the balance.

Cries rang out from the jungle as the nocturnal animals started to stir. A harpy eagle screeched as it made a fresh kill. Coridan had traveled several hundred yards before he tripped and once again found himself face down in the warm earth. This time no amount of persuasion could convince his body to rise. With a long exhalation, he succumbed to mind numbing sleep, his last thoughts of the sensual aroma that was drawing him home.

* * * * *

The vision was hazy…a blonde woman stood naked with her hands planted on the wall of a small hut. He could not see her face because her back was to him. Tall, she had long hair that seemed to snake its way to her shapely bare bottom, curling lovingly around the firm globes of flesh. The woman shifted restlessly as if in anticipation. Need slammed into Coridan, nearly knocking the breath from his lungs. His cock expanded, growing impossibly hard until he'd reached full erection. The urge to claim raged through him.

The woman quivered, sensing his presence. He stepped closer, still unable to touch her. She moaned and bent slightly at the waist, exposing the lips of her dew-covered pussy like a flower spreading its pedals waiting to be plucked. Coridan closed the distance between them. His arms encircled her small waist, pulling her flush against him. Her body melted into his seamlessly like the last piece of a missing puzzle. The woman released a shuddering breath.

Forgive me, fair one but I must have what you appear to offer freely. He groaned, sliding his hand over her taut stomach until he reached her pussy. His fingers gently parted her, seeking her hidden pearl. He stroked the tender flesh until her hips rocked rhythmically. Her breath came out in pants as she drew nearer her release. The need to feast upon her flesh, taste her, overwhelmed him. Coridan dropped to his knees, sliding his hands between her legs to give him better access. His thumb continued its torturous play circling and flicking her clit, encouraging her wetness.

From behind he plunged his phallus-like tongue into her cunt. Her taste exploded in his mouth, nectar and honey, tart and spicy. He'd never had a woman's essence intoxicate him so. He swirled and probed, stroking the channel where his near-bursting cock would soon be. Her juices ran down his chin and still he fed. She tried to pull away as the first orgasm rocked her but his grip firmed keeping her in place. He growled against her cunt like a feral beast refusing to give up its prey.

She was his.

As the pulsing inside her slowed, Coridan pulled himself away. He stood quickly, ripping at the ties of his loincloth with one hand and holding her with the other. His massive cock sprang free. It took mere seconds for him to position the plum-like head at her entrance and drive home, sinking his aching flesh in all the way to his balls. The woman shrieked coming hard again. Her body convulsed around him drenching his cock in new wetness as he began to grind his hips against her heart-shaped ass.

Her pussy clutched him, drawing him deeper, refusing to release him from its moist grip. Not that Coridan wanted to go anywhere. He closed his eyes, inhaling the exotic aroma that emanated from her body, relishing the slide of her warm skin against his chest, honing in on the sound of flesh slapping flesh. Coridan decided this experience was as close as he'd ever get to meeting the goddess in the flesh.

Little mewing noises came from her throat encouraging him without words. He drove hard inside her, lifting her feet from the floor as he speared deep nudging her womb. He wanted to make this moment as memorable for her as it was going to be for him. Coridan fought the urge to mark her but the need was too powerful. He leaned over, gathering her tender flesh between his teeth at the curve of her neck and began to suck, drawing at her soft tissue. Thrust for thrust, he matched the pull of his mouth with his cock. She whimpered, her knees trembling and threatening to give out.

Coridan reached around her once more, one hand supporting her at the waist while the other found her clit. It only took a flick of his nail for her to shatter, her pussy slamming down around him like a vise sending him spiraling in her wake.

He bellowed as his fluids pumped out of his body in an endless milky stream. Coridan opened his eyes and jerked upright, his hand still gripping his cock. Drenched in sweat, he blinked as the jungle around him came into focus. The fragrance of orchids perfumed the night air along with the musky odor of sex. He groaned and released his shaft, fisting his hands in frustration. It had all been a dream. The woman was gone taking with her the best fuck of his life.

He fell back onto the ferns, his breathing still ragged. In his mind he knew she was not real yet his body refused to accept that fact. Her skin had felt as soft as feathers to the touch while at the same time her flesh practically scalded him from the heat contained within. The silk of her sunshine-scented hair had caressed his face in loving strokes causing his flat disc-like nipples to bead.

Hell, he was getting hard just thinking about the mysterious woman again. To his embarrassment he had been so motivated by lust that he hadn't bothered stealing a glance at the woman's features. She could be a toothless, shrivel-faced hag for all he knew not that it would have mattered to him one way or the other at this point. Coridan knew he would gladly sacrifice beauty for the kind of connection he'd had with the woman in his dream.

If only she were real and not a figment of his imagination...

* * * * *

Ariel lay upon the bed of furs her mind calculating her chances of escape. It would be easier if Coridan was alive, not that she expected to be rescued but it would certainly help in the fight. She felt fevered and it was difficult to concentrate with the Atlantean heat coursing through her body like a chariot of fire.

Raoul and Santo hadn't returned since the professor interrupted their little pleasure session. Not that she truly cared. They couldn't satisfy her, only Coridan could. Unfortunately she couldn't allow that to happen with her people counting on her.

Fear sliced through her as she considered the fact that he might be dead. Her body trembled unable to accept that as even a remote possibility. There was no way a dead man set off her hormones like this. Coridan had to be alive and well somewhere. It was just a matter of reaching him telepathically. If her first theory was correct and he could sense her pheromones, then there was a real good chance that he was on his way.

Her body grew restless at the thought of taking in his massive cock. Ariel tried to ignore the ache within her womb. She needed that man or at least her body thought she did and it demanded she listen. Ariel imagined him standing before her naked, his glorious cock rising to attention under her hungry gaze. Her mouth watered at the thought of wrapping her lips around his shaft and sucking until she could taste his salty fluids and feel his spray as he came in her mouth and down her throat.

She groaned and licked her parched lips. Her nipples throbbed and beaded, demanding to be suckled and stroked. Ariel felt as if she'd explode if she weren't able to gain release soon. The fur beneath her bottom tickled her anus causing her pussy to weep with need. The feelings were strange, alien, like she'd awakened inside a cocoon and had finally broken free. She inhaled deeply, slowly releasing the air from her lungs. The exhalation glowed gold in the dim lighting. No! She blinked to try to clear her vision yet the gold remained.

Ariel gasped. Seers were able to experience the energy bind that bonded Atlantean women to their mates!

Goddess bless!

She had to pull herself together. Fight this need with all of her power. Night had fallen on the jungle like a thick blanket, shrouding all who dwelled within its lush realm. The red-devil would come for her first thing in the morning to begin his interrogation. She had no doubt this was true.

Ariel tested her bonds once more. The vines chaffed her skin causing her flesh to turn pink and raw. She sent an energy burst through herself to heal her wounds. Ariel recalled the professor's hatred radiating out through his eyes. He may not turn her over to his men but he would derive great pleasure in her pain. Tomorrow she'd have to be prepared for anything.

Once she refused to tell him where her people were located the torture would begin. At the same time she would need to use all the energy at her disposal to deflect his men from discovering the transport. Hopefully by the time night fell tomorrow she'd have enough psychic strength left to attempt contact with Coridan again.

* * * * *

Morning came sooner than Ariel would have liked. Her neck stung as if her flesh had been bitten during the night. At first light, as promised, the professor stepped across the threshold of the hut and ordered Raoul and Santo to untie her.

The guards yanked at the vines with unusual dramatic flair. It took Ariel a minute to realize their actions were for show.

The professor watched closely, his face shining with pleasure at the guides' exaggerated movements. They pulled Ariel off the furs allowing her to grab her sheer blue skirt and slip it on before being dragged out of the hut. Raoul and Santo lifted her under the arms to alleviate any pain she might suffer by their actions. This confirmed her earlier suspicions. The men were trying to go easy on her despite their fear of the professor.

They placed her in the basket, the softness in their eyes the only thing revealing their true discomfort. The professor stepped in behind them then ordered the men to lower the basket. Upon reaching the ground, Raoul and Santo picked Ariel up hoisting her above their heads to a table that had been placed on end.

The men lowered her to her feet when they neared the erect table. She stood facing the wooden structure. The professor walked up and spun Ariel around slamming her back against the hard boards.

The warm memories of the meals she'd shared with her people flooded her, so much happiness, so much laughter. The Atlanteans never meant for this object to be used as a tool of torture. Sadness filled Ariel as she realized she might never experience those things again. It was for that laughter, for her people, she would endure whatever this man subjected her to today.

He ordered Raoul and Santo to tie her hands behind her securing them to the top legs of the table. Similarly they tied her feet securing them to the bottom legs of the structure until they'd stretched her wide in a standing 'X' position.

There was no way she could fire a shot and hit anyone unless they stepped directly in front of her hands. She couldn't see behind her and therefore couldn't aim. Besides, taking out one or two people would in no way ensure her escape. If anything it would bring the red-devil down on her like a rain of fire.

The professor watched, a wicked smile on his chubby face.

"What do you really want, professor?"

"My due."

Ariel shook her head. Some men never learned. "I've told you everything I know."

Rumsinger snorted. "I doubt that very much. In fact you've told me nothing at all. It's as if your tribe has disappeared off the face of the Earth." He crossed his arms over his chest and stepped to within inches of her body. "And since we both know that's not possible they have to be here somewhere."

Ariel felt his warm breath upon her cheek. The rancid smell that followed had her fighting the urge to gag. "I told you, I know nothing." She swallowed hard.

He arched a furry caterpillar-like brow. "There are few, if any, tracks leading away from this compound. My men have scoured the land and the only thing we've found is a drinking cup." The professor fisted his hands. "Now I'm going to ask you again, once more nicely, where are your people?"

Ariel swallowed hard. "I cannot tell you what I do not know."

"Have it your way." Rumsinger turned to face Raoul. "Go to my hut and retrieve my knife."

Raoul's eyes widened. His gaze darted from the professor to Ariel, then back.

"Move now!"

Raoul jumped and darted to Ariel's old hut. He returned in short order carrying a knife that looked more like a sword to her. He handed the blade to the professor, who proceeded to run his finger along the edge. A drop of blood pearled on the tip of his thumb. He brought the digit to his mouth and sucked before turning his attention back to Ariel.

"Where are they?" He raised the knife to her outstretched arm.

Ariel bit her lower lip and shook her head.

The professor ran the edge of the blade over her biceps. Pain seared her, sapping some of her strength as she fought the urge to cry out. A streak of red followed the sharp metal's trail. Ariel winced as he drew the knife away blood dripping down her arm.

The professor stared at her arm for a moment then turned his attention back to his blade. "Once more, my dear. Where is your tribe?"

"I don't know," she spat, the copper taste of blood filling her mouth as she fought the pain.

"Have it your way." He shrugged and raised the knife again. This time the blade came down on her leg, its razor edge leaving a clean slice behind. "Get me the salt, Santo."

The guard's nostrils flared but he did as ordered.

The professor grabbed a handful of the white granules and rubbed them into Ariel's wounds. She screamed, the raw flesh burning like fire under the abrasive seasoning. Damn him. She would die before she led him to her people.

Coridan, she screamed in her head repeatedly as she fought the urge to heal herself.

* * * * *

Coridan froze as pain sliced through him, driving him to the ground. The garbled cry resonated in his head, echoing over his senses, demanding help without words. He pressed his hands to his limbs trying to figure out if he'd suffered any injuries. None were visible.

The next wave of pain had him rising and sprinting through the jungle. He was still a day and a half away from the encampment. Whoever communicated to him psychically was in dire need. The contact had vibrated through him like a sound wave echoing the pain the individual felt.

The being hadn't used a traditional Atlantean route of communication. This led Coridan to believe he dealt with someone or something different. He pushed himself harder, his heart slamming in his chest. Muscles bunched as he leapt over fallen trees and ducked around lianas. Snakes scurried to escape his approach along with a few bug-eyed iguanas.

He'd traveled a few miles when he heard a faint whisper. The wind rushing past his head from running created enough interference that he'd been unable to make out what had been said. Coridan stopped, his breathing harsh as he listened again, waiting. *Please, speak to me...*he asked no one in particular.

Coridan...Coridan...

His name was repeated like a mantra, barely audible but there nonetheless. Someone called him by name...but who? Coridan's brows furrowed. Who could be calling him on his private frequency, the one reserved solely for true-mates? The blonde from his vision flashed through his mind. Excitement and fear lanced through him as he concentrated so he could answer back.

Who are you?

*Please...*the voice whispered.

I am coming. Fear not. He sent the thoughts out using the same frequency and then tried to hold onto his patience which was rapidly slipping from his grasp. For several minutes he heard nothing. He debated whether to continue his journey and try again in another mile or so. Coridan released a strangled breath. Whoever had contacted him was gone. Fear clutched at his throat as he considered the possibility that they'd been killed.

He would have felt it, wouldn't he?

No! He shouted the thought. *I demand that you speak to me.* He had meant the command to sound firm, unforgiving. Instead it had come out like a plea from a desperate man which he supposed he was. Coridan took a step and heard a whispered response. It sounded faintly like the tickling trill of a woman's laughter albeit one who fought pain.

You know who I am. You have known me all your life. You think me a stranger. It wasn't exactly a question yet the words floated weightlessly, suspended in the ether.

Stop speaking in riddles, woman, and tell me who you are.

I am your seer and I demand your respect and allegiance. Her voice broke off on an angry gasp.

Feeling as if he'd been kicked, Coridan's stomach clenched. The seer... It was not possible, was it? *How is it that you come to communicate with me in this manner?*

'Tis not important.

Was this some kind of cruel joke? Seers didn't have true-mates, everyone knew that. *Is there anyone else there with you?* he asked, hoping his vision woman was there with Ariel.

Not of our people if that is what you ask. There was an edge to Ariel's voice as she spoke, the tenor not nearly as teasing as it had been moments ago.

Coridan's brows rose. That explained the sudden shift. He snorted and shook his head. For a moment he'd actually thought she'd been jealous.

The time for reunions is over. I am here with our old friend and enemy, the professor.

Coridan tensed every muscle on alert. *What does he want?*

He is seeking our people. I will allow him to kill me before that will happen but I need your help.

No! The thought of Ariel dying stabbed at his chest like a blunt sword. He would not allow her to die, could not. Forsaken by his people Coridan cared not what happened to the Atlanteans but she was a different matter.

Ariel groaned in pain. *You will have to be careful once you near the compound. The professor has his men seeking the tribal members.*

The Atlantean people are not my problem, he growled.

Ariel hesitated. *I'm not sure how long I can keep them from the transport.* Fear rang out in her voice. *They must not reach the transport…aahh!*

Ariel! Coridan's heart skidded to a halt a second before slamming into his ribs. His hands flew to his chest protectively. *What is he doing to you?*

He likes to play with knives. I will heal myself once he returns me to Eros' hut. Until then I must take the pain. He is unaware of our true powers. Remember, he's only witnessed Eros' rescue of Queen Rachel.

I will kill him. Coridan's voice came out ferocious like a caged animal inside his head. Rage filled him, tainting his blood.

No! Ariel laughed but the sound held no humor. *I will take care of this slug when the time comes.*

Amongst your people women do not kill. Or have you forgotten, seer?

You claim to have no people so my actions should not concern you. As for my memory, I have forgotten nothing including your past deeds so do not lecture me, warrior. I'm in no mood. Just come.

Coridan gritted his teeth. He didn't like being commanded. But he could not stay away, even if he'd wished to do so. Reluctantly he responded. *As you wish…*

Before she could refuse or break contact with him Coridan sent her an energy surge along the same path she'd communicated with him on. He knew she'd be surprised he could do so for the Atlantean people were unaware of his true power. He wished he could see the look on Ariel's face when she received it. The thought made him smile.

In her weakened state the energy would temporarily give her enough strength to continue her fight. She could use it to struggle in the name of the people. She could use it to struggle to save herself. He didn't care how she chose to justify her actions for he knew the truth. She was doing it...

For them.

He surged into the jungle, racing through the brush, mentally replaying what had been said. Ariel had become defensive when he'd questioned her about her ability to reach him, defiantly hiding behind her title. 'Twas a pity she didn't know her title no longer held sway over him.

He was a tribe of one now.

However, the fact remained she had communicated to him on his private channel like a true-mate. His mind latched onto that thought as his imagination took over. For a moment he pictured their limbs entwined, writhing as they experienced an energy bind. His body tightened in anticipation, his heart hammering in his chest. Coridan pushed himself harder than he'd ever done before.

She may deserve his respect due to her position but if it turned out she truly was his mate and the female behind the enchanting fragrance that still haunted him, then their conversation was far from over.

In fact it had just begun.

Chapter Four

ℬ

Professor Rumsinger leaned over Ariel's bleeding body. He'd been torturing her for hours. The light in the sky had begun to fade, casting the jungle in deep shadow. "You'd make it so much easier on yourself if you'd just tell me what I want to know."

"Go to Hades, slug," she growled out as she strained against her bonds.

Rumsinger glared, then hauled off and backhanded Ariel across the cheek. Pain exploded in her head as she fought to keep it from reaching Coridan. He was still too far away to be of assistance. The world tilted as she tried to focus on the red-devil's face. She could feel her lip starting to swell, taste fresh blood in her mouth. She glared, hoping the bastard would return her to the hut soon. She needed to heal her wounds before she bled to death.

As if reading her thoughts the professor spoke. "Raoul and Santo, get her bandaged up. I don't want the bitch bleeding to death before I get the answers I seek."

The two guards jumped, scurrying off to retrieve what she could only imagine to be supplies for tending her wounds. They returned moments later carrying clean bandages and some kind of bottled elixir. Ariel swallowed hard as they approached her with the unknown liquid which they'd dabbed onto a piece of cotton.

The second the medicine hit her skin it burned not quite as bad as the salt but close. Ariel gasped and fought the urge to struggle, the cure worse than the cause. To their credit the two men tried to be gentle attempting not to harm her only help.

46

The professor stood in the background overseeing the men's progress. "That's good enough." He pulled Santo away then shot Raoul a warning glare.

Raoul moved away from Ariel reluctantly, the hand holding the cotton trembling with controlled rage. From the expression on his face he didn't like the professor any more than she did.

Perhaps these two men weren't quite as bad as she'd first suspected. Ariel couldn't think about it now. She fought the urge to slip into unconsciousness. She needed to remain alert so she could continue confusing the professor's men who came dangerously near the transport. Just as she thought she'd not make it a moment longer, an energy surge burst through her, revitalizing her senses, fueling her aching muscles.

Coridan...but how?

He didn't have the power to reach her from this distance, did he? She considered her case of Atlantean heat. Perhaps there was more to the young warrior than first met the eye. The thought both frightened and intrigued Ariel. Could a warrior with such power have existed under her nose the whole time without her sensing any shift in energy? If he did, what did that mean? Could they experience an energy bind without either of them losing any power? Was he stronger than she was? The thought gave her pause.

Ariel didn't like the possibility that Coridan could somehow be more powerful than her. She was the seer after all. She'd never encountered a male much less a warrior with the ability to send energy or communicate from great distances. Nor one who could heal without effort. She had no doubt the action hadn't strained him in the least.

Despite her knowledge to the contrary, there was no denying where the energy her drained body had just received had come from. Coridan had sent it to her as he continued to shorten the distance between them. Her gaze flicked to the red-devil before her. He looked weary. With any luck he'd drop dead.

She sent a thought to his mind, dragging his muscles down, weakening his ability to concentrate. She'd convince him he was too tired to continue. Her gaze darted to Santo and Raoul, their expressions guarded. The professor yawned loudly drawing her attention back to him.

"I've had enough," he said, scratching his ass. "We'll pick this up tomorrow. For now take her back to the hut." The professor took a step toward her old hut then stopped. His gaze locked on her would-be guards. "This time make sure I find you at your posts or there won't be a next time." The silence that followed the statement spoke volumes.

The men's expressions dropped, their coloring deepened as the professor's meaning sank into their heads. They gave Rumsinger a curt nod and then moved to Ariel. Brown hands worked quickly to untie her. Ariel slumped the second they released her limbs. The men caught her, grasping her beneath the arms, dragging her to the lift basket.

Raoul and Santo placed her into the basket following close behind. They glanced back now and again to ensure the professor had gone into his hut. The basket lifted from the ground, rising into the air, putting distance between her and the red-devil for the first time today. The men who had been searching the jungle were now returning and began to settle around a fire that at this moment was being built in the center of the compound.

Ariel turned her gaze away. It seemed like a lifetime since her people had eaten and danced around the center flame yet it had only been days. The basket stopped with a jerk and her guards walked her to Eros' hut. Raoul and Santo immediately gave her water and allowed her to wash up quickly.

Raoul handed her some fresh fruit then encouraged her without words to eat. Ariel did so, rapidly, wolfing down the mangoes and bananas as if they were her last meal. Perhaps the fruit would be if the professor had his way. Afterwards she cleaned herself once more, removing the blood soaked bandages as she did so then walked to the bed of furs. Ariel removed her skirt and laid down before the men asked her to do so and then spread her limbs wide giving them enough space to tie her to the bed.

The men grabbed vines and had her bound within moments. She was tired and in no mood to entertain the two natives tonight no matter how much kindness they'd shown her today. Not that she need worry. The professor had put the fear of the goddess into them only moments ago. As soon as the men finished their task they gave her one last look of longing before slipping out of the hut and allowing the flap to drop behind them.

Alone at last… Ariel sent an energy burst through her body. Every place the professor had sliced started to tingle and then burn as the healing began. Ariel relaxed into the growing warmth, her mind at ease. She was no longer alone. Coridan was alive and with him a growing hope. It didn't change her apprehension about the young warrior but there was every possibility he would get her out of this predicament and then they could be on their way.

Ariel settled into the furs, her thoughts turning to Coridan. His muscled form rippled beneath her eyelids, teasing her, taunting, his golden skin slick with sweat as he raced toward his destiny. Ariel opened her eyes, squelching the feelings threatening to rise.

She could not afford to feel anything toward Coridan other than respect and gratitude. She could not lie with the warrior and perform the energy bind. There was no sense leading him to believe otherwise.

He'd been foolish in his actions against Ares. The jealousy Coridan had felt wounded not only himself but her too. His pride kept him from seeing the way of his folly. Coridan was arrogant and his arrogance had gotten him banished from the tribe. He needed her guidance and nothing more whether he realized it or not and as his seer she would give it to him.

Her pussy clenched demanding release. The woman in her railed against her decision. Now that she'd healed herself the Atlantean heat was back with a vengeance. How would she ever survive this ordeal? Between the professor and Coridan she wasn't sure which one would kill her first.

* * * * *

Night fell upon the jungle. Muscles quaking, Coridan stumbled further falling only to rise again. His vision blurred and the trail before him all but disappeared. He knew he'd have to rest. He staked out a soft spot on the ground and then lay down. A new vision was upon him the second he closed his eyes.

His body flexed as his cock slid in and out of the tight cunt gripping him. The woman beneath him moaned as her orgasm rocked her body, pulsing and throbbing, milking his cock of his life-giving fluids. Coridan had taken her from behind as before, her face shielded from his seeking gaze.

Her soft moans reached his ears, her body undulating as she coaxed him back to life. This time he wanted to see her face, taste her nipples, suck her tongue into his mouth as his cock impaled her. He had to know for sure. Coridan rose until his weight no longer pinned her in place. He reached down and carefully turned her body, allowing her enough time to lift her leg over him until she was laying flat on her back.

The head of his cock rested just inside her entrance because he couldn't bear the loss of contact. Her blonde curls hid her face. With trembling fingers he reached for her hair and brushed it aside, his heart pounding with anticipation.

The second the hair parted, Ariel's lust-filled aqua-blue eyes stared at him. Coridan's breath caught in his throat and he couldn't seem to swallow. It was true but how could this be? The seer couldn't mate, could she? And if not why was she here now lying beneath him spreading her thighs, allowing a warrior such as himself entrance into her scorching cunt?

Coridan didn't know all the answers but he trusted what his body told him. Her eyes widened as he slid inside her slowly, inch by inch, impaling her again on his rigid cock. Once he'd seated himself he made no move to thrust. His gaze stayed locked on her face, taking in her expression, gauging her need. Ariel shifted restlessly beneath him as her body expanded to accommodate his massive size. Her hips bucked in encouragement.

Seer, I do not understand how this can be.

She did not answer. Instead she reached up, looping her arms around his neck and pulling his head down to her breasts. Coridan couldn't think, only react. His mouth opened, closing over one turgid peak. He suckled the fevered flesh, flicking his tongue back and forth, worrying it with his teeth. She moaned, her fingers lacing through his hair. His free hand slipped between their bodies seeking her engorged clit. He circled it with his thumb all the while laving her flesh.

Ariel quivered, her body tightening for another release.

Coridan followed her every nuance. Felt the second she moved to the brink of the abyss. He released one nipple and then attacked the other. His thumb continued its teasing circles, guiding her on, winding her up. Ariel's body began to move in time with the draw of his mouth. It wouldn't be long now.

She whimpered. He thrust forward. Her breath caught as his hips began to move. Her nails scored his back, marking him. Coridan bellowed, releasing her clit so he could clamp down on her hips holding her in place. He rolled his hips, thrusting and rocking, spearing her deep.

You…thrust…are…thrust…mine.

He bucked hard riding her body as if she were a horse bent on throwing him. His fingers dug into the tender flesh of her flanks showing her with enough force who was in charge.

Ariel's head thrashed from side to side. Her whimpering moans held Coridan's name. She let out a keening cry a second before she came.

Coridan became like a man possessed, driving into her body, demanding more. He wanted her surrender. He wanted her promise that she'd be only his. He wanted her. A cry ripped from his throat and he closed his eyes to the exquisite torture that was her body. His cock pulsed, his balls emptied yet he continued to thrust, branding her—claiming her for all time. The next time she released a breath for exchange he would be prepared to act.

Sweat covered Coridan's body as he rolled off Ariel. His mind reeled from the implications. His breath came out in panting gasps from the exertion. After a few moments he was able to regain some of his senses. Coridan opened his eyes to look at his prize only to find himself alone in the jungle. He jolted, searching for any sign the seer had been there. Come clung to his hand and trickled over his rippled abdomen, dripping down onto his loincloth.

Damn, another dream. *No!* his mind screamed. It had been a vision, a clear, very vivid vision of things to come. He growled in frustration, dropping back down upon the vegetation. The second his lower back made contact with the ground his flesh stung. He frowned then glanced over his shoulder at his skin.

Red furrows marred his back almost as if he'd been scratched. He stared in disbelief. Had he scratched himself in the frenzy of reaching climax or was more going on than he'd first imagined? The visions were becoming more frequent the closer he got to Ariel.

What would happen when he finally reached her?

* * * * *

Ariel's eyes flew open the second she felt his cock enter her. Her breath froze in her lungs. She glanced down at her body, panic lacing through her as the tightness and heat increased. Her gaze locked onto her pussy as she felt the first thrust. She gasped as intense pleasure built and exploded inside of her. She couldn't sense Coridan trying to contact her. Yet Ariel knew instantly he was behind this magical moment. The question was…did he know?

Coridan, she whispered in his mind. She received no answer. Perhaps he was sleeping. Fear swept through her once again, his power was growing. Soon it would be greater than any Atlantean who'd come before him.

He slid in and out of her. Ariel's body flamed instantly and her clit pulsed. She threw her head back and squeezed her eyes closed. The sensations were too much. Logically she knew she could never accept a man inside her body without the urge to experience an energy bind. Nevertheless there was no denying the stretched, full feeling she experienced now. Invisible hips rolled, rocking her into submission, daring her to cross over the edge. Ariel whimpered, her nipples beading into diamond-like points. Never in her life had she felt anything nearly as enticing, exhilarating — right.

Ariel ignored that last thought, bucking her hips against the invisible force. She'd often dreamt what it would feel like to have a man between her thighs and now she knew. Her thoughts hadn't even come close to describing what she felt. It was too bad this was all she could allow herself to ever experience. He thrust repeatedly, driving deep within her pussy, his hard cock showing no mercy.

Ariel groaned, attempting to clamp her legs together, feeling as if she were stretched to the point of ripping. Her pussy wept as her need grew and still he filled her. A cry spilled from Ariel's lips as she shattered. Her body convulsed, her channel pulsing and clenching around his thick shaft.

She laid there on the furs, her heart stuttering in her chest. Liquid from her release ran down her leg, dripping onto the fur beneath her bottom. Her breath infused with gold energy glittering in the thick air like fine jewelry. Ariel called on the goddess for strength because she did not think that by the time Coridan arrived she would be able to refuse him.

Yet she must.

* * * * *

Ariel spent much of the night staring at the ceiling. She'd thought of Coridan, her people and what she must do. He no longer recognized the Atlantean people as his own yet he was still coming to her rescue. Somehow she had to figure out a way to convince Coridan he'd always be a part of the tribe despite the mistakes he'd made with Ares and Jac.

Her resolve solidified about an hour before dawn. They would continue with her plan. Coridan would help her escape, then they would make their way to the transport, while keeping the professor's men at bay. If need be she would force Coridan through the portal.

Once they reached Zaron they could figure out how to dismantle the transport so their people would remain safe from the warlike people of Earth. After that, well she didn't want to think about what would happen after that. Coridan was difficult under normal circumstances. Under duress he'd be positively lethal.

Dawn broke, shattering the relative silence of the sleeping jungle. Santo and Raoul entered the hut, their gazes averted. They untied her, giving her a few moments to freshen up, dress and eat before leading her once again to the center of the compound.

The professor stood off to one side speaking to another man she'd never seen before. The native's body held thousands of little sores where it appeared mosquitoes had eaten him alive. His black hair lay plastered to his head, an impression of a wide band clearly visible from where his hat had been sitting.

The guide pointed to the jungle, his voice raised in excitement. Ariel's stomach dropped. Her mind reached out scanning the men around her. Anticipation curled within their bellies. No doubt they believed a great treasure had been uncovered. Ariel's lips thinned as she grimaced. The discovery was treasure just not in the form the men expected.

Impressions of a great stone arch filled her head. The guide speaking with the professor had indeed found the transport but had not yet revealed the location to the red-devil. The man opened his mouth to speak. Ariel closed her eyes and sent out a mental probe, scrambling the guide's mind until he could not remember what he had said or what they'd been discussing.

Her efforts pulled too much energy. Ariel fell, collapsing into Raoul and Santo's arms. Her head pounded, sweat beaded her body. She could hear excited voices all around but wasn't able to focus, her mind a myriad of impressions. A shadow passed before her eyes a second before she felt the blow.

The ensuing pain caused Ariel's vision to clear enough to see the professor standing over her. Her cheek throbbed and stung where he had slapped her. Ariel didn't have to see her cheek to know that his handprint remained behind clearly visible upon her flesh. She could feel it pulsing, red and angry.

Before she could control herself, Ariel lunged forward just missing the professor's throat. Her fingernails slashed the side of his face before Raoul and Santo jerked her back. Ariel screamed in frustration, her body tensing from being denied her prey.

The professor touched his face, flinching from the pain as he pulled his fingers back far enough to gaze upon the blood she'd drawn. His vision narrowed, zeroing in on hers. "You'd like to get your hands on me, wouldn't you, bitch?"

Ariel glared at him in defiance then spat on his shoes.

"What happened there?" He pointed to the spot where in her vision Coridan had marked her. Panic surged through her. Ariel's gaze went to the man swatting away the pesky mosquitoes.

"Like your man I've been bitten by the creatures that inhabit the jungle."

The professor's face hardened and he stepped forward with his fist raised. She braced herself for the incoming blow and closed her eyes.

"*Señor* Rumsinger, we tie her up for you." The guards shuffled the vines as if trying to get them under control.

Ariel peeked out from beneath her lashes. Rumsinger's face twisted in rage, his attention distracted by the guard's suggestion.

"Fine! Get her out of my face before I decide she is no longer of use."

Raoul and Santo pulled Ariel back toward the upended table temporarily protecting her from the professor's wrath. They tied her quickly, their eyes pleading with her to keep quiet and not do anything so stupid again. Ariel gave the men a quick nod then cast her gaze in the professor's direction.

Rumsinger turned back to the guide he'd been speaking to before the interruption. Ariel listened to the guide's thoughts. They were a blur of colors and images, none of which made sense enough to express. In fact, he couldn't seem to remember what he'd told the professor earlier. She breathed a sigh of relief. He also could not remember the location of the unusual thing he'd found. The man kept mumbling about the trees, big trees in a clearing. The mind scramble had worked.

The professor's gaze left the guide and immediately moved to Ariel once more, before narrowing into razor slits. Rumsinger's thoughts were clear. *Bitch, I know you are behind this somehow but I can't prove it.* He snarled. *Eventually you'll screw up and I'll be there.*

Ariel visibly trembled then allowed her gaze to drop away. As long as he wasn't certain, she and her people were safe.

* * * * *

Coridan knew he'd reach the compound by nightfall after finding a trail which cut a half day from his journey. He'd been traveling all morning, stopping only long enough to grab a handful of bananas from the trees. His body needed nourishment.

He'd mentally located several of the professor's men, some of whom would never find their way back to camp now that he'd played upon their fears. His muscles burned as he pushed on. Ariel was once more in pain which meant the professor tortured her to get her to spill her secrets.

He knew the seer had been serious when she'd spoken of death before betrayal. Unfortunately, Coridan could not allow her to die. Not now—not ever, since he'd discovered their connection. He wasn't sure where this bond would lead but he wouldn't find out if she died.

Coridan leapt over fallen trees and snaked around lianas, his feet silent as they fell upon the soft earth. His mind continued to scan, locating and cataloguing each individual to ensure they stayed far away from the transport. When he turned his attention back to the compound he connected with Ariel.

Seer, are you well?

I'm fine warrior, just take care of yourself.

I would like to do that, seer, but you know that is not possible.

Have you chosen to accept your people once more?

No. I do not come for my people. He paused. *I've returned because you called.* He didn't need to add *to me* at the end of his statement, they both knew that was the real reason.

Come to me when night has sunk its talons into the jungle… Ariel's voice dropped in his mind.

That I will. The smoky tone of his voice could not be disguised in his thoughts.

He sensed her frustration before she spoke. *You know we cannot join, warrior.*

Coridan shrugged to himself and then pressed on. *I know what you have told me.*

I've spoken the truth. Anger…and something else tinged her words. If he hadn't known any better he would have believed the emotion to be desire.

I will see you tonight, Ariel. With that said, Coridan broke contact. She would be fuming at the intimate use of her name. It had been his intention. He knew Ariel wasn't lying to him but he also knew she wasn't speaking the whole truth. He could sense it. Yet his gut told him he should not reveal this fact to Ariel. She would be even less pleased by the revelation than he was.

Chapter Five

ဢ

After a day of torturing Ariel, the professor once again ordered her returned to Eros' hut. Ariel healed herself once more after Santo and Raoul took their leave. Coridan hadn't contacted her since that afternoon yet she could sense his nearness. The Atlantean heat was unbearable. Her lungs labored in the stagnant air as she waited. Heat infused every pore leaving glistening sweat in its wake. She refused to acknowledge the anticipation that lay nestled in her belly like a hive of bees.

He was a warrior, a disgraced warrior at that. She was the seer, theirs was a match that could not be. Before she could stop herself Ariel's mind reached out, searching. Silence greeted her. Was he ignoring her call? The thought sent anger surging through her. How dare he ignore her? Who did he think he was?

He was not of royal blood or of the spiritual line. Ariel pulled at her restraints, her breasts bobbing back and forth with the effort. The influx of adrenaline seemed to feed the heat, stoking the fires, coaxing the flame.

Ariel groaned in frustration before stopping her struggles. Her body pulsed and throbbed with an undulating rhythm of its own. She had to get in control. He would be here any moment. It wouldn't do to be seen in this condition. So…so out of control. Ariel glanced down at her flushed skin and marbled nipples. She knew without looking that moisture glistened between her legs like a welcoming spring. She could smell her own arousal in the air. It called out to the warrior, beckoning him.

A quiet thud reached her ears followed by bits of palm floating down from the ceiling. Her gaze locked onto the thatched roof. Coridan had arrived. Ariel's heart tripped then sped up. Her hips moved of their own volition against the silky furs beneath her bottom, teasing her back orifice. She strained to listen. Silently, leaves parted near the window and in the next moment Ariel saw him. Her breath stilled in her lungs as she watched Coridan peer in and then slip through the small opening. Amazing, considering his size.

He looked even better than she recalled. His body fierce, proud and oh so muscle bound. Ariel swallowed hard as he smiled, his white teeth gleaming against his tanned skin. His eyes sparkled then turned molten as he inhaled, taking in her feminine musk. The change in his expression was dramatic. He was now certain she was the one calling to him, that it was her pheromones that wafted in the air covering the miles until they'd reached his senses.

Ariel pulled at the vines binding her. She was vulnerable should he choose to act upon those instincts. His gaze followed her ripe nipples before slowly making its way down to the liquid molten treasure between her thighs. Her pussy wept openly. His nostrils flared a second time before he focused on her face. He could smell her heat. *Her Atlantean heat.*

Ariel didn't have to read his mind to know he was remembering the dream from last night. She recalled it with clarity. She glanced down at the front of his loincloth and saw the evidence of his memory, bulging hard and thick, behind the hide confines.

Coridan, we mustn't. Our people are counting on us.

Our people… His gaze bore into hers. *You forget, seer, I have no people.*

Ariel licked her suddenly dry lips. *You have…*

His lids narrowed.

It doesn't matter. She swallowed. *I need your assistance.*

And you'll have it. First, I want to know why is it that your fragrance can reach me over the miles, inflame my blood, draw me like the flowers call to the bees? Why is it you are in Atlantean heat when I am the only Atlantean male left on the planet? Tell me, seer, am I your mate?

It matters not, for I am the seer.

It matters to me.

I cannot mate with anyone or I will lose my powers. You know this as I do.

So you've told me but it doesn't explain how you can reach me on my private channel of communication when we both know only true-mates can do so.

I do not have a true-mate. And I will not stay here and listen to this.

Coridan snorted. *It seems to me you have little choice.* He purposely allowed his gaze to wander to the vines binding her.

Ariel growled in warning. Coridan took that moment to grin down at her.

Answer my questions, seer and I will be happy to free you.

No!

He shrugged. *Well then it seems to me we are at an impasse.*

Goddess bless, Coridan, release me. Ariel knew she sounded desperate and she didn't care.

He moved closer to the bed, his gaze roaming over her ample curves mapping, memorizing. His gaze froze as he focused on the side of her neck where she'd been bitten the night before. *You bear my mark as I bear yours.* Coridan twisted just enough so Ariel could see the claw marks on his back.

Ariel's breath caught at the sight. *This still means nothing.* Her voice quaked.

Your stubbornness is showing, seer. Perhaps there is another way I can get the answers I seek.

Don't even think about it. Ariel glared at Coridan with every intention of making him back down but she couldn't stop a quiver of excitement from coursing through her body, racing through her veins. And from the look on his face, Coridan had noticed it too. Damn his warrior heart. *Coridan, listen to reason. You know my power's based on the fact that I have not joined with a man and experienced the energy binding process.*

You had better not have joined with another warrior. Menace laced his words causing Ariel to start. He sounded determined, possessive—all warrior.

You must listen to reason. She begged him, half hoping he ignored everything and claimed her. Her body writhed against the restraints, a womanly invitation if there ever was one.

Coridan's eyes flashed as if he fought his baser instincts. *Do not worry, seer, I will not join with you while we are dependent upon your powers.*

We will not join – ever. Ariel's voice quavered in her mind.

Never is a very long time, seer. Do not make vows you will not be able to keep. He shifted, his gaze releasing her.

You heard me. We will not join. Ariel realized her mistake too late. Her words smacked of challenge to a warrior's ears.

Coridan simply smiled and then moved to the end of the bed.

Ariel bit back a moan as she remembered her vision. His head had been buried in her pussy, feeding from her, devouring her. She tried to squeeze her legs together to ease the sudden ache but it was impossible with the vines binding her feet.

Her body recalled the pleasure and her skin flushed, heating to fever. Her nipples resembled ripe berries ready to be sucked into an eager mouth. Ariel gazed at Coridan from beneath heavy lids. She had never been so aroused in her life. It took all she had not to beg him to fuck her.

From the hungry expression on his face, Coridan had been following her thoughts. He dropped to his knees between her spread legs. His gaze left her face, gingerly traveling south over her gently rounded belly, sliding to her mons and then down to the moist crevice below.

You may say otherwise, seer, but your body calls to me. I hear it. My body recognizes yours as my other half. In the end, I will not be denied.

His vow made her tremble.

Coridan leaned forward until his mouth hovered mere inches from her cunt, his moist breath licking over her skin. Ariel couldn't seem to be able to think clearly. Her thighs trembled, her pussy wept and her desire rose to a level bordering madness.

Tell me what you desire, seer, and I shall give it to you and more.

Let me go.

Coridan blew hot air across her cunt and Ariel's back arched.

Tell me what you desire. Do not think to deny this…us.

I can--

Coridan's lips pressed against her bare pussy in a tender kiss. Ariel screamed inside her head.

Please…

You taste as I remember in my dream. My back still burns from the scrape of your nails. Do you recall what we were doing when you marked me, seer?

Please, Coridan.

Please what, seer?

Ariel's lungs heaved. *Please pleasure me…warrior.*

Coridan exhaled heavily as if he'd been holding his breath waiting for her response. His tongue swept along the slit of her entrance, enticing. He moaned. Ariel's sole focus zeroed in on the man between her thighs. Her body thrummed as his phallus-like tongue dipped beneath her folds, finding her clit, stabbing it once in promise before retreating.

He was trying to kill her. There could be no other explanation for this torture. Her mind splintered as he entered her, his stiffened tongue surging forward caressing her woman's barrier then swirling a second before repeating the process. Ariel's fingers dug into the tight vines holding her, gripping, hanging on as her body soared toward completion.

His tongue flicked over her clit again at the same time he reached for her breasts. This time Ariel did moan aloud. Luckily, Raoul and Santo were used to her strange noises and seemed to purposely ignore anything that sounded sexual since the day the professor had discovered them pleasuring her. Ariel thought back on the men's untutored groping. How could she have compared their actions to what Coridan was doing to her now?

She had been a fool.

Coridan speared her once more, a second before he sent a power surge bursting through her. Ariel cried out as her body convulsed in an orgasm. Her womb pulsed, raking her with pleasure and pain. It took several moments before Ariel returned to any semblance of normalcy. Once she had, she realized Coridan had waited, watching her every movement.

Ariel calmed and opened her eyes wider. As soon as he captured her gaze Coridan stuck out his tongue. Slowly, ever so slowly, he licked her from clit to anus, circling the back orifice a couple of times before retracing his path. Ariel shuddered at the erotic sight and came again.

I must go now, seer. I have to locate the rest of the professor's men so I can determine how best to plan our escape. Sleep well. Coridan gave her a knowing grin that told her without words he knew she'd be thinking about him tonight.

You can't leave me like this, she whimpered, pulling at the vines.

He moved up her body, his hard muscles gliding across her soft flesh and nearing her mouth.

What are you doing? Ariel hated the fact she sounded breathless in his mind.

What does it look like? He stopped, his brows furrowing.

No! We mustn't kiss. I mean… Ariel jerked her head away as panic filled her. If he kissed her she didn't think she'd be able to hold to her resolve and resist him. Worse yet, he'd know. He'd know she was lying about her feelings toward him, about the depth of their connection.

Why not? His voice sounded suspicious.

Because…I said so. She knew it wasn't a valid reason. She knew she sounded petulant but as seer she didn't need a reason. *Now untie me so we can go.*

No. Coridan paused, his questioning gaze straying to her lips a moment before he slid down her body resting once more between her thighs. *If they discover you're missing without us developing a plan, it may be more than difficult to escape this planet, it may be impossible.* He lazily stroked the fleshy area on the inside of her thigh with one hand while holding her gaze. *I will return as soon as I can. I must ensure the transport is fine but rest assured I would not leave you. I promise you this upon my honor as a warrior.*

If I remember correctly, you have no honor. The words were out of Ariel's proverbial mouth before she had a chance to think. She closed her eyes for a second before seeking his gaze once again.

Coridan's face hardened and his jaw locked. He stood and quickly stepped away from Ariel as if being near her caused physical pain. Ariel's stomach clenched along with something that felt suspiciously like her heart.

Remember, seer, you called me. His nostrils flared. *I will return.*

He left the same way he'd come, like a whisper on the wind. Ariel shivered at the loss. There was no sense berating herself but why had she said that to him? She hadn't meant it yet it had fallen from her lips like the rain tumbles from the sky. She'd hurt him, purposely so. Ariel had no doubt she'd hit her mark.

She sighed. Maybe it was for the best. This way they'd be able to focus on what was important, saving the Atlantean people—their people. There was no time for physical pleasures although her sated body told her otherwise.

It was for the best.

Unfortunately, the ache in her heart didn't agree.

* * * * *

Anger coiled around Coridan's chest, choking his breath until he had to stop his descent from the trees or risk falling. Ariel purposely reminded him of the shame he'd brought upon his family name to enrage him. Coridan was most certain. Yet had she not spoken the truth? His heart clenched, refusing to accept the emotions bombarding it. Had he screwed up so mightily that his own true-mate would want nothing to do with him?

Coridan didn't like the answer he received. He'd have to change her mind. Convince her he was not the man who'd so foolishly endangered Ares only days before. He had to let her see and experience his growth for herself.

His heart clenched. Did that growth include returning to a people who'd shunned him?

If it meant being near Ariel then the answer was yes.

However there would be no point of him stepping through the transport if he could not change her mind enough to get her to give him another chance. Not that he'd decided one way or the other whether to return. He may be a man without a people but he wasn't without a mate. The sooner she accepted that fact the better off they'd be.

In the darkness, he wound his way through the vegetation locating several guides along the way. As he neared the transport he felt the energy shift. No one had disturbed the portal—yet. But it wouldn't be long. The professor's men camped only five hundred yards or so away. The only reason they hadn't spotted the stones already was because of the dense trees growing around the clearing. In a day or less, they would find the secret Ariel fought so hard to protect and lay siege to his people.

His people... Despite Ariel's assurances, he wasn't convinced his people would welcome him back with open arms. If they did would Ariel go back to her rightful place as seer leaving him to walk the planet Zaron alone, unmated? Ariel was his true-mate, wasn't she? All signs pointed to yes but he'd been wrong before. Only an offer of an energy bind could confirm his suspicions.

Coridan's emotions stilled. He couldn't bear the thought of Ariel turning away. He would not allow his past deeds to cloud his judgment. He sent out an energy burst, scaring away the men nearest the location. In their minds they'd only see wild beasts and spirits from the beyond. That would only hold them at bay for a short while. He needed to get Ariel and escape but not before she answered his questions.

Coridan peered into the darkness. Whether they joined or not he had to know the truth. There could be no other way. He would not allow her to escape to Zaron without revealing her secrets to him. He could not. His heart, his very soul, depended on her answers. Coridan replayed her words. They had been said in haste, in fear.

His mind stilled. Had he gotten too close? When he'd stroked her body she'd been ready to comply with his every whim. He knew he could have pressed her to give herself to him and she would have accepted, eventually. She may not have wanted to but her urges and need were stronger. Ariel had wanted his cock as much as he'd longed to give it to her.

She was a complicated woman who would not be easily controlled, not that he intended to do so. Yet in order for them to mate successfully and raise enough energy to perform an energy bind she'd have to compromise. Yield her body and mind. Open for him so he could bury his shaft in her body and plant his seed.

The thought of Ariel carrying his child sobered Coridan for a moment. Tenderness and fierceness collided in a firestorm of emotion causing his body to tense. He rolled his shoulders until the muscles eased. He needn't worry about what didn't exist. She had not agreed to become his mate yet much less bear his children. First came convincing then he'd move on from there.

A grin split across Coridan's face as he imagined all the ways he could go about convincing Ariel to see things his way. As long as her body remained bound she was at his mercy. She had to listen to whatever he had to say. Ariel had no idea what power he could wield if necessary. And the more he considered the situation the more necessary he found it to be. The seer had met her match whether she realized it or not. Now all he had to do was convince her of the fact.

Chapter Six

ℰℴ

Coridan didn't return that night. Ariel waited as patiently as she could. She had no idea what he'd done for the rest of the night while her body had thrummed in need but she'd hoped he'd been just as uncomfortable.

He was an arrogant, self-centered bastard. Jac had it right when she'd called Ares the same thing. Ariel finally understood how Jac had felt. Being dominated was not something she had any experience with at all. Coridan had left her tied here all night. He could have easily untied her and they could have made their escape, but no, he wanted his questions answered. It didn't matter that he'd said he was doing surveillance. If she wasn't tired of all this crap she'd make him wait for the answers until he rotted.

Of course, that was not only illogical it was impossible. She'd give just about anything to wipe that smug smirk from his handsome face. Ariel fisted her hands. How that man could infuriate her and inflame her at the same time she did not know.

Birds chirped heralding morning. Confused, frustrated and horny, Ariel was in no mood to put up with the professor's crap today. If he gave her too much trouble she'd figure out a way to castrate him.

Excited voices reached her ears and her muscles tensed. Santo and Raoul threw the hide flap back and stepped inside the small hut, their faces ripe with excitement.

"They've found it." Their eyes gleamed and smiles split their faces.

"Release me! Release me now!" Ariel panicked.

"I'm afraid, *señorita*, we cannot do that."

She tugged at the vines willing them to break.

"Going somewhere, my dear?"

Ariel didn't have to glance up to know who stood in the doorway. The patronizingly droll voice could come from no one but the professor.

"No." She glared. "I'm not going anywhere. I'm tired of being confined."

"We've found your little secret." He smiled and stepped deeper into the room.

Ariel's stomach rolled and tears threatened to spill from her lids.

"It will be quite a discovery once you tell me what it's used for."

Ariel choked, strangling on her tumultuous emotions. The fool had no idea what he'd found. "I'll tell you nothing."

"Don't be like that. You know how much pleasure I derive from your pain." His thick lips separated slightly to expose yellowing teeth. "Perhaps my men could convince you to cooperate."

Santo and Raoul's expressions perked with interest.

Fear clutched Ariel's breast sending its needle-like tentacles burrowing into her flesh. Her mind raced to Coridan. He'd kill them all if they touched her, destroying himself in the process. She couldn't let that happen, not as long as she drew breath.

* * * * *

They have discovered the transport. Coridan's voice boomed in her mind.

I know. The professor is here now inquiring about its use. What do you want me to do?

70

Stay away. Ariel's voice sounded defeated.

He snorted. *You know I cannot do that. You are my tru –* He let the words die knowing she was not ready to hear them. She had yet to admit the truth. *I have managed to remove a stone from the transport. I did so after I realized they'd discovered the sacred crystals. I know not whether that will be enough to stop its use.*

Coridan, you bring your family name great honor and justice. The transport is disabled. You have done well.

He smiled even though she could not see him do so. Her words touched him deeply. *I will come and get you. It may take a while to dispatch so many men but I will, know this, seer.*

No! Stay in hiding. I may be able to convince the red-devil I know nothing.

Has he harmed you?

No...

Coridan heard the unspoken *not yet.* It hung in the air like the humidity. He couldn't force Ariel to tell him what the professor was doing. He growled in frustration. She was too stubborn for her own good. She would not be able to keep pain from him. If the professor touched her he'd know it instantly. Coridan knew himself well enough to know he wouldn't be able to hide in the jungle while Ariel was tortured. The warrior in him would fight to the death.

He may be labeled an outcast but some things were ingrained. Protecting the Atlantean women was one even if it turned out to be the seer. Coridan pressed deeper into the jungle, searching for a hiding place to conceal the stone he'd removed from the transport. He didn't want the stone to be too far from its rightful place but he couldn't afford for the precious item to be discovered.

Coridan found a hollowed-out tree stump three hundred yards from the transport and placed the stone inside, concealing it from prying eyes. He covered the area in leaves then carefully removed all trace of his presence. If only Ares were still here. He could use some assistance although it would kill him to ask for help from his mentor. He'd gladly accept the mighty warrior's skills now. Everything Coridan had learned about fighting had come from Ares.

The warrior had taken him under his wing and raised him as if he were part of his family. Coridan had repaid him with jealousy and deceit. If he ever laid eyes on the fierce, raven-haired warrior again he'd beg his forgiveness. For Ariel's sake, he would do anything…including give his life.

* * * * *

The vines binding Ariel's limbs were cut away. Santo and Raoul helped her up while the professor stood in the corner of the hut watching her. Ariel dressed in her sheer skirt and washed quickly, taking only a couple of sips of water before turning to face her enemy.

"You know my dear, I'm a very observant man." He exhaled heavily. "And I've noticed you don't seem to need food or water often. Why is that?"

"I know not what you speak of." Ariel's gaze darted around the room looking for a means to escape.

"I think you know exactly what I'm talking about." He took a step toward her.

Ariel forced energy to build then raised her palm ready to fire. At the last second Raoul yanked her hands painfully behind her back.

"Thank you, Raoul." The professor acknowledged the guide. "I do believe she was about to harm me. The question is how?"

"Let me go." Ariel struggled as Raoul and Santo bound her once again.

"I think we should take her down below where I can run some tests on her hands." The professor walked to the door glancing over his shoulder to make sure she followed before stepping beyond the threshold.

They reached the bottom in moments. Raoul and Santo practically dragged Ariel to the table in the center of the compound. Instead of tying both hands behind the table, they only tied one. The other they jerked forward palm up so the professor could examine it closer. He pulled out a magnifying glass and went over her palm slowly, carefully. Ariel knew he'd find nothing out of the ordinary for Atlantean power emanated from the inside out.

Rumsinger grabbed a swab, dipped it into some kind of chemical and then ran it over the length of her hand before returning it to a small plastic test tube. He sealed the tube and then placed it inside of a dark container. He then picked up a syringe and approached Ariel.

She swallowed hard. She didn't know what the substance was he'd used on her but her skin began to tingle. Her gaze caught the professor's. He gave her a lascivious grin.

"Keep still. I wouldn't want to harm you."

A small prick followed and within a minute he'd obtained some of her blood.

"Santo, bind her hands behind her back and bring her along. She needs to explain to us what it is we've found."

Ariel's heart hit her knees as they freed her hands and then yanked them behind her back once more. Raoul held her by one elbow while Santo held the other. They walked her down the familiar trail that led to the transport. Ariel didn't know where Coridan was but prayed he'd stay far away.

A gentle breeze caused the treetops to sway. She inhaled the sweet air, sensing the approach of rain. Animals chattered in the foliage, scurrying about, yet not venturing far from their homes. They sensed the storm too.

They reached the clearing within a few minutes. Ariel stared at the transport, dread filling the pit of her stomach. It looked so harmless when deactivated. The Atlantean people waited for her on the other side. Once Coridan returned the stone he'd conveniently pilfered they could take the last step in their own journey. The trick was to keep these men from reaching Zaron in the process.

The professor approached her with a scowl upon his face. "Don't even think about lying. I want to know what this is and I want to know now."

Ariel blanked her face. "I've never seen this before." She didn't see the blow coming but she felt it. Her lip split as the professor drew his hand back. The coppery taste of blood filled her mouth. The flavor was becoming familiar.

"One more time, what is this?"

Ariel struggled in Raoul's and Santo's arms. "I told you, I know nothing about the transport." The second the words left her mouth Ariel realized her mistake. How could she betray the Atlantean people like this? She'd failed.

The professor's mud brown eyes widened giving him an insect-like quality. "So this is a transport." He turned and surveyed the stones. "It doesn't look like it is working. How do you turn it on?"

Ariel clamped her lips shut. She'd said too much already. She would not help the slug anymore.

Rumsinger approached her. He stuck his hand out and gently stroked over her mouth, pressing just enough to cause pain in her split lip. "How do you turn it on?"

"You don't and I cannot activate it." A necessary lie. The wind around them picked up blowing loose debris.

"Who can?"

Ariel smiled, her lip smarting from the effort. "I believe you know her as Dr. Rachel Evans."

The professor's smug expression faded like the last wisps of sunlight as the storm approached heralding the rain. "Are you telling me you know Dr. Evans?"

"I know Rachel."

"Where in the hell is she?" His hands fisted at his sides and his ruddy complexion turned beet red in the growing dimness.

"Gone." It was a word that said nothing and everything.

The professor glanced over his shoulder at the transport, his demeanor shifting, growing uneasy. The first splattering of rain fell. The big drops bounced to the ground landing on fat outstretched leaves. Rumsinger looked to the sky, his expression darkening to match the weather. Rain began to fall in earnest. Wetness covered his glasses, running down his face in torrents.

"Let's return to camp. Nothing more can be done until this storm blows over."

The men promptly returned Ariel to Eros' hut. She didn't bother fighting. Raoul and Santo undressed her and bound her to the bed then stepped to the door. They threw the flap back in time to see lightning flash. The two men looked at each other and then hurried out the door. Ariel heard raised voices and then the basket lowering to the ground. Apparently, they'd left her up here alone until the rain stopped.

Rain came down in scathing sheets, thunder cracked, shaking the limbs supporting the tiny hut. The tree swayed under the storm's fury. Ariel tried to think of other things. She'd never liked living up in the trees which was why she'd chosen to have her hut on the ground. Another flash of lightning flared through the window. Ariel's heart thudded and her limbs trembled. She never liked storms. They reminded her too much of the destruction that occurred on Atlantis when she was a child.

Thunderous booms shook the walls. Ariel closed her eyes and concentrated on breathing. *Everything will be all right,* she told herself repeatedly. Drops slapped the leaves tossing them from side to side like a wave upon the ocean. She heard a dull splat as something dropped to the floor.

Ariel peeked out from beneath one lid and saw Coridan's loincloth lying on the floor. Her eyes flew open. Her gaze met a pair of large feet. She allowed it to roam up long tanned legs, over thick muscled thighs to…oh dear goddess.

Ariel's gaze jumped to Coridan's drenched face. Heat spread over her cheeks and down her body until every nerve stood at attention. His golden hair lay plastered to his soaked head. Coridan's expression remained unreadable as he sent an energy burst through his body to dry himself. Ariel couldn't seem to be able to catch her breath. Her lips prickled so she licked them.

Coridan approached the bed, his gaze hardening as he took in her swollen face. His nostrils flared, his muscles tensing as he reached out to touch her. Before his fingertips made contact he pulled back, afraid. *What did the red-devil do to you?*

Ariel tried to turn away but Coridan gently caught her chin before she could do so, tilting her face so he could get a good look at her. His fingers were tender as they traced her injuries. *I swear to the goddess, seer, I will kill the monster who has done this to you.*

No. She shook her head. *You mustn't.*

Why? He stroked her chin a moment longer then raised his hands a few inches above her face sending healing energy coursing through her body.

Tears stung the back of Ariel's eyes. *I must finish what he started.* And she wanted more than anything to keep him safe.

What does that mean?

One drop fell sliding down her cheek and onto the fur below. Coridan traced the wet trail with his fingertips reverently. *I have betrayed our people.* She dropped her gaze unable to look into his eyes, not wanting him to see her shame.

Seer, I know not of what you speak but I do know you could no more betray your people than stop the sun from rising.

Ariel glared at him. *You know nothing, warrior. I tell you I have.*

If I know nothing then tell me how this betrayal occurred.

She jerked her face from his touch unable to bear his tenderness. Her gaze pinned him. *I have told the professor what the stones he found are used for. He now knows it's a transport thanks to my betrayal.*

Coridan watched her. There was no judgment, no accusation, only understanding. *You made a mistake.* He shrugged. *It happens to us all.*

Did you not hear me?

I heard every word.

And?

And what, seer?

She groaned in frustration. *Are you not listening? I have betrayed our people. If you hadn't removed one of the stones the professor and his men would already be on Zaron.*

Coridan laughed but it held little humor. *You call that a betrayal? I attacked the only man who ever cared for me, Ares. The man who took me under his protection and showed me what being a warrior really meant, although from my actions you wouldn't think I'd learned a thing.*

I was jealous of Ares' accomplishments, his power – his mate. And because of my stupidity he almost died. I came this close, he squeezed his fingers together for emphasis, *to letting him drown. Do you have any idea what that feels like? I feel the pain every day. The shame burns in my heart, tainting my soul until nothing is left but blackness.*

Coridan began to pace. *Forgive my impertinence but you have no idea what betrayal is.* He threw his arms up in the air, his hands fisted tight as if cursing the heavens. *I live with my mistakes and will continue to do so for the rest of my life…alone.* He swung around to face her. *A slip of the tongue does not equal betrayal.*

Are you quite finished feeling sorry for yourself?

His eyes widened at her words. *Feeling sorry for myself...* Coridan approached the bed, his eyes sparking blue fire. *How dare you? I should untie you so I can turn you over my knee and spank that luscious bottom of yours.*

You wouldn't dare. Ariel knew better than to goad him but she couldn't stop herself. The thought of his hands upon her ass titillated her.

Oh wouldn't I? I suggest you don't tempt me further, seer. You might be surprised at just what I'd do given the opportunity.

That sounds like a threat. Ariel's temper flared, sparked easily by Coridan's domineering presence. His nearness was all the fuel needed to set her body aflame. Their combined pheromones drove her on making her feel reckless.

I don't need to threaten you, seer. He ran his finger down her side. Ariel shuddered. *You know I speak the truth.*

I know nothing of the sort.

Coridan smiled a very knowing, very masculine smile that told her she'd just crossed that invisible line. *Coridan, think before you do anything rash.*

His smile widened. *Rash? You will find, seer, that since the incident that got me exiled from your tribe I rarely do anything one would call rash.* Coridan dropped to his knees at the foot of the bed and spread her legs wider ignoring the tug of the vines as he insinuated himself between her thighs. His broad shoulders separated her, opening her pussy lips like a flower for him to view, scent or pluck, depending on his whim.

Ariel gasped as ripples of excitement spread over her skin, puckering her nipples, engorging her clit. And he hadn't even touched her — yet.

I will teach you not to tease a warrior, seer, especially a warrior intent on claiming you as mate.

Ariel opened her mouth to protest but closed it as Coridan's gaze seared her.

He lowered his head and inhaled. *Your nectar calls to m,e begging me to sip from it. Can you hear it, Ariel?*

No. Her answer came out throaty, breathless. Ariel's lungs labored. Her nipples quivered as need lanced through her. She wanted this man, wanted his touch and wanted his thick cock buried deep within her cunt.

He flicked his tongue, spearing her clit. Ariel cried out, her voice quickly drowned out by the storm's intensity.

You like that?

Her gaze locked with his. *You know I do.*

He smiled. *I just wanted to hear you say so.* Coridan dipped his head, flattening his tongue over her nether lips. Ariel's hips bucked and her eyes rolled back in her head, as she fought for control over the insatiable need, scoring her body.

We cannot join, she grit out between clenched teeth.

Coridan raised his head. *I told you I would not sheath myself in your channel. But...* He flicked his tongue.

Ariel gasped. *What?*

I'm curious...are your powers solely tied to your cunt and the energy bind process? His long fingers began to circle her anus spreading the moisture seeping from her pussy around the entrance.

Yes, both. She nodded. *What are you suggesting, warrior?* Ariel knew but couldn't bring herself to say the words. Her body tightened in anticipation. Her clit throbbed.

I could untie you and pleasure you in other ways...

Their gazes remained locked as they each considered Coridan's offer. He continued playing in her juices, spreading them over her sensitive flesh. Once his finger was thoroughly lubricated he circled the tight back muscle slowly working his way inside.

Ariel mewed as her body began to convulse. She came hard as a second finger joined the first. She was vaguely aware of being untied and turned onto her stomach. Her limbs were then retied spreading her legs further apart. Her awareness didn't snap back until she felt Coridan's weight upon her, pressing her into the soft furs.

What are you doing, warrior?

You know what I'm doing. Do not tell me you do not want this also. Your body weeps for mine. As if to prove a point he reached between their bodies and ran a finger through her wetness.

Ariel opened her mouth to deny him but a moan came out instead. He spoke the truth. She did want him, any way she could get him, and since they couldn't join or energy bind like a mated couple, this would have to do. Fear and anticipation raced over her.

"I thought so," he all but growled in her ear. Coridan stroked his cock, his hand brushing the back of her thighs. *We need more fluid.*

Ariel glanced over her shoulder. She could see thick pearl liquid bead up on the tip of his plum-sized head. Coridan scraped the liquid from his cock and began to massage it into her skin, around her anus and just inside her entry. Ariel shivered and then lifted her bottom slightly to allow him better access. His gaze caught hers once more.

Do you welcome me into your body, seer?

Yes…

Are you ready for me?

Ariel knew she was but wasn't about to admit as much. She'd imagined what joining with a warrior would be like for most of her life. This may not be exactly as she'd imagined but she looked forward to the experience. She didn't want to think about this being the only opportunity she'd ever get to join with Coridan but knew it must be so, the laws were clear.

That thought depressed her more than she cared to admit. Ariel's gaze dropped to Coridan's sensual mouth a second before she nodded her approval and laid her head on the bed.

* * * * *

Forbidden echoed in Coridan's mind as he rubbed the head of his cock around her back orifice attempting to get her sphincter muscle to relax. Ariel moaned as he pressed the tip inside, squeezing past the tight ring that squeezed, trying to keep him out. He'd never felt anything so tight and utterly delicious in his life. His body heated along with her own.

Energy arced between them dancing in the air almost as if a mating ceremony were taking place. He shuddered at the intensity, accepting the goddess' gift, knowing that without the energy bind the joining remained incomplete.

This wasn't how he'd planned to claim her but it was a start. He pushed deeper, burying another couple of inches into her virgin body. He groaned as Ariel's anus cradled him.

Muscles shook, his skin heated as he fought the urge to thrust. Ariel would be the death of him. *Are you all right, seer?*

I…uh…fine, she gasped.

Coridan flexed gently, loosening the muscle that held him. His cock slid in further. He was now half way. *Relax, seer. Breathe.* He encouraged, knowing he held his breath.

Do not tell me what to do, warrior, she commanded. *Shut up and fuck me.*

Ariel shifted, her hips grinding into the bed. Her rounded bottom tickled his abdomen and her well-developed thighs caressed his balls. *Forgive me, seer.* Coridan surged forward burying himself to the hilt inside her hot body. She shrieked.

For a few moments neither moved. Stars floated in front of Coridan's eyes at the exquisite torture of her untried body. His thrusts started out slow. He didn't want to damage her on her first time of joining. Ariel's fingers dug into the furs and her body's rhythm reached out to match his own.

Seer, do not. Coridan gripped her hips. *I fear I shall lose myself if you do.*

Ariel ground her mound into the bed. *I can't help it. The Atlantean heat is upon me. I need you to fuck me, Coridan…now!*

Coridan groaned as his resistance snapped like string before his eyes. He knew she was forbidden by Atlantean law but it wouldn't stop him from taking, claiming.

His grip on her hips tightened as he pulled back several inches and then thrust forward. Ariel screamed, her cries driving him as the storm raged on outside. Goddess bless, he was fucking her. The thought had him digging in, spearing her deep, staking his claim on her ripe virgin ass like the one he'd eventually make on her cunt.

His body shook as Coridan fucked her hard, plundered her body, demanding she accept his cock—accept him.

* * * * *

Ariel moaned as her body stretched to accommodate his massive size. She felt full, overflowing. Heat infused her. She closed her eyes as energy surrounded them sparking like lightning in the air. This wasn't possible. There'd been no ceremony, no raising of energy, yet that is exactly what appeared to be happening. They hadn't performed the energy bind or joined as woman and warrior. Coridan drove into her, demanding, dominating—scattering Ariel's thoughts to the wind.

She bit down on her lip as he rolled his hips. Coridan reached around her until his questing fingers found her engorged clit. He squeezed and pulled while angling her hips for deeper penetration.

She gave a keening cry like a panther whose mate had just pinned her to the ground with its barbed cock. She wanted to scratch and bite him, resist his frenzied mating, but she couldn't. This was more than pleasure, more than mutual attraction. This was joining in its most primitive form.

Ariel came at the same time Coridan pumped his hot semen into her body. His cock pulsed, filling her to the brim with his fluids. Moments later he collapsed onto her back. The weight of his body felt good. It felt right.

Ariel nuzzled deeper into the furs. Her ass stung a little but the pain was easily overpowered by the overwhelming sensation of pleasure coursing through her body. Coridan slipped from her anus removing his weight from her back. Instantly she felt empty, alone. He lay on the bed beside her stroking her damp hair away from her face.

Forgive me, seer. He shook. *I know by law that shouldn't have occurred.*

Ariel laughed. *I'm fine, warrior.*

He seemed to relax a bit. *I meant not to crush you.*

You didn't. Ariel smiled.

Good, I want my mate to be happy.

Ariel froze and her smile faded. She couldn't seem to speak. He'd felt it too. Goddess bless, had he just called her his mate? His earlier claim slammed back into her consciousness. She couldn't take a mate. She'd told him that.

Seer?

I am no man's mate, especially a warrior. 'Tis forbidden.

He tensed.

Ariel turned to face him. *I've told you I can take no mate.*

Coridan's face hardened. *I kno,w yet you allowed me into your body willingly.*

So? Heat infused Ariel's face. *We did not perform an energy bind or proper joining. My pussy is still untouched.*

His muscles tensed. *I am the only warrior who has ever been allowed to enter or touch you—anywhere.* He paused as if grappling with his temper. *I am the first—and last.*

Ariel swallowed past the lump forming in her throat. *I cannot mate.*

You just did. I shall not argue the semantics, he bellowed in her head. *Does my seed not fill your body?*

Yes but —

I may not follow all our laws, but I recognize when I join with a true-mate.

No! I have not offered to perform the energy bind or a proper joining and you know it. You have seen no gold come from my body. That should be all the proof you need.

Coridan stood. He quickly untied her and flipped her onto her back before returning the vines to the stakes at the ends of the bed. *I am your true-mate despite the lack of gold in your breath. You know it and now I know it. 'Tis beyond refute. The sooner you accept the fact, the better off we'll be.*

And what of my power? Our people?

I told you, I have no people. As for your power I notice no other change in you. Without the energy bind you remain the same. Coridan padded across the floor and picked up his wet loincloth. He slipped the material on, leaving a puddle behind. Once dressed, he turned back to Ariel. *You have a choice to make, seer, accept me as I am or leave this place and never return.*

Ariel watched in disbelief as he walked to the window leaving footprints behind on the wooden floor and then disappeared without looking back. She pulled against the ties as angry tears fell from her eyes. She was not his mate. Could not be.

She was no man's mate. Goddess blessing be damned. Ariel exhaled and gold filled the air.

Chapter Seven

ဆ

The rain stopped several hours later. Raoul and Santo returned to the hut to retrieve her. Apparently, the professor wasn't finished. They'd made it to the door when Raoul shouted something in his native language. Ariel and Santo swung around in time to see Raoul pointing to the floor, his eyes the size of saucers.

Comprehension struck Ariel like a blow, her gaze beaded to the floor. Coridan's footprints led to the window before disappearing. She had to do something and fast. She reached for Raoul's mind but before she could act, Santo pulled at the vines binding her hands. His expression had grown cold, jealous. He flipped back the hide covering the door and shouted to the professor below.

As if in a dream, Ariel listened to the basket creak as it rose in the electrified air nearing the branch that would lead the red-devil to Eros' hut. Her heart sank and she realized there would be no more lying. She'd be lucky if the professor didn't kill her immediately. At least she'd gotten to experience a taste of what joining with a true-mate could be like before she left this primitive world to bond with the goddess.

Rumsinger burst into the room, anticipation and excitement oozing from his oily pores. "So there's no one left, eh? I suppose you want me to believe those footprints appeared like magic."

"Believe whatever you want." Ariel didn't bother hiding her contempt. The game had ended.

The professor smiled and rubbed his hands together like a praying mantis as he moved closer to examine the prints. "Definitely male and from the looks of these prints he's large, very large." He leered at Ariel. His thoughts had already taken a turn for the worse. He imagined himself dominating Coridan, breaking his spirit before leading him back to civilization. His thoughts were vile, oozing venom, like the man.

Ariel laughed. "You will not capture him."

Rumsinger turned back and glared at Ariel. "We'll see, my dear. After all we have the perfect bait." He allowed his gaze to wander over her body, pausing at her pussy before continuing to her ample breasts. "I think whoever he is he will come to your rescue once he realizes my men are taking advantage of your…" he quirked a bushy brow, "charms."

"You bastard!" Ariel pulled against Santo's grip to no avail.

Rumsinger glanced out the window. "Nightfall nears. It's too late to go back to the transport." He pointed at the fur bed. "Tie the slut to the bed, Santo. Tomorrow we go hunting."

Rumsinger stepped away from the prints, his eyes gleaming wickedly in the fading light. Ariel watched as hatred replaced anticipation. He smiled once more at her. "You do realize you are no longer of use to me, don't you?" He laughed then an evil cackle that sent shivers darting along her spine.

She was going to die and so was Coridan if she didn't warn him.

* * * * *

Ariel could hear snoring coming from just outside the hut door. One of the guards was now fast asleep. She didn't think Coridan would risk returning tonight. He'd been too angry with her when he'd left. Ariel ignored the sudden pain in her chest. Never in her life had she felt guilt and she wouldn't start now.

Coridan, can you hear me?

Nothing.

Coridan, this is Ariel.

Nothing.

Coridan, answer me now and stop this foolish game.

She thought she heard a slight chuckle but couldn't be sure. *Coridan, you must listen. The professor has seen your tracks. He knows you are here somewhere. It's only a matter of time before he finds you.*

So that's why there has been so many guides scouring the jungle. Pure male amusement colored his voice.

Goddess bless. Stop acting the fool. Take the stone, get to the transport and leave this place at once. You are in danger. Ariel took a deep breath, hoping to get a grip on her frustration and at the same time mask her fear.

No! I am not afraid of these mortals. I am a warrior, remember?

She groaned. *I know what you are but you must listen. Tomorrow the professor plans to trap you.*

And just how does he plan to do that? He sounded smug, unconcerned.

By using me as bait. Ariel knew the implications had struck home. Coridan stopped speaking and may very well have stopped breathing. It was a moment before he responded.

What does he plan to do? he asked, all smugness gone.

Ariel debated whether to tell him the truth. He couldn't read her if she did not allow it, at least she didn't think he could.

Do not think to lie to me, mate. You forget it is not possible after the semi-joining.

Ariel growled and slammed her fist down on the bed, pulling the vines as far as they would go. *There was no such thing as a semi-joining.* Damn his tanned hide.

Tell me! The voice was an outright command leaving little room for disagreement.

His tone girded Ariel, but she complied. *He plans to turn me over to his men.*

Why?

He knows my cries as they rape me will draw you out from hiding.

Again there was silence.

You know I cannot allow his men to touch you. His tone was soft, deadly. *I will kill every last one of them if need be. You are mine.*

The stark possession in his voice shattered the wall surrounding Ariel's heart. She did not want him to die for her. She did not want him to die, period. *You cannot come here no matter what you sense is occurring. I am strong. I will survive.* The lie slipped from her lips before she could stop it. She had to protect him. *Please, Coridan, return the stone to the transport and leave this place. Go to our people, warn them. Do this for me — for us.*

His gravelly voice cracked as he spoke. *You know I cannot do that.*

* * * * *

Dawn came swiftly after another sleepless night. Ariel was wide-awake when Raoul and Santo entered the hut to retrieve her. Their brown gazes wandered lustfully over her body like hungry caiman that had just spotted their morning meal. She was no longer off limits and they knew it.

They left Eros' hut after Ariel dressed and consumed fruit and water. Light dappled through the leaves casting shadows upon the ground below. The day, already stifling, would only get hotter. Sweat dripped down Ariel's back, the droplets clinging to her butt-cheeks. Despite the fact she'd healed herself, her anus still prickled with sensation from Coridan's intrusion. Raoul and Santo glared at her, their gazes no longer holding any compassion. They would take their turn with her body just like the others. Ariel had no doubt the two men would be first in line.

By the time the basket reached the jungle floor a small crowd of native men had gathered around the professor. Their gazes locked on Ariel at the same time that their voices rose with anticipation.

The professor stepped away from the crowd and approached her. His gaze strayed to the jungle repeatedly before finally settling upon her. "The men are looking forward to this, my dear. You should be flattered."

Ariel laughed. "I should be flattered that your men look forward to raping me. Hmm…you are a strange people."

He grinned lasciviously. "Of course, if your friend shows up we'll have to delay the day's entertainments."

"I'd hate to ruin your fun." Ariel straightened to her full height dwarfing the professor. "My friend is well aware this is a trap. He will not appear."

"All the more pity for you." Rumsinger shrugged then turned away from her to address his men. "Gentlemen, quiet please." The professor held up his hands and the crowd hushed. "We're going to do this in an organized manner. Who would like to be first?"

The men's voices rose as they argued amongst themselves. Pushing and shoving ensued. A couple of the natives stepped forward at the same time a deep, masculine voice boomed from the tree line. "I will be first—and last."

Ariel's heart dropped and sang at the same time. She didn't know it was possible to be elated and furious at once but that was exactly how she felt. She knew that voice without looking. She glanced in the direction the voice had come and sure enough, Coridan stood with his arms crossed over his wide chest, a mischievous grin planted on his face. The smile in no way reached his aqua eyes which were at this moment glacial in appearance.

He looked magnificent, an angry god-like warrior in his prime who was about to smite these men. Ariel glared at Coridan but he'd yet to spare her a glance. She swore under her breath. If the professor didn't kill him, she would.

* * * * *

Coridan surveyed the clearing. He considered the group and the easiest way to extract Ariel from their clutches. There were approximately fifteen men standing in what once had been the tribal gathering place. Instead of a communal meal, they were contemplating a crime against an Atlantean woman. Coridan's muscles flexed. That he could not allow.

Since he was the only warrior left he would serve as judge and jury for the Atlantean people. His gaze locked onto the red-haired devil, the monster behind these actions. It would be so easy to kill him. One strong blast of energy and his heart would no longer beat in his chest…if he had a heart. Coridan had his doubts.

One of the guides raised a rifle and pointed it in Coridan's direction. Before the man could blink, a blast hit him in the throat knocking him off his feet stunning him for at least a few days. The fight had begun. Coridan fired with both hands into the crowd downing two more men. Angry shouts rang out as the men scattered. The professor stood for a few seconds gaping like a fool.

Guns fired missing Coridan by inches. He shot back with energy bursts.

"Get to the transport," the professor shouted over the chaos. The guides leapt like dogs answering their master's call.

Several men darted into the jungle before Coridan could fire off a shot to stop them. Some of the men dared to attack him directly. They ran toward Coridan with fists flaying. If the situation had not been so serious he would have laughed. He easily knocked them to the ground as he met them halfway. His body rolled forward, immediately coming to his feet a couple yards from Ariel. She strained against her bonds, her face a mask of horror.

The professor shouted one final order before disappearing into the thick underbrush. "Kill her!"

One man drew out a knife, its blade jagged and angry and approached Ariel. Coridan dove for the man tackling him around the knees. The blade came down slicing into his shoulder taking a deep bite from his flesh. Ariel screamed. Coridan didn't stop to think about the wound. He twisted around easily and with a flick of his wrist rendered the man unconscious. Two men remained in the compound until they caught a glimpse of their *compadre's* limp body.

Coridan's gaze raked over them letting them know without words exactly what he'd do to them if they challenged him. He held up the unconscious man beneath him for emphasis and then sent an energy burst through his own body healing himself instantly. The guides' eyes widened a second before they dropped their weapons and raced into the jungle. Coridan threw his head back and roared to the heavens before rising to his feet. He grabbed the knife the man had threatened Ariel with and slipped it in the waistband of his loincloth.

Ariel's limbs trembled and her normally golden face had paled. *You are insane, warrior. You could have been killed.* Thick emotion choked her words.

Coridan smiled as he covered the short distance separating them. *You were worried about me.*

Don't let it go to your head. Ariel's gaze narrowed. *I would have worried about anyone who'd been in your position.* She snorted. *But then again, most Atlanteans wouldn't have been stupid enough to pull a stunt like that.*

Coridan arched a brow. He kept his expression purposely blank. He would not let her see just how worried he'd been when those two men first approached her. He unsheathed the knife and quickly sliced through the vines binding her limbs.

Come, we must get away from this place. The professor will not stay away for long, once he realizes we have not followed. He reached out and slipped his hand around her wrist before Ariel had a chance to answer and began dragging her to the opposite side of the compound.

Aren't we going to try to get to the transport?

No. The professor's orders were clear. His men will be guarding it like angry vipers. Coridan strode into the jungle. His long legs covering distance easily. Ariel had to jog to keep up.

What are we going to do? She tried to tug her hand free but he refused to release her.

Coridan glanced back over his shoulder before looking ahead once more. *We are going to regroup for a day or so. Come up with a plan of attack so that when we make our way to the transport we'll be able to exit this planet and never come back.* His jaw clenched at the thought of leaving.

This planet had been all he'd ever known. He hadn't been born when his parents left Zaron to settle here. Would he like his home planet? Would the Atlantean people accept him or would he be shunned again?

The thought of returning to Earth to die alone was almost beyond his comprehension. It was possible the unwanted citizens of Atlantis were now transported off Zaron and placed upon another distant planet. Both were very real possibilities. Fear and uncertainty beat at his brow, grabbing the muscles of his abdomen and knotting them into a tight fist.

Coridan weaved his way through the jungle working them deeper into the thick vegetation. Here they would be able to rest, gather food and remain relatively safe until the time came to battle once more. He spotted what he'd been searching for amongst the foliage, striding toward a dense crop of trees.

At first glance, they'd seemed impenetrable, but once he made it through the thick limbs, he found himself standing in a tiny twenty-foot-by-twenty-foot clearing. The ground lay covered in lush grass, soft enough to form a comfortable bed.

Stay here. Coridan released Ariel's wrist. She rubbed it as if his touch had left an impression on her skin. He took in her actions, his eyes roaming over her body, checking for any injuries. *I will return in a few moments with food and water. We can even build a pit fire because it will be impossible to locate in the dense growth.* He didn't give Ariel a chance to respond before he once more slipped through an invisible opening.

* * * * *

Ariel watched his wide back disappear. Her heart thudded rapidly in her chest and she slowly turned examining their temporary home. Tall trees surrounded the area, forming a natural canopy should the weather decide to turn inclement. The lower vegetation circled the area creating a natural wall that neither side could see through. She slipped off her skirt then sat before she collapsed. Her legs had been trembling ever since Coridan had battled the professor's men.

Fear had gripped Ariel with its razor sharp talons ripping at pieces of her soul with each crack of gunfire. It was a miracle they had survived. She'd been so frightened for Coridan's welfare that it hadn't occurred to her that she could have been killed. At the time of the altercation she would have gladly given her life to save his. Luckily it hadn't come down to that in the end.

She was still amazed at the power Coridan had wielded. He fought like ten warriors, firing energy bursts at several different opponents all the while watching what happened to her. After the battle had ended he still managed to heal himself.

Ariel shook her head. She'd truly misjudged his power. He had kept much hidden from the tribe, from her. The thought excited and scared her. Was her power up to the challenge of Coridan's or had she just encountered a warrior far beyond her psychic abilities as a seer?

Ariel wasn't sure. Many questions remained unanswered. However, before anything could be decided she needed to make one thing perfectly clear. She was not any man's mate. As soon as Coridan returned, she'd let him know.

Ariel closed her eyes and lay back onto the soft grass. The green blades tickled her shoulders, stroking her back, cupping her firm ass like loving hands. Her mind easily slipped back into the night before as she remembered Coridan's caresses. How he'd pleasured her body, filling her with his rigid cock. She groaned, her hand moving of its own volition to her nipples.

Ariel stroked herself feeling the familiar warmth rise in her body. She needed to release some of the tension caused by the day's events. She pictured Coridan's muscular form, imagined his weight pressing down upon her.

Their semi-joining had given her some relief from the symptoms of Atlantean heat but she was wise enough to know the feeling was only temporary. Soon the heat would return with a vengeance. She had to reach release before Coridan returned. Without her firm grip on her control Ariel knew she'd be unable to resist his advances. Ariel didn't want to consider what would happen if he sank his cock into her scalding pussy.

Ariel's clit twitched and her channel flooded at the thought of Coridan's cock filling her woman's center, planting his seed deep within her belly until she grew ripe with his child. Her eyes flew open as the last thought flitted through her mind. She waited for a negative reaction but it never came. Her heart fluttered but in a good way. She was shocked to find that the thought of having Coridan's babe didn't disturb her in the least.

That fact scared her senseless. She should be disturbed. She should be fighting their attraction with every fiber of her being but she wasn't. Instead, Ariel clamored for his touch, longed for him to stroke the fire burning within her, wanted him to claim her. Her breath caught as her nipples engorged. She pulled at the tender flesh, pinching the peaks between her thumb and forefinger.

Ariel moaned as wetness trickled between her legs giving the humid air a musky odor. She bit her lip as she released one nipple and then stroked her hand over her abdomen until she reached the area causing her so much discomfort. Her fingers splayed over her mons, caressing her lower lips until they took on a healthy pout beneath her questing fingertips.

Ariel's hips moved with the swipe of her hands. She spread her petals seeking the tiny nub hidden beneath. The first scrape of her nails had her seeing rainbows. She bit back a cry as she circled the sensitive flesh gently squeezing it between her fingertips. Her body shook, balancing on the precipice of release.

Chapter Eight

** හ**

Coridan scented Ariel's musk the second he neared the hidden clearing, the same glorious aroma that had drawn him to her in the first place. He'd been so preoccupied with gathering supplies that he hadn't noticed sooner. Her gentle moans now reached his ears, the sound burning into his senses, transforming him from sated to ravenous in seconds.

He pushed through the brush until he could see her. Ariel writhed on the ground, one hand pulling at her stabbing nipples while the other lay buried between her spread thighs, slick from her womanly juices. Her full lips parted slightly as she drew in a heated breath.

Coridan groaned at the sight. His cock immediately leapt to attention, stretching the material of his loincloth until it became painful to remain clothed. He stepped into the clearing, dropping the fruit and gourds filled with water on the ground. In one swift movement he'd untied his loincloth and let it slip to the ground. His cock sprang free, bowing slightly from its massive size.

His nostrils flared as he inhaled her womanly scent, the aroma sweet enough to almost cause him to spill his seed before he had a chance to touch her. She hadn't noticed him yet. Not that he was surprised. Her eyes remained closed, her face a mask of sexual ecstasy. Unable to control his pleasure, he growled.

Ariel's eyes flew open, pinning him in place. *We cannot.* She murmured in his mind all the while her hands continued to torture her flesh.

Why do you punish yourself — and me?

I — ahhh...

Coridan's body shook as she cried out in rapture, her orgasm crashing over her goddess-like body. He closed his eyes, fighting for what little control he could muster. His mate did not want to join with him. Ariel was killing him one release at a time and she did not care. The last thought hurt the most. He opened his eyes and gazed down upon her. A healthy pink blush covered Ariel's lush body, a gentle reminder of her recent orgasm. Coridan willed himself to back away but his feet would not obey.

Ariel's gaze traveled from his face, over his chest, before landing upon his painful erection. She licked her lips as she rose to her knees before him, tossing her long blonde hair over her shoulder. Coridan tried to swallow but all the moisture had abandoned his mouth. Tentatively she reached out, her hand encircling his shaft. Coridan bit down hard enough to make his jaw ache. If this was another ploy to manipulate him she'd be sorry.

Her grip tightened on his cock and she had his full attention. Ariel smiled as she slowly stroked up his length and back down, while her free hand reached beneath him to cup his sac. Coridan's muscles locked and his lungs refused to allow air inside. His body swayed as she released his sac to clasp his shaft with both hands. He swore under his breath. If he got any harder he'd explode. Ariel's hands moved in tandem up and down while adding a slight twist of her wrist.

He leaned forward in an attempt to capture her mouth. She pulled away.

If you try kissing me in order to bring about an energy bind, I'll be forced to stop.

You are impossible.

She smiled. Her movements continued until a pearl of liquid appeared at the eye of his cock. Ariel paused a second before bringing her finger up to swipe the seed away. Instead of wiping it on the grass, she brought her finger to her lips and sucked on his essence. Mewing sounds escaped from her throat as she relished his taste. Coridan groaned at the same time his knees nearly gave out.

She hadn't released his cock and he prayed she never did. Ariel smiled, drawing her hand away from her mouth. The fingers around his shaft tightened as she slowly lowered her head. Coridan held his breath, waiting. The second her lips surrounded his crown it was all over. He'd promise her anything, even that he would leave her alone once they reached Zaron if that was what she wished. Ariel slipped more of his cock into her hot, velvet mouth and began the delicious up and down movement she'd done only moments ago with her hands.

Coridan's fingers sank into her hair, grasping the soft tendrils as she pleasured him as no one ever had. His body tensed and his hips bucked against her downward movements, extending the sweet torture. She may refute it but with each swipe of her tongue Ariel bound herself to him a little more.

Soon she wouldn't be able to resist his pull. Her body already trembled with need. He could sense her hunger, feel it goading his own. Soon her resistance would be gone and he'd be there waiting.

Coridan smiled as his sac drew up next to his body. Within seconds he was coming. He bellowed as his seed shot out, draining him of energy. Ariel drank deep, the column of her throat working as she lapped up every drop of his essence before releasing his cock. They fell back onto the ground, their lungs heaving with the effort. Coridan tucked Ariel close, her body tensing for a moment before she relaxed into his embrace.

* * * * *

Ariel curled up into Coridan's warmth, her sated body limp from her earlier release. Her lips still tingled from taking his impressive cock into her mouth and she could still taste his salty essence. Her hunger for him was growing no matter her attempts to stave it off. Soon she'd be unable to resist Coridan's advances even though he'd made no effort to force himself upon her. In fact, she no longer worried about her warrior, only herself.

She'd wanted his kiss to seal their fate. She'd wanted to feel his lips upon hers as they performed the energy bind. The intimacy of that simple act would have been too much. Ariel knew she couldn't handle the emotions that would ultimately come with it.

As it was her people's welfare had begun to take second place in her heart and the realization scared her to death. Coridan claimed to have no people yet he offered himself to her at every turn. Was it truly possible for a seer to have a true-mate? Not according to Atlantean law. Moreover, what might happen to her power if they performed the energy bind?

She hadn't examined how she felt since their escape from the professor. In doing so now she couldn't detect any difference. Was it possible for her to join with Coridan and keep her magic? Of all the tales that had been passed down through the ages, she'd never heard of this being so but...what if?

Ariel's hand brushed along Coridan's chest, tracing the hills and valleys which made up his ribcage before finally settling on his firm abdomen. Her fingers followed the rise and fall of his chest with each breath he took. Coridan's skin remained hot beneath her touch, as heated as her own. It was as if the Atlantean heat had transferred over and engulfed them both. Ariel shivered at the thought. If Coridan had somehow caught Atlantean heat he'd be uncontrollable.

With you, seer, I'm always in heat. His voice held a teasing lilt.

Ariel closed her eyes and willed herself to feel nothing for the man beside her. They needed rest if they were to do battle tomorrow. Later they'd figure out a plan of attack that would allow them to reach the transport unharmed.

She hoped.

* * * * *

"What do you mean you can't find them?" The professor turned to face Santo and Raoul. The men cowered beneath his gaze moving out of striking range.

"*Señor* professor, we have searched everywhere. It's as if they've disappeared."

Rumsinger growled. "The guards are still positioned at the transport, correct?"

Raoul shifted nervously. "*Si, señor.* They are exactly where you ordered them to be."

"Good. Then they're still here somewhere." Rumsinger locked the men into his gaze, daring Raoul and Santo to move. His foul mood stretched out ensnarling them. "I suggest you search again. I'm not a man who appreciates disappointment." He stepped closer, menacing. "If you disappoint me again…" He smiled. "I'll kill you both."

Raoul and Santo's eyes widened as fear gripped their features, twisting their semi-handsome faces into macabre masks. "*Si, señor.* Right away, señor. You can count on us."

The professor laughed. "Your lives depend on it."

The men scurried into the jungle. The professor watched until he could no longer see the whites of their shirts. "Damn incompetent bastards," he grumbled. "I'm going to have to do everything myself."

Rumsinger strolled into the jungle leaving the security of his hut behind. The light in the afternoon sky had begun to fade leaving much of the brush in deep shadow. A slight breeze ruffled the treetops but didn't quite make it down to ground level. The place was like hell but with humidity.

He tapped the pistol strapped to his hip for reassurance before reaching into his pocket to retrieve a flashlight. Rumsinger shined the beam on the trail ahead. Iguanas slithered off the path, their clawed feet taking them up the side of the trees with no effort. The professor snorted, paying little or no attention to the slinking reptiles, his mind too busy working out a plan to get the stones and crystals loaded and back to New York for further study.

The seer had called the stone contraption a transport. He was certain that's what she'd said. Which meant that despite the fact it didn't look like it, this object was some kind of transportation device. A thrill raced up Rumsinger's spine as he reached the clearing that contained the transport. Visions of space and time-travel flashed in his mind. There was no telling where you'd end up when you stepped through the device. If the bitch told the truth, he'd just made the discovery of a lifetime.

Nobel Prize, here I come.

Rumsinger covered the small distance remaining until he could clearly gaze upon the stone symbols that made up the transport. Guards stood at the ready nearby. He crushed the vegetation growing around the device as he paced back and forth examining the object. The stones and crystals all seemed in order yet it obviously didn't work.

His beam followed the etchings around the circle as he carefully pieced them together in his mind. He reached the bottom of the transport a few minutes later. Rumsinger stared at the stones and frowned before stepping closer. Although it had been made to appear otherwise, one of the stones was missing.

"Damn it," he spat out to no one in particular. "There's something wrong with this thing."

The men looked at each other.

"Have any of you moved anything?"

Negative replies echoed in the clearing.

"How many stones were there?"

"Don't know, *señor*."

Rumsinger turned on them, his thoughts murderous. "One of you has to have written the information down."

A small man stepped forward with a piece of paper all but tossing it into the professor's hands. Rumsinger peered over the notes pausing long enough to look up at the device and then back down at the paper.

"There's supposed to be thirteen stones here. I only count twelve."

His breath came in angry gasps as he glared at the men around him. "I won't be mad, just tell me which one of you moved a stone."

Hushed whispers spread in rapid fire throughout the group.

"No one has touched a thing, *el professor*."

"Damn it all to hell!" Rumsinger stilled as quickly as he'd exploded. The male must have taken the missing fragment. No wonder the thing wasn't working, it couldn't as was. He had to find the male of the tribe. The woman was of no use to him. She'd been nothing but trouble since her initial capture. Women truly were filthy creatures.

Rumsinger turned to the guards who looked uneasy. "Has anyone been here since I sent you to stand guard?"

The men stepped back. "No *señor*, you are the first person we have seen."

The professor snorted. Surrounded by incompetence, Rumsinger knew there was nothing he could do to change the situation. He shook his head and then turned back to the trail he'd just traversed. He strolled back through the jungle replaying the earlier battle scene in his mind. The missing piece was not small and the male hadn't been wearing enough clothing to conceal anything, which meant he'd hidden the missing stone somewhere nearby.

Rumsinger swung his light around looking for any place obvious that could be used for hiding an object of that size. Nothing jumped out at him. A bird squawked above him as if the light had disturbed its beauty rest. The animal was lucky he didn't kill it. Given the mood he was in it wouldn't take much to kill man or beast.

Rumsinger picked up a nearby branch and threw it blindly at the creature. Within a matter of seconds he'd lost everything, the woman, the warrior and the stone needed to operate the transport. Without the latter he had nothing to show the world. Nothing to proclaim for his superior intelligence. Nothing to garner the respect he ultimately deserved.

Tomorrow he'd order the men to fan out and begin the search for the missing stone. He had to find it before the giant Tarzan-looking man did or all would be lost. Rumsinger gritted his teeth. He'd sacrificed too much on this bloody trip for all to be lost now. He'd kill every individual if necessary. No one was going to keep his treasure from him.

No one.

* * * * *

Ariel awoke to the sound of Coridan tossing logs onto a fire. She blinked but wasn't initially able to see the flames due to the depth of the pit he'd dug. Fruit had been placed next to the fire as Coridan prepared what looked to be a feast for them. Ariel stood and walked the small distance separating them.

Can I help?

He glanced up at her and smiled, causing Ariel's heart to do a curious little flip in her chest. *I believe all is in order. Sit. It'll be ready to eat in a moment.*

Ariel did as she was told making herself comfortable on the soft grass. *Have you been awake long?*

Long enough. He didn't look up from the task at hand, just continued to work slicing through the papaya and mango fruit and removing any seeds. Once finished Coridan turned to face her, his sticky hands extended, offering her the bounty he'd reaped from the jungle.

Ariel nodded her thanks before accepting a big slice of mango. She took a bite, the juices exploding down her chin. She wiped the sticky evidence away and continued to eat. Coridan watched her for many moments until she grew uneasy under his gaze. She cleared her throat and stared back. Then and only then did he pick up a piece of fruit for himself and take a bite.

The rest of the meal was eaten in companionable silence. They finished most of the fruit saving a few bananas for the morning meal. They washed down the delicious bounty with the water he'd stored in the gourds. Coridan then raised his hands above her before she could stop him sending a cleansing energy burst through her body. The intimacy of the act did not go unnoticed.

His aqua eyes stared at her lovingly. Ariel wondered if he knew how much his eyes gave away. Probably not. She smiled to herself. She didn't want to think about how that look made her feel. It was too…unnerving. Ariel thought it best to strike up a conversation, anything to take her mind off the man.

So how are we going to get to the transport without encountering the professor's men?

Coridan's gaze narrowed turning him instantly back into the warrior she knew…and loved? *We aren't. There is no way we can approach the transport without encountering a battle.*

Ariel tried to keep her voice calm as she spoke to him but worry crept in like a thief in the night. *Then what are we going to do?*

We're going to fight. Well, I'm going to fight. You are going to make your way to the transport with the missing stone and escape. I'll hold his men back for as long as I can.

He wasn't coming. Ariel's mind rebelled. *No!*

No?

No! That plan is not acceptable to me.

Coridan crossed his arms over his muscled chest. *Why not?* he asked, his brow arching in what could only be male incredulity.

The only way I plan to leave this planet is together. Otherwise, 'tis impossible.

That is not true, seer, and you know it. He swiped a hand through the air. *You are being foolish.*

Foolish?

Yes! You're acting like a...like a woman. He released a bent-up breath.

Ariel's eyes narrowed on him and her lips thinned. *You may not have noticed,* her voice hissed in their heads as she glanced down over her body for emphasis, *but I am a woman!*

Coridan glared back at her, hot and male. His gaze lazily caressed her bare skin leaving molten heat behind. *I'm well aware of your gender, seer.* He swallowed hard. *In fact, there hasn't been a second I've been able to forget it. My body makes me painfully aware of our differences every second I'm in your presence. The question is, how long can I go before my baser instincts get the best of me?*

Despite his harsh tone the threat in his words thrilled her, delighting Ariel to her toes. Coridan turned away and poked the fire, stirring the embers. Ariel exhaled, filling the air with shimmering gold. Her eyes widened, her gaze shooting to the warrior's broad back. Ariel fanned the air in front of her face madly praying the gold dispersed quickly. Coridan turned back to her, his gaze narrowing as he took in her frantic movements.

In one breath she could have unwittingly given him his answer.

Chapter Nine

ഇ

What are you doing?

Nothing. Ariel stirred the air.

Is that gold?

What are you talking about? Ariel glanced around.

Coridan squinted in the low light. Whatever it had been was gone now. *I thought I saw gold in the air.*

Ridiculous. Even if you had it would change nothing.

It would change everything…

Well it's a good thing it wasn't, then. Ariel shrugged. *Obviously what you saw was a trick of the light, an illusion.* She held her hands out as if to show him she had nothing to hide. *This can change nothing, not until we leave this place and warn our people.*

Her last statement gave Coridan reason to pause. Exhaustion beat at his body. Had he seen gold? Between the firelight and the flicker of glow bugs he wasn't sure. Yet Ariel's words seemed to be offering them a modicum of hope. He latched onto that bright speck, however distant, refusing to let go. He kept his face purposely blank so as not to draw attention to her words. Not only was her body coming around but her mind also.

We need to come up with a plan we can both live with. She sounded exasperated.

Coridan didn't miss the double meaning of her words. *Fine.* He conceded. *The professor will not be expecting a frontal attack. You will go to the tree stump where I've hidden the transport stone and retrieve it before we strike.*

All right but we must not underestimate the professor.

Coridan's face hardened. *I underestimate no one.*

Ariel nodded.

You'll come in from the south carrying the stone. I'll enter the clearing from the north.

Then what?

Coridan released a heavy breath. *While I'm holding the professor and his men at bay, you'll slip to the transport and replace the missing piece.*

Ariel smiled. *And then I'll join in the fight?*

His brows furrowed. *No!* Coridan shook his head.

Ariel's smile slipped to a frown. *I'm not going to just stand there as the red-devil tries to kill you.*

Coridan felt his lips thin. *Try being the operative word. He will not kill me and you will not join in the fight. Is that understood?*

For a moment Ariel said nothing.

If you do not agree to my plan then I will take you far from this place and claim you as my mate with or without the energy bind, as is my right. We will never see the Atlantean people or Zaron again. Is this what you wish? The part of Coridan that feared returning to his home planet prayed she'd disagree, give him the excuse he needed to act.

Ariel scowled. *You know something, you are such a…a…warrior!*

Coridan smiled letting her feel the heat her words brought to his blood. He was sure she'd been about to call him something else far more unpleasant. He was indeed a warrior, an Atlantean warrior to be exact. Few were fiercer in this world when called upon to do battle.

As I was saying… He arched a brow, knowing it would annoy her even more. He couldn't resist. The pout that came to her luscious lips when she didn't get her way held him in thrall. As if on cue Ariel crossed her arms over her ample breasts and stuck her lower lip out in a perfect pout. Coridan laughed to himself and then thanked the goddess for blessing him so.

Once you've put the stone in place and made sure the transport works you will send me a signal letting me know it is safe to make my way to the portal. His gaze locked to hers willing her compliance. *At which time you will slip through the transport and I will follow.*

I don't like it.

You don't have to like it, you just have to do it. I cannot do battle and worry about your safety at the same time.

Ariel's shoulders squared. *I am perfectly capable of taking care of myself.*

That's not what it looked like when I found you.

Her nostrils flared. *The professor had gotten the jump on me. You would have fared no better.*

He snorted. *You think not.*

Ariel's jaw closed with a slight clank. *What kind of signal should I send?* she asked, easily avoiding the subject.

Any will do. Coridan waved his hand in the air. In the end, it wouldn't matter. It was basically the same plan he'd suggested earlier but wrapped in a nicer package. He didn't bother to tell her that once she was safely through the other side he would stay behind and destroy the transport ensuring the safety of the Atlantean people and his reluctant mate. Hopefully his last heroic deed would change his family's reputation from disgrace to honor.

* * * * *

There was something about Coridan's plan that didn't sit well with Ariel. She knew he wasn't revealing all and it sounded suspiciously like the old plan reworded. Did he think her a fool? There had to be another way other than direct assault. A full frontal battle would amount to death. Before she could formulate her own plan, he spoke.

'Tis best we rest while we can. Tomorrow will be a busy day fraught with much danger and peril.

Ariel returned to where they'd lain together. She settled once more into the soft grass and willed herself to close her eyes. Her mind churned with ideas that she gradually dismissed one by one. She was no strategist. Ariel glanced at her warrior. Coridan crouched near the fire, feeding the hungry flame, his gaze distant tinged with what appeared to be sadness.

The last thing Ariel saw before exhaustion claimed her was the resolve chiseled in Coridan's expression as if he'd made a monumental decision. One which Ariel was sure she would not like or agree with.

* * * * *

Ariel awoke as dawn stretched like a lion's claws across the horizon. She immediately closed her eyes against the light. Her body felt snug and warm tucked protectively next to Coridan's bulk. She shifted her legs and then her arms feeling a wonderful stretch. Her mind focused on each movement as her lashes fluttered open. Her fingers flexed, clasping a nearby branch. Ariel's mind stilled. At least she thought it was a branch.

Ariel frowned a second before her eyes opened fully. Coridan's aqua gaze bore into her, his jaw was set and his nostrils flared as she moved her hand. Her gaze traveled from his chin over his chest to where her hand rested. Somehow during the night she'd clasped his cock. Her eyes widened as she started to uncurl her fingertips.

Do not! Coridan bit out as if he were in an extraordinary amount of pain. He took a deep breath and cleared his throat. *If we are to die today then I ask one request.*

Her gaze met his, steady and strong. *We will not die.* The trouble was Ariel could not be sure what their fate held. She didn't have the herbs needed to bring about a vision.

Be that as it may, his voiced hissed in their minds, *I'd like to experience the sensation of being inside you before we go.*

You've already been inside of my body.

You know what I mean.

Ariel's stomach clenched. She'd denied him and herself for so long. What if they died today and never got to experience the pleasure of a real joining? Her heart stammered at the thought. There was a good possibility they would not succeed. Could she meet the goddess without knowing the pleasure of having Coridan's, her true-mate's, cock inside her aching pussy? She didn't think so.

Moreover, what of the energy bind that would bond them for eternity? No, she must stand firm on the binding. As for the other, she'd denied him and herself for long enough. Her mind made up, she focused once more on Coridan.

Come to me, warrior. She exhaled sending gold floating in the air.

* * * * *

The second Ariel acquiesced Coridan practically pounced on her. He pinned her body to the ground allowing his weight to settle upon her feminine curves. With a simple exhalation she'd confirmed his suspicions. The sun made the gold sparkle. This was no trick of the light. No wonder she'd not allowed him to kiss her earlier. She'd mentioned the energy bind as being something possible, not probable. He'd seen the gold last night but his mind had refused to accept the truth.

You've lied to me, seer. His voice was harsh, his body demanding.

I've never lied to you. I simply withheld the facts. There is a difference.

His gaze pinned her as he shifted his hips so she could feel his growing erection.

The time for games is over.

Ariel's eyes widened. *Coridan, we must not perform the energy bind. Remember our people.*

This is no longer about our people, seer. He reached between their bodies and untied his loincloth pulling the material away until they lay skin to skin. *This is about a warrior and his mate. You know it and I know it.*

Ariel held up her hand gently covering his lips with her fingertips. *I want you but you'll have to promise me there'll be no energy bind or I won't be able to go through with this no matter how much I long to do so. You know as I do if we joined and anything happened to either one of us it would be like sentencing the other to death.*

Coridan felt his face harden. She still denied him the final step in their ultimate joining. Yet he knew she spoke the truth. He knew that whether they joined or not if anything happened to Ariel his life would not be worth living. Coridan didn't want to consider what Ariel's life would be like on Zaron if he didn't make it through this battle. Would her pain be as great? If they joined he knew that would be the case. He debated whether to stop their physical pleasure before it continued any further. Just then Ariel shifted her hips taking all his decision-making abilities out of his hands.

You have my word. He groaned, nuzzling her neck, nibbling her lobe. Her body burned like lava beneath his fingertips, his lips. Coridan traced the gentle dip of her waist as it flared into full hips. He ran his palms along her outer thighs relishing the feel of her long legs, the slight trembling his touch ignited.

Her breath came out in short, gasping pants as he found her rock-hard nipples and rolled them between his thumb and forefinger. Gold filled the air and energy sizzled around them. Coridan closed his eyes, shutting out the temptation of claiming all. He didn't want to force himself on his mate. He wanted Ariel to come to him willingly.

Ariel spread her thighs wider, enveloping him. Coridan's cock dropped, immediately immersed in the slit. His body

111

shook. He had to taste her. He released her earlobe and slid down her body palming her rounded globes one last time before settling between her legs.

* * * * *

Coridan's tongue snaked out, taking Ariel's breath from her lungs. He undulated the muscle, teasing closer to her clit. Her body screamed in anticipation tightening to a razor's edge where she remained balanced and waiting to fall. This was it. In a few moments she would know what it felt like to embrace a warrior and hold him deep within her cunt.

Coridan dipped his head and began to nibble on her clit like he'd been nibbling on her ear only moments ago. His lips were excruciatingly soft as he feasted upon the tiny bud, building her need, driving her desire. He flicked his tongue once, then twice, before plunging inside her saturated channel.

Ariel bit her lower lip to keep from screaming aloud. Energy pulsed within her, dancing and caressing the sensitive inner walls of her woman's center. Pressure began building inside unlike anything she'd ever experienced. If felt bigger than herself, than them, greater than all the things she'd ever accomplished for the tribe.

Coridan pulsed energy sending it rippling through her pussy and vibrating her clit at the same time. Ariel shattered as wave after wave of delicious release roared through her. As soon as the last pulse fluttered her body Coridan's weight was upon her his thick cock sliding to her entrance.

Ariel's eyes widened, locking to his as he slipped the tip of his cock inside her pussy. The sensation scalded as her body gripped him, drawing him deeper. Sweat dotted Coridan's forehead and his aqua eyes turned molten like an underwater lava flow. His gaze held hers as his hands slid away from her body, his palms brushing her skin electrifying her as he neared her hips. Ariel tilted her pelvis instinctively as Coridan slid his cock an inch deeper into her cunt.

Her breath caught as he nudged the natural barrier guarding her innocence. Coridan's gaze never wavered.

I am honored to be granted this gift you give me now, seer.

Ariel… My name is Ariel.

Ariel. He repeated, smiling down upon her. Pure male satisfaction rumbled in his voice sending shivering darts of pleasure over her skin.

After this no other warrior will be able to pleasure you. Know this Ariel, for 'tis the truth I speak.

Coridan…I – Ariel shrieked.

In an act of dominance Coridan thrust forward, tearing through her feminine barrier, imbedding himself to the hilt.

* * * * *

Her body fisted around his cock gloving him. The time for arguments was over. Coridan's breath strangled in his throat as he tried to speak. *You are mine, Ariel.* He punctuated the statement with a roll of his hips.

Ariel's lips parted as her body stretched to accommodate him. *I belong to no man.*

Coridan arched a brow. *That is correct.* He smiled once more into her determined face. *You belong to a warrior – not a man.* Ariel's jaw set. Before she could say anything to deny his words, Coridan started to move taking all protest away.

Their bodies merged and melded twisting in an act men and women have performed since time immortal. Nails raked, skin scraped and still they fucked until all energy from the universe converged and exploded sending them into eternal orbit. By the time their bodies separated their position in each other's lives had solidified. An hour later they departed the tiny sanctuary sated and ready for battle.

Ariel and Coridan worked their way through the jungle taking care to remain undetected. Rumsinger's men stalked through the vegetation flushing out all living creatures from their hiding places in an attempt to locate them. Trees were felled and animals killed as the guides' search became frantic.

Worry creased Ariel's delicate brow as they neared the transport. Coridan stopped halting her movements. *From here, we'll take to the trees.* He pulled a liana free, cupped his hands to give her a leg up and waited for Ariel to climb. They reached the treetops safely.

I want you to go south for seventy-five yards. There you'll find the missing stone hidden in a rotting tree stump surrounded by wild ginger. The flowers disguise the stump and I've covered the top with dried leaves.

Ariel nodded. *What are you going to do?* Worry crept into her voice.

I'm going to diminish their numbers giving us a better chance of escaping with our lives. Once I've accomplished that I'll come in from the north meeting you in front of the transport.

Okay. Ariel hesitated, glancing over her shoulder one last time. Her gaze caressed Coridan lovingly before she grabbed a liana and swung away, heading in the direction of the stone.

Coridan watched until she'd disappeared. His heart slammed against his ribs as the call for battle rushed through his blood burning his veins. It was time to end the professor's reign of terror for the last time.

* * * * *

Ariel found two men resting nearby the stone's hiding place. She debated whether to call Coridan assistance but decided against it. She was an Atlantean woman, more powerful than a human male and at least ten times smarter. Her thoughts turned to her warrior. He already had his hands full with the men guarding the transport and with Rumsinger.

The men lingered, in no hurry to continue their search. Ariel knew she didn't have time to wait them out. She needed a plan. Her gaze scanned the area looking for anything that she could use as a weapon. She couldn't afford to waste an energy blast on these two and besides, she was going for stealth. Locating the perfect item she swung silently to a nearby tree which possessed exactly what she'd been searching for a moment ago.

Ariel plucked two coconuts, weighing their heaviness in her hands before deciding they'd make the perfect weapons. Not too heavy yet not too light, she'd easily be able to hurl her makeshift weapons at the unsuspecting targets. Ariel launched the first coconut at the native man closest to her. The fruit made contact, slamming into his head. A strange hollow thud sounded a second before the man dropped to his knees.

The other man rushed forward to help his friend, not suspecting foul play only to be on the receiving end of a coconut to the face. Ariel heard a crack and then saw a gush of blood as the man's nose rained crimson. He too fell a moment later, a look of shock clearly etched in his wide-browed features.

With the two guides disposed of Ariel dropped from her hiding place and rushed toward the leaf-covered stump. Her heart raced in her chest as she uncovered the stony prize that she and Coridan were prepared to die for. Ariel strained to hear any sign of struggle yet the jungle remained ominously silent, as if holding its collective breath.

She gathered the stone near her body tucking it into her ribcage as she made her way toward the clearing. If all went well, there would be no men surrounding the transport. If not, she would be walking into her execution. She stood taller, throwing her shoulders back as she prepared to face either possibility. Ariel knew that she and Coridan were all that stood between their people's destruction. Ariel did not fear death.

Her stomach clenched as she realized what she feared most was something happening to Coridan. That possibility ate at her insides like scavengers picking over bones. She threaded her way through the jungle, taking care to ensure her footsteps remained silent. She imagined herself as the wind gently rustling leaves while leaving no trace behind. Ariel reached the clearing within moments.

Blood coursed through her veins almost deafening in its thunderous journey. She kept to the tree line as she worked her way to the transport. The area looked as if she'd just left it—deceptively undisturbed. Her heart tripped then stuttered. If all went as planned Coridan should be waiting for her.

Fear sliced through her, freezing her in her tracks. With instant clarity, Ariel realized despite her resolve to return to her people she couldn't leave this planet unless Coridan came with her. If he chose to stay then so would she. Leaves skipped across the open area as a warm breeze stirred the air. Ariel swallowed hard, listening. Silence ensued. Forcing herself to move, Ariel stalked to the transport. It only took a minute to figure out where to place the stone but it felt like an eternity.

The second the missing piece slid into place the machine began to rumble. Like a giant puzzle it needed all of its pieces to create the entire picture or, in this case, place. The center dimmed turning the once see-through space into what looked like growing clouds. The mist thickened again churning like a killer storm. Ariel stared entranced, forgetting for a moment why she was here. A thunderous noise cracked behind her. Ariel jumped. She spun around her hands fisting at her sides in preparation.

Coridan swung down using a thick brown liana, rivulets of blood streaming from one massive biceps. Angry shouts came from behind him as the professor and a few of his men followed in close pursuit.

"Run," he shouted aloud.

The noise shocked Ariel and gave testament to how critical the situation had become.

"Stop them!" Rumsinger bellowed. "Don't let them get through the transport or it'll be your heads."

Shots rang out. Coridan dove for Ariel taking her to the hard ground. The air rushed from her lungs as he rolled attempting to shield her with his body. It took a moment before Ariel could catch her breath. It didn't help having a warrior's body resting upon her like a leaden weight.

Coridan's face was a mask of undisguised rage as he leapt to his feet and prepared for battle. Ariel scrambled to her knees in time to see Santo raise a gun and point it at Coridan's back. There was no time to think or scream only act. Her hand flew up and energy burst out knocking the man and herself to the ground at the same time.

She lay there momentarily stunned. Coridan spun for a second, noting the scene long enough to grit his teeth. He then turned to face the professor once again. Ariel knew what he was thinking without him having to utter a word. She also knew she'd never hear the end of this if they made it out alive.

Atlantean women were forbidden from fighting not because they couldn't fire an energy burst but because it took such a physical toll on their health. She'd rendered herself defenseless but Ariel knew she'd do it again in a heartbeat if it meant saving Coridan's life.

Ariel floundered on the ground listening to the sounds of Hades raining down upon their heads. *Pows* and *zaps* slashed through the silence of the jungle as bullets made contact with bark. Coridan fired burst after burst from his hands until they glowed a constant yellow. Men screamed, their sounds unnatural as the energy bursts hit their targets. Gunfire cracked and popped sending animals scurrying for their lives.

What felt like an hour was truly only a matter of minutes, Ariel was finally able to rise and although weak she could at least warn Coridan of any other sneak attack.

"Get to the transport, it should be ready," he hollered over the cacophonous noise.

I shall not leave you, Ariel whispered in his mind.

Coridan growled. *We had a plan. Stick to it, seer.* His arm shot out and Raoul fell.

Ariel shook her head. It mattered not that he could not see her. She took a step toward Coridan at the same time Rumsinger raised his pistol and fired. She never saw the shot coming. The bullet ripped through her shoulder tearing the tender flesh to shreds. She screamed and reached for Coridan as the world dimmed around her.

Chapter Ten

ଛ

The scream shattered the ice surrounding Coridan's heart. He turned, catching Ariel a second before she dropped to the ground. Blood was everywhere, striking terror in his heart. Crimson flowed freely from the wound dotting the ground with a splash of vibrant color. Fury clouded Coridan's vision as blood covered his hand.

He gathered Ariel close then spun around and felled the last few men remaining. He then sent out a wide burst of energy to ensure everyone who was down stayed down, knocking the pistol from Rumsinger's hands in the process. The professor stood on the periphery, his normally ruddy complexion ghostly white. He gripped the hand that had once held the pistol, his trembling fingers assessing the injury.

Coridan raised his hand building energy for what he knew would be a death blow. Anger surged. His body shook, trembling under the strain. Golden energy swirled around him like frenzied fireflies.

Rumsinger's eyes widened as he watched the energy rotate and crackle. Coridan held Ariel around the waist as he brought his free hand back against his body. He'd need all the support he could get once he released the flow.

"Prepare to die, you black-hearted bastard," Coridan roared.

His muscles tensed as he anchored his hand. Energy singed his skin, making the hair at the nape of his neck stand on end. He took a deep breath and aimed. The professor stared like doe-eyed prey right before a predator pounces upon it. Sweat drenched Coridan's body as his arm shook in the ready. He released his breath and prepared to fire.

The energy roused Ariel. Her hand snapped up encircling his wrist in a velvet touch that felt more like a shackle. Coridan's gaze flickered to hers and locked at what he saw there.

No... She murmured in his mind. *You have done enough. Do not allow this slug to drag your renewed honor down to his level of hatred.*

He has injured you, abused you and threatened to kill us both. For that I cannot let him live.

Ariel's fingers released his wrist and gently stroked the side of his face. He could feel the strain ease with each pass, each caress.

I do not debate that he deserves to die but as seer, I cannot allow my true-mate to come to me with tainted blood upon his hands.

Coridan opened his mouth to argue. Her words fought their way through his muddled mind. *Did you say true-mate?* He had to ask. He had to know if his mind had simply wanted to hear the words so desperately that it had created them.

She smiled, her full lips parting enough to expose the gold in her breath. *The gold does not lie.*

Coridan's eyes widened, his gaze snapping to Rumsinger for a second to ensure he'd not moved before returning to the angelic woman in his arms. *Are you offering me what I think you're offering, seer?*

Ariel's aqua gaze turned molten for a moment despite her obvious pain. *I shall only offer it once. The choice is yours.*

Coridan felt as if he were being split in two. The warrior in him demanded justice. While the man wanted nothing more than to draw his mate near in a searing embrace which would seal their fate forever.

In the end there was no decision to be made. He glanced at the professor, then raised his hand sending an energy blast shooting through the air. Rumsinger flew off his feet landing hard on his back.

Ariel frowned. *You…you…*

Stunned him. Coridan smiled then raised Ariel up in his arms taking care to avoid her injury.

The kiss was tentative at first, tasting and nibbling the plump flesh of her mouth as if she was a rare delicacy. In his case, that's exactly what she was, a rare delicacy, a gift from the goddess, a second chance all rolled into one woman.

Ariel's tongue darted out flicking against his lips, urging him to take a deeper taste. Coridan sank into the kiss devouring her essence as she released her magic so they could perform an energy bind.

Flames shot through his blood healing his wounds both inside and out. His once shattered heart stitched itself back together as Ariel's love flowed through him. Coridan inhaled as much of the gold breath as his lungs could hold, allowing it to mingle with his essence before returning it fully to the woman he now called mate.

* * * * *

Ariel's lungs filled with the spicy male scent that could only be Coridan. The wound at her shoulder began to burn as the binding energy spiraled through her system, bonding and healing. She would have cried out but Coridan refused to release her captured mouth. He fed, he supped, drawing her deeper into a world of pleasure. Her body came alive with a craving for his cock which bordered on insanity. Would she ever get enough of him? She didn't think so.

He was her warrior, her man—her mate.

Reluctantly Ariel broke the embrace. Coridan's nostrils flared, his chest heaving in an effort to draw breath. Gold floated in the air between them, circling, spiraling—binding. His gaze remained unfocused, heated.

'Tis time we leave this place.

At her suggestion his mind seemed to clear. He still hadn't released her but Ariel didn't care. She found comfort in the warmth of his body, in the bond that now existed between them. That somehow had always existed between them.

Rumsinger groaned, his pudgy hand groping at his chest. He sat up and then quickly rose albeit on wobbly legs. His mouth opened and closed like a gaping carp.

"You are not worth our time," Coridan's voice growled menacingly at the professor.

Ariel and Coridan turned away and took the final steps needed to reach the transport. With one final glance over their shoulders at the professor, they stepped into the swirling mass and left the only world they'd ever known behind.

* * * * *

"It's about fucking time you guys got here," Jac's voice broke through Ariel and Coridan's harmonic connection.

Coridan stumbled, barely righting himself while Ariel found her feet. Ariel's gaze narrowed on the band of people gathered around them. Guards dressed in black uniforms flanked familiar faces, surrounding them with sword-like weapons drawn. The guards' faces were harsh as their gazes locked on the intruders. Ariel dismissed them with a glance, turning away to address the familiar faces.

Rachel stood to the side, dressed in a gown of white, a band of jewels woven into her long brown hair. Jac wore a single emerald at her forehead with a gold band holding it in place. Her skirt, which was a lovely shade of jade, was much shorter, showing off her long lean legs. For a second, Ariel experienced a flash of jealousy, then as if realizing her foolishness, she relaxed. Coridan was her mate, not Jac's mate.

She turned to her old nemesis. "It's nice to see you too, Jac." Amusement filled Ariel's voice as she watched Jac's gaze narrow in suspicion.

"Lower your weapons." Rachel commanded as she stepped forward. The guards only did so to half-mast. "What took you guys so long?" she asked idly stroking her protruding stomach.

Ariel's gaze locked onto the Queen's abdomen, then focused on the slight bulge appearing in Jac's stomach. "How long has it been?" Her brows furrowed as she calculated the days on Earth.

"Months," Jac and Rachel answered in unison.

Coridan stiffened beside her, his discomfort rolling off him in waves. Ariel reached down and took his hand in hers. Rachel and Jac's eyes widened a second before matching smiles appeared on their faces. Their brows arched as they assessed them.

Jac turned to Rachel, who met her knowing gaze. "Well at least now we know what they've been up to lately." The women burst into giggles before stepping forward to embrace Ariel. They remained in the group hug for several moments.

* * * * *

Coridan warily watched the exchange, his gaze darting from face to face. From the Queen's and Jac's expressions, he knew Ariel was relating their adventure but she'd purposely blocked him, keeping him from hearing the tale. The women pulled apart then looked at Coridan.

"You didn't think you were getting off that easy, did you?" Jac asked accusingly.

Coridan's face flushed, his muscles tensing for the worst. It was too much to have expected things to change concerning his people. He'd made a mistake and now Ariel would pay.

There was only a slight hesitation before they pulled him into their embrace. For a second Coridan's mind froze. His breath caught as he tried to assimilate the information he received from the women. He immediately relaxed, his body trembling beneath their caring touch. He dropped to his knees, giving the women a traditional Atlantean greeting. Two loud voices barked orders and the guards parted like water when a boat slices over its surface.

Ares and Eros approached, their stern gazes taking in the homecoming scene. The two warriors assessed him, his tattered clothes, his battle-worn appearance, with cold eyes.

Coridan rose to his feet, prepared to face any punishment they saw fit to give him. At least he had his true-mate by his side. The men looked from him to Ariel and back again.

Our wives tell us you should be looked upon as a hero.

Coridan shook his head in denial. *I acted as any warrior would have given the circumstances.*

Ares stepped forward until he stood toe to toe with Coridan, his jade eyes giving nothing away about his true emotions. Coridan braced himself. He deserved any blow the warrior bestowed upon him.

Jac tells me you had the opportunity to kill that bastard professor and you let him go in favor of experiencing an energy bind with your true-mate. Ares' harsh voice boomed in Coridan's head, demanding answers.

Coridan fought the urge to flinch under Ares' accurate appraisal. *'Tis true.* He whispered in the warrior's mind. *I chose to accept my true-mate's offer of bond over protecting my people. I shall accept any punishment deemed necessary.* The admission burned like acid in Coridan's throat even though he knew he'd do so again without question.

Ares' eyes flared a second before a smile broke out across his face. *'Tis about time you learned priorities.* He threw his head back and laughed, clapping Coridan on the shoulder in a brotherly embrace.

Eros joined the men. *Welcome home, warrior.* He clamped Coridan on the other shoulder and drew him away from the transport. *So when can we expect to have a little seer added to the family?*

Coridan's face heated, his gaze seeking Ariel. Jac and Rachel, who chattered enough to give monkeys pause, were leading her in the same direction. For a second their gazes locked and heated. In that moment, a promise was exchanged. Coridan broke the contact and turned his attention back to the two men.

So 'tis all right that I've taken the seer as mate? He held his breath waiting for their reply.

Ares and Eros laughed. *It had better be since 'tis already done.*

What about Atlantean law?

Eros faced Coridan, stopping their progress. *Much has changed with the Atlantean people over the years of our separation. There are no longer preparation rituals or laws forbidding seers from joining. Our people have diversified much on this planet. We even have alien races amongst us. They all live in harmony despite their differences. You have much to see and even more to learn but all in due time.*

Coridan nodded, relief streaming through his body. They walked on and made it another thirty feet or so from the transport when the machine started to rattle. All turned as one to face the noise. Coridan caught Ares' eye, questions filling his mind.

'Tis what happens when someone comes through the transport. 'Tis probably my half-brother Orion, we sent him to find you after retrieving Queen Rachel's and Jac's friend Brigit.

Coridan arched a brow. Ares' half-brother? He said nothing, saving the question for later. He knew Ares would eventually tell him about everything that had occurred since he and Ariel had been away. The guards stepped forward positioning their bodies between the transport and the royals.

The machine thundered, growing blacker by the minute. Suddenly a hazy form appeared. A second later Rumsinger tumbled forward, the force of the transport hurling him into the room. He stumbled a second before falling to his knees. The guards stepped forward weapons held at ready.

Rumsinger stood, brushing his hands off, his mud brown eyes slowly taking in his surroundings while a combination of awe and shock flitted across his face. He looked at Jac, Ariel and then Rachel, his eyes widening on the last.

"You're dead," he gurgled, not appearing to realize he'd said the words aloud.

"Let me at the bastard." Jac stepped forward, only to be swept up in Ares' strong arms. "Put me down this instant, damn you!"

"No!" Ares' face remained a hard unrelenting mask.

"Let me go so I can kick his ass." Jac struggled, arms and legs flailing, in her mate's arms.

"I will not allow you to harm yourself or our child." With those words spoken, Ares' stride grew longer.

Coridan watched his one-time mentor make his way toward a set of jewel encrusted double doors which appeared to be made out of crimson colored crystals. He could still hear Jac's murmured grumbles but she no longer fought Ares' hold. The doors opened as the couple approached. Ares stepped through and disappeared with Jac down a hallway leading to the right.

"How dare you?" Rachel approached the professor, her hands planted on her hips.

Queen Rachel's question drew Coridan back to the immediate problem. Stunning the red-devil had not been enough. Coridan reached out and snatched Ariel from the place rooting her, enclosing her within the safety of his arms.

"Stay back!" Eros commanded.

Rachel jumped but took a step closer to Rumsinger.

Before the guards could fire a weapon, the professor closed the distance, his hand snaking around Rachel's throat in what could easily become a death grip.

Ariel and Coridan tensed. Eros stopped all movement, his face displaying for a second the fear Coridan knew the King felt.

"Stand down, men," Eros ordered. "No one is to harm the Queen."

"That's right," Rumsinger shouted. "Behave and I won't have to kill her." He squeezed his fingers together to emphasize his point, causing Rachel to cough.

Coridan's blood boiled. He glanced down into Ariel's terrified face and pressed a chaste kiss upon her forehead before placing her behind his large body. Rachel's eyes rounded with fright, her fingers clutched protectively over her abdomen.

"I want to get out of here." Rumsinger bellowed, stepping back toward the transport. "Let me leave and she'll return unharmed."

"You can't leave." Eros' muscles bunched as if ready to pounce.

The professor's grip on Rachel's throat tightened once more and she gagged. Coridan took a step forward and stopped, drawing Rumsinger's attention momentarily away from the Queen. Once again his mind screamed out for vengeance. It was in that moment he felt Ariel's hand cling to his wrist. The touch brought him back, allowed him to focus.

The professor and his madness must be stopped.

The transport began to whirl and shudder. Eros' eyes widened. His voice slammed into Coridan's mind. *The transport only works one way.*

Then what is happening?

I know not. The King stared, waiting.

The crystal doors behind them slammed open and Jac came striding forward with Ares hot on her heels. "What the f—?"

The transport's swirling and sputtering was followed by a loud scream. All eyes locked on the device as a red-haired woman fell through the transport. Off balance and out of control, she shrieked again as her body collided with Rumsinger and Rachel sending him sailing forward and the Queen falling to the side. Coridan barely tracked Eros' movements as he swept forward, catching Queen Rachel before she landed belly first onto the floor.

The woman's actions sent the professor barreling head-first into the guards. The men didn't have time to avert their weapons. Rumsinger cried out as his skull impaled on a crystal sword. His body flopped for a few seconds before going limp. The guard holding the weapon tilted the sword until the professor slipped from its blade and onto the floor. Blood pooled on the opaque tiles. No one could have survived a blow like Rumsinger received.

Silence reigned in the room for a few moments as everyone took in the remarkable scene. Relief flooded every fiber of Coridan's being as he swept Ariel into his arms.

"I'm sorry. I didn't mean to—" the red-haired woman sputtered as a frown took up residence on her face. She squinted. "Who is that?" She pointed to the body on the floor lying twenty feet from her.

"Brigit!" Jac's and Rachel's voices cried out in unison, struggling to escape their mates' grips.

Coridan and Ariel watched the red-haired woman stand. She picked up a pair of wire-rimmed glasses from the floor and then wiped the lenses on her clothing before putting them on. The transport once again whirled and the guards braced for an attack.

A striking warrior appeared in the gloom and stepped through the transport. He resembled Ares a little but appeared far wilder with his facial tattoo. He had one aqua eye and one jade colored eye. His gaze locked onto the red-haired woman Jac and Rachel had called Brigit.

"Orion?" Ares and Eros called out, their voices filled with a myriad of questions.

"Honey, what have you done?" Orion asked as his gaze went to the man on the floor. "I told you to lean back, transports always throw you forward."

The woman glanced at the body once more then over her shoulder at Orion. "Oh shut up. I don't want to hear 'I told you so' from you. This is bad, very bad." She began to wring her hands.

Rachel and Jac pulled free from their mates' grasps and rushed forward. "Brigit, it is you."

The woman's eyes widened as her gaze absorbed Jac and Rachel. "Who were you expecting?"

"Only you." Rachel and Jac embraced Brigit for a moment before releasing her. Curious glances shot to the warrior beyond.

Brigit followed their gazes. "Don't ask." She shook her head and then spoke as if reading Jac and Rachel's minds. "It's a long story."

Brigit stepped forward ignoring Jac and Rachel as the group converged to surround the lifeless body. "Is that Professor Rumsinger?"

Rachel nodded.

"Is he dead?" Brigit asked, her body trembling.

Coridan crouched down, touching his fingers to the repulsive man's neck. The body twitched one final time and the professor's head cracked open, splitting down the middle like a melon.

Coridan turned to look at the group, their faces an equal part hope mixed with fear. The woman known as Brigit swayed on her feet, her face pale as she waited for the answer to her question. The tattooed warrior stepped behind her, resting his hands lightly upon her small shoulders.

Coridan stood and nodded his head, confirming the obvious.

Brigit swayed again, her gaze beading on the professor's twisted face. She leaned forward tentatively as if to see for herself then stepped back against Orion's body. Her eyes closed momentarily as she took a couple of deep breaths and swallowed hard. Brigit nodded to herself, opening her eyes to glance back at the group. "It's about goddamned time."

The statement exploded the tension in the air as readily as if she'd detonated a bomb. Nervous giggles tittered from the women and the men barked with laughter.

"Come. 'Tis over," Eros said, herding everyone away from the grizzly scene. "I believe this is cause for celebration."

The King led the group away from the man who'd caused them all so much pain and suffering. Coridan gathered Ariel to him, his body vibrating with emotion.

So what do you think?

Her gaze fluttered to his face. *I care not what has happened to the professor.*

His lips quirked as he fought the urge to smile. *That's not what I'm speaking of.*

Ariel's brows furrowed in confusion.

Coridan slid his hands to her stomach and gently caressed her bare skin. *Would you like to carry my babe?*

Ariel's eyes flashed, love turning the blue into the color of a fathomless sea. *You know I would.*

Coridan's smile flashed wide and his heart swelled. He waggled his eyebrows. *Then I suggest we get started.* They laughed, an intimate sound filled with smoky promises and desires to come.

They were home, where they should be.

The End

ATLANTEAN HEAT

Trademarks Acknowledgement

The author acknowledges the trademarked status and trademark owners of the following wordmarks mentioned in this work of fiction:

Reeboks: Reebok International Limited Corp. U K
Star Trek: Paramount Pictures Corp.

Chapter One

෨

Cassandra stared out the small viewing hole watching stars and distant galaxies go by. The blackness was comforting, like a favorite outfit or a baby's toy. She'd longed for this moment since the day her people had left Earth.

Unlike the majority of the Atlantean people, Cassandra had wanted to explore outside of their jungle borders, experience the rest of what Earth had to offer. After meeting Queen Rachel, she'd become positively fascinated by humans. If her queen was indicative of a human female what were the males like? Cassandra knew they couldn't all be molded in the form of the professor.

She would have left her people long ago if it hadn't been for the fact that Atlantean warriors watched Atlantean women like hungry raptors protecting their kill, not allowing them to wander too far out of their sight. Cassandra understood the reasons but knowing this hadn't curbed her wanderlust.

The stars twinkled like the fireflies that used to swarm in the balmy jungle. She pressed her hand against the tiny window, remembering the simple joy she'd gotten from chasing the glowing bugs around, capturing them, only to release them once again.

Cassandra glanced at the amazing-looking warrior beside her. Orion was one of the few she hadn't dallied with. Out of sheer boredom she'd chosen to share company with several of the warriors on Zaron. They'd served their purpose at the time. Perhaps if the trip was long enough and they got bored...

She quickly dismissed the thought.

She'd heard rumors about the striking warrior, some of which had certainly piqued her curiosity but not enough to act on it. He was after all an Atlantean warrior first and foremost. Moreover, Orion was not her true-mate which, from the looks of his body, was a pity. Her gaze caressed his muscled form focusing on the impressive bulge filling his pants.

As if sensing her gaze on him, Orion turned. The impact of his dual-colored eyes, one jade and one aqua, knowingly assessing her told Cassandra without words he'd read her thoughts. *Don't worry.* He smiled. *I'm not interested in you either and I think I can contain my boredom until we reach Earth.* Mirth simmered in his voice.

Cassandra laughed. His candor was refreshing. *It was just a thought not a proposition. I'm looking for something…different.*

And you think you'll find it in an Earthling?

Perhaps…

Orion flicked switches, transferring fuel into their reserve tanks. *Where is it you wish me to take you once we reach the planet?*

I've longed to see the ocean again. Cassandra sighed, picturing the blue-green water with its white foamy crests gently lapping at a sandy shore. *Queen Rachel has told me I might enjoy a place called California.*

Orion frowned and punched another button, bringing up holographic maps of planet Earth. *Where did she say this place is located?*

The same piece of land you need to be on to find Brigit. Cassandra stared at the swirling map, her eyes widening as she saw how close the water was to this California place. If she reached out she could almost touch the wetness, feel the refreshing spray on her face. She resisted the urge to touch the spot on the map that held so many possibilities for her.

What do the glowing lights represent on the map?

Colonies. He pointed to a spot on the west coast of the North American continent. *The brighter the light the more populated the area.*

Cassandra stared entranced as the colonies lit up like the stars, each one glowing brighter than the next. One stood out, far outshining the rest. *I want you to take me there.*

Orion glanced then pressed a button to draw closer to the spot she'd pointed to. *The place you wish to visit is called Los Angeles.*

Cassandra smiled. "Los Angeles," she murmured aloud, testing the name on her tongue. The words rolled off easing past her lips like a gentle kiss. Her skin prickled, leaving gooseflesh behind. This was the place. The place she'd begin her search. Even the name left a shiver of excitement shimmying up her spine.

Queen Rachel has said you will need something called money. I have researched this item. It is what the humans use to barter with in exchange for goods and food.

Do we have any of this...money?

Yes. The replicator has managed to reproduce a travel sack full of the stuff. You should have more than enough for what you need. I've also taken the liberty of placing a deciphering unit in your sack. You'll be able to find any meaning or item by just thinking about it. It should help when it comes to talking to the humans.

Orion pressed a panel to his side, which had been all but hidden from view seconds ago. He pulled out a metal device Cassandra had never seen before. *What is that?*

A communication device. He flipped a switch on the side of the thin rectangular object and a tiny screen appeared. *If you need assistance or are ready to come back home, just flip this switch and hold the device next to your head. It will pick up your thoughts in the same way we're having this conversation and transport you to the ship. Make sure you allow yourself plenty of space, because the device is powerful enough to transport the objects around you.*

Cassandra nodded and reached for the device. Orion pulled it just out of her reach.

Are you sure you want to do this? 'Tis not too late to change your mind. His voice was serious and held more than a little concern.

Cassandra forced a smile. Inside she was terrified. She'd never been away from her people—ever. Nevertheless, she was absolutely sure this was what she wanted so she swallowed her fear and faced Orion unflinchingly. *I've never been so sure of anything in my life.*

He stared for a few moments, his gaze assessing, deciding. Cassandra held her breath waiting, praying that whatever he could see in her face would be enough to allow her this time of discovery.

Finally he nodded. *California it is.*

* * * * *

They landed without incident two days later. Cassandra had never seen so many lights in all her life. It was as if the stars had fallen from the sky and lay like a blanket upon the hillsides, shining, twinkling, beckoning to her. She'd asked Orion to drop her near the water. In her black flight suit, with her blonde hair braided down her back, Cassandra watched as the first rays of light hit the ocean illuminating its murky depths.

She took a deep breath and inhaled the salty air into her lungs. Tears of joy burned behind her eyelids. It was as beautiful and awe inspiring as she'd remembered. The waves rolled in lapping at the beach, their gentle roar like music to her Atlantean ears. She sat down on the beach to watch the waves roll in. She hugged her sides and just breathed. The peace that had eluded her so easily on Zaron engulfed her here. The muscles in her tense shoulders relaxed. She slipped her boots off and dug her toes in the sand, flexing and releasing the grainy substance.

The humans were beginning to awaken. A few had stumbled onto the beach, shattering the tranquility of the moment with their huffing and puffing. Cassandra had no idea why they were running. From what she could see no predator chased them. Obviously one of the strange behaviors they naturally displayed. Dressed in baggy clothing a few glanced her way eyeing her flight suit.

After they'd left, Cassandra reached into the sack and rummaged around until she'd located her deciphering unit. She needed to find a place to stay since the beach was not an option. She held the unit next to her head, much like how the communication device worked, and pictured the object she wanted to locate.

The device hummed a second later flashing the words hotel and motel across the screen. Ah, shelter was in a hotel or motel. She hoped. Cassandra had no idea which direction to travel in so she decided to follow the next human who ran past.

She gazed at the shoreline, waiting, but it appeared she was alone. Cassandra glanced at the water once more, the vast openness calling to her, daring her to enter its depths. She stood. There was no sense resisting what was inevitable. Stripping off her flight suit, she faced the ocean. Her naked flesh puckered under the cool air relishing its cold-fingered touch.

Cassandra raced into the surf with a reckless abandon that harkened back to her childhood. The cool water momentarily took her breath away. The water near Atlantis had been warm year around. It took Cassandra a couple of minutes to adjust to the change. The frothy brine lapped at her skin as she dove headfirst into an oncoming wave.

* * * * *

Buzz Rittner jogged harder on the wet sand. Anger surged through him as he recalled his commander's orders. *You will take your leave effective immediately.* He figured he was the only Ground Training Officer at the Marine Corps Air Station in Miramar ever forced into a leave.

Well that wasn't exactly true. He had been commanded but the leave was permanent. At least that's what the early retirement papers he'd received yesterday had said. He'd immediately phoned his sister Carrie for support. She was the only woman in his life whom he trusted. Unfortunately this time Carrie's advice had mirrored the military's.

He growled in frustration and ran harder, ignoring the pain and slight weakness that now accompanied his workouts. At forty-three he considered himself in prime physical shape. *Just not good enough to go back into space after exposure to radiation poisoning* the little voice inside his head whispered. It had been the fucking kiss of death to his career.

Buzz knew his attitude of late hadn't been the best. Frustration did that to a man. He knew he was a tough man to train under but he hadn't thought he'd been that bad.

Asking him to leave had probably tickled the commander pink. The bastards had finally gotten rid of their damaged goods. Damn them all!

He pushed on, eating up miles on the sand. Malibu was gorgeous this time of the morning, no people, only sand, ocean—and the naked blonde who'd just broken through the surf in front of him.

Naked blonde? Where in the hell had she come from? His speed slowed as he neared her.

Buzz came close to tripping when she turned her head to stare at him with those striking blue eyes of hers. Still quite a few yards away, he knew there'd been no mistake. Her eyes were the brightest blue he'd ever seen, the color of the ocean when he'd viewed it from space.

He glanced over his shoulder to ensure there wasn't another runner behind him. Nope. It was just the two of them, completely alone. Every muscle in his body tightened as he neared what he could now see was the most beautiful woman he'd ever laid eyes on.

His gaze traveled down the length of her, taking in her slim waist and perfect navel, before zeroing in on her world-class breasts. Her rose-colored nipples alone were enough to give him erotic dreams for a month.

She didn't have movie star looks like most of the women in Los Angeles. Hers was an earthy beauty, one that didn't need makeup or surgery to create. She had a wide, full mouth that held a hint of color he knew instinctively had not come from a tube. Her height was impressive, damn near six feet give or take an inch if where the surf hit her was any indication. Buzz was suddenly glad he had reached six-foot-four. She was lush, her curves round and firm, made for exploring. The woman was like sex on a stick just waiting to be devoured by the right man.

Buzz's cock leapt to attention. Thank God for baggy sweats. He debated whether to stop as he got closer but the truth was the last thing he needed was an entanglement. He had enough problems without adding a woman, albeit a beautiful naked woman, into the mix. But damn, he was tempted—oh so tempted.

"Down boy," he muttered to himself as he passed the woman, giving her a quick nod and a flash of a smile.

Seemingly unbothered by her state of undress the woman's eyes lit up as she warmly returned his smile. Buzz's heart did a little flip in his chest. He ignored it and pressed on. She probably recognized him from his cereal box cover. Buzz frowned. He hated the fact that he missed the attention and that one look from her had kicked his libido into high gear. The latter made him all the more determined not to wait around for her to get out of the water.

Buzz prided himself on being a noble guy but one look at her silky pussy and he knew all bets would be off. There was only so much temptation a guy could take before caving.

It was a few moments before Buzz realized the woman was following him. Her soft footfalls were near-silent against the crash of the surf. It had been the sensation of being watched that had tipped him off. He glanced over his shoulder. Sure enough, the woman trotted behind, now dressed in a black skin-tight outfit with a sack thrown across her back, easily keeping pace with him. Buzz's muscles tightened, his heart rate doubled. Her effect on him was like a kite trying to fly in a tornado. He broke out in a cold sweat. He had to get the hell away from her.

Buzz glanced forward once more and picked up speed. Maybe it was coincidence, maybe she was crazy, most of the truly beautiful ones were. He'd encountered numerous groupies throughout the years but hadn't bothered dallying with any of them. He didn't want to be anyone's checklist conquest.

Buzz jogged a bit further before looking back again. She'd fallen slightly further behind but she was still there. Her expression... Well her expression was open like a child's when they first discover a playground.

As much as he told himself to keep on running and not look back, he couldn't. He needed the attention as much as she longed to give it.

Against his better judgment Buzz slowed to a stopped. Something drew him to her, something beyond primal need. His hands casually rested on his hips as he attempted to catch his breath. Her sexuality was natural, fresh, not feigned like many of the groupies he'd met. She slowed as she neared, her gaze running over the length of him. Buzz's jaw tightened. He hadn't had a woman look at him like that since—well since he'd been NASA's flavor of the month pinup boy.

His cock twitched, beginning to grow under her heated stare. This was odd since he'd never really responded to any of the groupies beyond being flattered by their attention. They were too aggressive for his taste. He liked to be the one to choose and so far it had worked out in his favor.

He'd kept the sex casual and the women at a distance. Buzz's heart damn near stopped when she smiled again. Strange, very strange. Space was his mistress, always had been and always would be even if NASA never allowed him to visit her again.

"Can I help you, darlin'? Would you like an autograph?" he asked, using his best Texas good ol' boy drawl, the one that had worked so well on the women outside of Houston when he'd been training for a space mission at NASA.

He swallowed hard as bitterness welled inside of him. There'd be no more missions. The solar flare he'd experienced while manning the International Space Station had made sure of that. Too much radiation they'd said. No more space flights. No more hope of being on the first manned mission to Mars. He snorted, shaking his head.

She shifted on her feet bringing his thoughts back from the dark place they so often traveled. He'd become so used to the despair he now considered the dark place home. His gaze narrowed on her as he realized she still hadn't answered him. "I guess that's a no." Disappointment welled inside his voice but he squelched it before it got out of hand. "Are you lost?"

Her eyes widened and she smiled, nodding her head.

Buzz's heart tripped in his chest and it had nothing to do with his run.

She cleared her throat. "I-I need to find a hotel or motel."

Her words hit his gut like a punch. Buzz blinked, that wasn't exactly what he'd thought she'd say. He didn't know what he'd expected — was she propositioning him? *Yeah, like she'd be interested in a washed up, unemployed astronaut.*

Her smile was warm. Buzz's mind raced at the possibilities, however remote. His gaze took in her clothing. It was black, made out of a strange material that melded to her body like a wet suit. Yet it was obvious that wasn't what her clothing was used for because she hadn't been wearing it in the surf. She was certainly dressed oddly for being on the beach but hell, this was L.A.

"There are several hotels right down the road in Santa Monica. I'm staying at a place called *Shutters on the Beach*. I could drop you off or you could walk." He pointed further down the beach. "It's quite a ways from here, past Gladstone's."

"Gladstone's?" She frowned, repeating his words like a child would mimic a parent.

Something wasn't right with this whole picture. He could tell from the blank look on her face she had no idea where he was talking about. His gut told him she wasn't stupid, only overwhelmed. Maybe she'd been injured and dumped on the beach. He'd heard of cases where people lost all memory during a traumatic event. The trouble was she didn't look injured. An injured person wouldn't have kept pace with his seven-minute miles.

Perhaps she was a foreign groupie. At the height of his fame, he'd received mail from thirty countries. "You're not from around here, are you?" he ventured.

"No, my home is many galaxies away, past the Pleiades." Her voice was clipped and strangely accented but her words were clear.

She might be foreign but he'd called it right. This chick was crazy. She didn't need a ride. She needed professional help. Why had he offered to give her a ride? He'd never done anything so stupid in the past especially with a groupie. Hell, she probably thought *Star Trek* was real.

Buzz chastised himself again, knowing if she accepted he'd honor his word. The forced leave must have scrambled his mind. He knew she was trouble—six feet of leggy, womanly trouble that he should be trying to stay far away from but damned if his cock didn't disagree. It wanted to get to know this woman a lot better.

Buzz's gaze locked onto her nipples which were clearly visible through her outfit. Because of the bare glimpse he'd caught earlier he didn't need to use much imagination. Her nipples were beaded and thick, like miniature thimbles. His mouth watered at the thought of sucking her deep, laving her with the rasp of his tongue, nibbling on her flesh. His nostrils flared as he bit back a curse. What in the hell was the matter with him? He was acting like he'd never been laid.

Her gaze zoomed in on his face a second before her smile widened. Heat filled her aqua eyes as if she knew exactly what he'd been thinking. Buzz stared back unabashedly. He half hoped she did know what he was thinking. It would save them both a lot of time and trouble when he stripped that outfit from her body and laid her across the thick, billowy linens *Shutters on the Beach* was known for draping across their beds.

Buzz didn't know when he'd decided to break his unwritten 'no groupies' rule and fuck her. Crazy or not, foreign or not, he just knew it was going to happen. He had no doubt. Something in him roared to reaffirm his position as a vital male and stake a claim on her luscious flesh—a purely primal reaction that he'd never experienced before.

He wanted to hear her soft moans as she came repeatedly. Taste the salt of her skin after they'd made love for hours. He could almost imagine the rich smell of musk that would emanate from her weeping pussy as she heated, waiting for his cock to fill her.

Damn. Buzz fisted his hands where they rested on his hips, resisting the urge to throw her on the beach and take her now. He was acting like a hormonally driven teenager. His need thrummed, the beat steady and strong in her presence. Muffled voices reached his ears. His mind halted as he saw several joggers coming their way. If he had a brain in his head he'd take her to the nearest hospital and drop her like a bad habit.

His gaze went to her mouth and then back to her soulful, hungry eyes. So much for good intentions. He blinked as her expression registered on his sex-filled mind. *Hungry?* God, he hoped like hell she was. He was ravenous.

He cleared his throat, willing his voice to be calm as he spoke. "My car is back down the beach. It'll take a while to get there. Do you want to come with me to get it or would you rather wait here?"

She glanced over her shoulder at the approaching people. "I want to *come...*with you."

The film broke in Buzz's mind as he imagined an emphasis on the word come that couldn't have been there. He didn't wait for her to repeat herself. He reached out and grabbed her slender wrist, striding briskly as he tugged her along behind him.

The warmth of her skin seared him, frying all reasoning. Even though groupies were game for almost anything Buzz prayed his caveman act didn't scare off this woman because right now he teetered on the edge of feral and was losing the battle.

Chapter Two

ഔ

Cassandra smiled as her skin heated to inferno at his touch. She couldn't help herself. This human was exactly what she'd been searching for in her dreams, a man who could trigger her Atlantean's heat. Oddly enough, she didn't even know his name.

What she did know was he was aggressive and male. Like a true warrior his finely developed muscles split in striated lines as he strode across the sand. She'd decided to follow him the second their eyes had met. She hadn't missed the hunger swimming in his gray-green depths. It was still there. Simmering just below the surface of his rigid self-control. She looked forward to shattering that control the first chance she got.

He had lean hips, a nice ass and long legs. She wondered if his cock was as impressive as the rest of him. She hoped so since she planned to be fondling the organ soon.

A day's growth of stubble covered his firm, square jaw. Long, dark lashes shielded his gray-green eyes. His brown hair was short, holding hints of blond and a smidge of gray. A welcome change from the longhaired Atlantean warriors she'd left back on Zaron.

This was no child.

This was a man.

The thoughts in his head ran from dark to aggressively sexual. For a moment she'd seen space. He'd floated above this planet in some crude manner and despite his deep-seated anger wished to return. Her smile widened as she considered his broad back clearly outlined in the thin damp shirt he wore.

If things worked out as she planned she'd grant him that wish and more.

Cassandra allowed him to pull her along, retracing the steps they'd taken only moments ago. He was going to give her a ride to a hotel called *Shutters on the Beach*. She needed to get her deciphering unit out to understand what his thoughts of *foreign groupie* and *crazy* meant but couldn't risk doing so in front of him. At least not yet.

Half an hour later, they reached a transportation device he'd called his car. Crude but effective, she noted several other humans seated inside the transports as they winged down the hard gray trail that had been carved from the land. Each transport seemed to come in different shapes and individual colors. The man walked to one side of the transport and opened a hatch.

"Step in," he said.

She eyed the machine for a moment before complying. This civilization was odd indeed.

The man shut the hatch behind her and then walked around the transport to the other side. He opened another hatch she hadn't noticed before and sat down beside her. His smell filled the car, crisp like the ocean with a hint of musky salt from his sweat. Cassandra inhaled as if the mere act of breathing in would draw the man into her body.

He took out a chain of dangly metal and fit one of the pieces into the side of a slim column in front of him. With a flick of his thick wrist the transport roared to life. The vibration beneath her bottom caused her clit to twitch. Cassandra dug her fingertips into her thighs to keep from moaning aloud.

Obviously pleased with the transport, the man patted a round object with his long fingers before reaching over his shoulder to secure a strap of some sort across his broad chest.

Cassandra glanced over her shoulder. She had a similar strap on her side. She repeated his actions and snapped her strap in place. The material of her flight uniform stretched and caressed her aching breasts, teasing her nipples into tight crests. His gaze strayed to the front of her flight uniform before glancing into her face. He smiled at her but the action appeared strained. Cassandra smiled back, pleased that he seemed affected by her body as he shifted a stick and the transport started to move. He eased onto the gray trail and headed south.

"My name is Buzz Rittner but I suppose you already know that." He smiled, glancing her way.

"I'm called Cassandra."

He watched the transports in front and slowed their transport when they'd gotten too close. They stopped for a moment and he turned to her expectantly.

Cassandra had no idea what he wanted.

"One of those one name kind of gals like Cher, eh?" Buzz laughed and then winked at her. "Only in L.A."

Cassandra smiled, nodding her head in agreement. She had no idea what he was talking about and she didn't care. If he thought she was like a Cher then so be it. She'd check on that item too, once they reached the hotel.

The transports began to move again. Cassandra settled back in her seat and enjoyed the ride. Buzz had opened something called a window and she'd been able to again experience the ocean air upon her skin. The wind blew tendrils of her hair free from its braid, kissing her face with its invisible lapping tongue. Cassandra loved this transport and from the look on the man's face so did he.

"We're here," he announced. "The valet will take care of the car." He squeezed her hand and winked. Cassandra's stomach did a little flop and her heart melted.

* * * * *

They pulled into the entry of *Shutters on the Beach*. Buzz stopped under the awning and waited for the valet parking attendant to approach. The man opened the car door for Cassandra. She stepped out, her wide-eyed gaze immediately seeking Buzz for reassurance. Buzz tried to ignore the pleasure he derived from that one little glance. He knew there was something different about this woman, something strange he should be noticing but was missing.

He reached for her sack but she beat him to it. She clutched the item to her chest as he walked around the car to join her. The action was strange but he quickly dismissed it as a cultural difference. Buzz slipped his hand around her arm and led her into the hotel. He bypassed the front desk and went straight for the elevators. A short elevator ride later they'd arrived on his floor. He'd reserved a room with an unobstructed view of the ocean. For some reason the depths of the abyss reminded him of space.

Buzz shook his head dismissing the fanciful thought. He had to stop comparing everything to his days as an astronaut. His sister Carrie had told him it wasn't healthy and he knew she was right. Hell, her love and support was the only reason he had any sanity left at all. Although from his spontaneous action today no one would believe that.

He led Cassandra down the hall until they reached his room. He pulled his arm free and slipped his hand into his pocket for the room key. A slight click later and the door swung open, exposing the impressive view. Buzz stepped inside and waited for her to join him, hardly believing he'd brought her here in the first place.

Cassandra gasped as her gaze swept the surroundings yet she made no move to come in. *What was she waiting for?* Maybe she was nervous. God knows he was. He rubbed his moist palms along his pants and then captured her gaze.

"Are you going to come inside?"

She smiled. "Are you inviting me into your dwelling?"

"I sure am darlin'." Buzz ignored the warning bells going off in his head and his immediate gut reaction telling him there was more to the question than met the eye. His lips quirked. He was probably just imagining things considering she had such an unusual way of phrasing things. *Definitely foreign.* It was the little things like that which made him want to learn more about this woman despite her being a groupie. That fact alone should have scared the daylights out of him but it didn't.

Her smile widened and her eyes seemed to light from within. She entered the room. Hell, if all she was looking for was an invitation he would have issued it earlier.

"Honey, I'm going to jump into the shower and rinse this sweat off my body. Make yourself at home."

* * * * *

Cassandra couldn't believe it! Buzz welcomed her into his dwelling. All that was left for them to do was experience the energy bind. Unfortunately it could not be rushed. She glanced around the light green colored room. The furs atop the bed matched the walls reminding her of the different colors the ocean reflected throughout the day. Sunshine filtered through the shuttered windows reflecting off the ocean beyond.

Her gaze followed the retreating male form as he walked down a short path and disappeared into another area. Alone, Cassandra took in her surroundings. The room was warm and welcoming with its soothing colors and soft materials. It would suit her needs perfectly. Here she would get to know her man intimately.

Cassandra heard water coming from the room Buzz had entered. She reached into her sack and brought out the deciphering device. Within seconds she understood what crazy, foreign groupie and a shower was. How dare he think she was insane and slept with a lot of men? Okay, she may have been a little wild back on Zaron, experiencing her fair share of warrior company, but there was nothing wrong with her thought processes. Cassandra's eyes narrowed as she considered her next move.

She knew what Buzz was doing inside that room. Her cunt ached as she pictured him naked, his skin covered in suds. Moisture pooled between her thighs. She dropped the sack onto the floor and then stripped out of her clothes before she lost her nerve.

She padded down the same path Buzz had taken earlier, her bare feet silent upon the carpeted floor. Cassandra didn't knock, she simply turned the handle and walked in. The small room was filled with steam. A curtain concealed the man she sought from view. His deep baritone rumbled from the other side as he hummed a musical tune.

Cassandra's belly fluttered and her clit twitched. This was it. She reached out and grabbed the edge of the curtain. Spray from the warm water splashed over her fingertips. Before she had a chance to pull the curtain aside, Buzz's hand grasped hers. Cassandra gasped as heat spread through her fingers, along her arm and over her body. Her nipples beaded in anticipation.

"I was wondering when you were going to join me."

His statement surprised and delighted her. "You were expecting me?"

Buzz pulled the curtain aside without releasing her hand. His hair, wet from the shower, looked darker. His tanned body glistened from a thousand tiny droplets. Moisture clung to his lashes hooding his gray-green eyes.

Cassandra swallowed hard, allowing her gaze to lower. His chest was wide, tapering into a slim waist. The image was even more impressive now that he'd removed his shirt. A smattering of crisp hair clung to his rippling abdomen leading down to the treasure trove below.

She followed the dark trail until it reached an impressive cock that jutted out from his body like a branch. He was thick and long just like she'd imagined. His plum-sized head flushed deep with color from his arousal. Her mouth watered as a drop of semen eased down his shaft. What would he taste like?

Her breath caught as all her dreams and fantasies merged into the man before her. She'd waited so long to encounter the one man who could ignite her body and fire her mind. Buzz was like a puzzle, the picture appeared perfect but there was a piece missing. Cassandra realized she'd gladly spend the rest of her life trying to find that one missing piece.

"See anything you like, darlin'?" he drawled, a hint of strained humor hanging in his voice.

Cassandra tore her gaze away from his cock and glanced back at his face. "I like everything that I see."

"That makes two of us." His eyes lit up as his hungry gaze devoured her nakedness. "Come on in, the water's just fine."

Cassandra stepped into the shower and Buzz pulled the curtain closed behind her. Warm spray filtered over his shoulders wetting her skin. She was surprised it didn't sizzle considering she felt as if she were on fire. He pulled her into his arms, breast to chest, cunt to cock, thigh to thigh. She moaned at the sudden sensate intrusion. Her nipples pebbled tighter. The ache in her cunt became excruciating. She needed to feel his hard cock inside of her, pumping.

Buzz's mouth came down upon hers. His tongue and teeth teased her bottom lip, lapping and nibbling until she opened for him. He plunged inside, tasting and devouring, a conflagration of heat and energy enveloping them, driving their need, pressing them closer. Cassandra's nails dug into his flesh as she slipped one leg up and around his muscled thigh. Buzz groaned a second before reaching down and holding her in place.

Everything happened at laser speed. Her nipples ached as she rubbed her breasts over the rough hair sparsely covering his chest. With his free hand Buzz reached up and grasped her nipple, rolling the marbled bud between his thumb and finger. Cassandra's channel flooded.

Buzz, I need you. Her fingers dug deeper into his shoulders and back. Cassandra was so far gone she hadn't realized until the statement had left her that she'd uttered it in his mind. Her body tensed waiting for his reaction.

Buzz pulled back from the kiss, his chest heaving to take in air. His face was a mask of raw hunger. "Slow down a minute." He appeared to be as far gone as she was. "I don't have any protection out."

"Protection?"

"Condoms." He gently put her leg down, pushed the curtain aside and reached for a small bag sitting on the side of the basin. He pulled out a foil wrapper, ripped it open with his teeth and tossed the wrapper on the floor.

Cassandra felt her eyes widen but she said nothing as she watched him roll the thin material over his shaft until he was completely covered.

"Now where were we?" he said as he smiled.

Chapter Three

ဢ

Buzz couldn't believe how close he'd come to fucking her without a condom. He'd never been so reckless. There was something about Cassandra that drove all logical thought from his mind—something about her that demanded a primal mating. Moreover, he'd been this close to forgetting she was a groupie and giving it to her.

Luckily his common sense had kicked in but he had to admit he was a tad bit disappointed. He longed to feel his cock slipping into her—skin on skin, the tight grip of her channel as she milked him. He was damn close to bursting just thinking about it.

He lifted Cassandra's long leg again, holding it against his hip, effectively opening her to his plunder. He palmed her breasts and caressed her thigh all the while rocking his cock against her swollen clit. She moaned, throwing her head back and exposing the long column of her throat for him to feast upon. Buzz grazed her neck, laving and nipping at the pulse beating erratically there. He blazed a trail over her collarbone, down to her breasts, until he was within a whisper of her kernelled nipples.

He flicked first one and then the other with his tongue, teasing her rosy flesh, tasting her. Buzz sucked one nipple into his mouth and almost came as sensation shot through him straight to his cock. Her skin held a hint of spice coupled with a honeyed sweetness. He had never experienced anything like it. Her fingers clung to his flesh, digging deep, spurring him on. He couldn't wait any longer.

"Darlin', I'm sorry but this time is going to have to be hard and fast." His voice came out on a harsh growl.

Cassandra smiled, her aqua eyes glowing with an emotion he refused to recognize. "I like it hard."

God give me strength. Buzz closed his eyes for a second as his resistance came crashing down. He released her breast, grabbed hold of his hard cock and then positioned the head at her entrance. He shifted her leg a bit higher until she wrapped it around his waist. With a roar Buzz plunged inside of her weeping pussy. His breath hissed out of his lungs as her velvet channel gripped him tight.

Oh man…

His hips began to pump, taking her deep, fucking her hard. He'd never felt anything like this. Anything like her. The last thought had him shaking his head and shackling his emotions. The last thing he needed was to confuse sex with a relationship especially since he didn't have relationships. Cassandra was just another woman, an astronaut groupie he'd share company with for a while and then move on.

No matter how many times he told himself that Buzz wasn't quite convinced. Their bodies melded, forming a perfect union between man and woman. He thrust again and Cassandra cried out.

Buzz felt the first of the tremors shudder through her body. He gripped her tighter and drove deeper, his cock nudging her womb with his thrust. Two more bucks of his hips and Cassandra shattered. She screamed, her nails taking out a strip of his flesh from his back as she came hard. He answered her scream with a bellow of his own, following her into sated bliss.

* * * * *

Cassandra's body thrummed as the last of the ripples from her orgasm fluttered through her. Never had she experienced anything like the joining she'd just had with Buzz. It was better than seeing the galaxies for the first time. Her heart thudded as she fought to catch her breath. She'd purposely monitored her breathing to keep the gold energy from escaping, especially after she'd glimpsed his thoughts on relationships. His expression hardened as his feelings wavered causing him to draw away from her. For some reason Buzz was as reluctant about facing his emotions as he was about discussing space.

The missing piece to her puzzle stood glaringly before her. Their connection had been far more than physical. She'd felt it and so had Buzz whether he was ready to admit it or not.

Buzz released her leg and slipped from her body. The emptiness left behind caused Cassandra to tremble. He turned the water off and then pulled the shower curtain back. Slipping the condom off, he tossed it into a container and then reached for two towels. He set one down on the rack, the other he placed around her shoulders and began to rub gently. His face softened as he caressed her body. Within a few minutes Cassandra was dry and her heart felt as if it had swelled to two times its normal size. So this was what finding your true-mate felt like. So this was love. He released the towel, allowing her to secure it around her body before reaching for the other one.

He wrapped the material around his hips, grabbed more foil wrappers and led her into the other room. Buzz tossed back the covers before guiding her back to the bed. Cassandra fell, pulling him on top of her. The weight of his body felt exquisite against her skin.

Cassandra relaxed, sinking deeper into the bed. She wiggled until she had managed to release the towel from around her body. Buzz's towel remained wrapped around his waist. His burgeoning erection pressed into her abdomen as his desire rose to match her own.

"I'm not sure what you're doing to me, darlin'." He smiled, rubbing his chin against the side of her cheek.

"Don't you like it?" Cassandra hated the fact that her voice sounded tentative.

His gray-green eyes widened before locking to hers. "I love it. That's the problem." He laughed but it held no humor. "Sooner or later we'll have to part. I have to look for a job and you'll have to get back home."

Cassandra fought the sadness welling inside of her. He had already planned for their departure. She allowed herself a few moments to wallow before determination took over. She had at least a day, perhaps two to change his mind.

She was an Atlantean woman experiencing full Atlantean heat. No man — warrior or human — in his right mind would be able to resist for long. The temptation was too great. Decision made, Cassandra reached up and grasped the back of his head, sinking her fingers into his hair and then pulling Buzz's lips down upon hers in a blistering kiss. She would not allow him to dismiss her — them — so easily. With her free hand she reached between them to loosen his towel separating their bodies.

It took her fingers but a moment to locate his throbbing cock. It came to life instantly. *'Tis my turn, I think.* Cassandra parted the towel and stroked the length of him relishing the feel of satin over steel in her palm.

Buzz broke the kiss, air rushing from his lungs. "Release me, I want to taste you."

His words seared her skin. She released him instantly and watched as Buzz slid down the length of her body until he was seated between her thighs. His face was mere inches from her shaven mons. He inhaled taking her fragrance into his body.

"God, you smell good, rich and spicy like a woman should yet sweet — succulent, good enough to eat. And I intend to." With that he lowered his face and began lapping at her nether lips drawing lazy figure eights over her swollen flesh all the while avoiding her aching clit.

"I don't know what it is," he murmured against her flesh, "but I can't seem to get enough of you."

Cassandra knew exactly what was occurring between them. They were true-mates whether he'd heard of the concept before or not. He flicked his tongue, rasping the hooded bundle of nerves once. Cassandra dug her fingers into the linens on the bed and gritted her teeth. She couldn't seem to catch her breath. His stubbled jaw rasped the inside of her thighs adding more sensation to his taunting mouth.

"Please, Buzz." She groaned.

He stilled his movements a moment as he watched her reactions. Instead of continuing with his carnal actions he blew warm air across her flesh and like kerosene to a flame she ignited. "Tell me what you want," he croaked, his voice so passion filled that it was barely understandable.

"I want… I want you to fuck me."

He laughed a pain-filled sound that told her with more than words that his control had reached its end. "I'll do just that in a moment right after I hear you scream out another orgasm."

He dove back into her needy flesh, sucking her clit between his lips, tasting her with his tongue. Cassandra's body stiffened as sensation shot through her, tightening her muscles, ratcheting her need. Her body clenched and unclenched as a pleasure-pain greater than any she'd felt before filled her and then she was tumbling. A keening cry ripped from her lungs and her body bowed on the bed. Buzz continued to feed, lapping at her cream as she came hard.

Spots floated behind her eyes as the blood rushed from her head to her cunt. Spasms rippled through her as her channel flooded anew. Cassandra felt Buzz's weight shift, heard the tearing of the foil wrapper and within seconds he was sliding home. The ache she'd felt only moments ago was now filled. Buzz's cock slid into her moist heat, rocking her gently.

He fucked her slowly this time, gliding maddeningly, savoring her body. His hands bracketed the side of her head keeping her focused on his face. "Do you have any idea how beautiful you are?" he asked on an upward thrust.

Cassandra fought the urge to close her eyes. She bit into her lower lip and shook her head.

"You are the most beautiful woman I've ever laid eyes on." He stared deep, drawing her into his gray-green depths.

Cassandra laughed. "You probably say that to all the women you lay with."

His brow furrowed. "No I don't." He snorted. "I say very little. We exchange pleasantries. We fuck once and then I'm gone. No fuss. No mess. No complications."

"So is that what you've got planned?" she asked, bracing for his answer.

Buzz stared at her for several minutes, his face a mask of unreadable emotions. Cassandra debated whether to intrude on his thoughts but decided against it. She wanted to hear his answer. If he was lying she'd know.

His jaw clenched and unclenched a couple of times as if he couldn't decide whether to tell the truth or not. Finally he spoke. "At first, yeah."

"And now?"

He scrubbed a hand over his face. "I'm not sure what I'm doing now. I sure as hell don't have a plan."

Good. Cassandra thought. At least that was a start.

* * * * *

They made love on and off over the next three days stopping only long enough to eat and shower. Cassandra couldn't seem to break through the shell separating her from Buzz's heart. She feared his emotional state was directly tied with his space journeys but she'd been unable as of yet to get him to speak of it. She trembled in the cool night air as she stood on the balcony.

Without a word, Buzz stood, grabbed a blanket from the bed, moved to stand beside her and wrapped it around them. Standing together outside, sated and replete, they stared out at the night sky like an old mated couple. The peace and comfort of the situation gave her the courage to broach the subject.

"Have you ever seen the Antares and Rho Ophiuchi?"

He nodded, a slight frown marring his features. Cassandra watched his jaw clench and then unclench. Finally he sighed and ran a hand through his spiky short hair. "I've seen it. The colors are spectacular like a rainbow that has burst."

"I love the blues, pinks and clouds of orange."

His muscles seemed to relax a bit and he smiled. "My favorite is Eta Carina. It reminds me of a big set of testicles." He laughed and she joined in.

"Trifid reminds me of a pink and blue dust storm, endless and powerful."

Buzz turned to face her now. His gaze roved over her face. So many questions filled his expression but he seemed to dismiss them one after the other. "How is it that you know so much about space? Are you an astronomer?"

"I do not study stars if that is what you ask. I simply like the colors, the power in those glowing beacons when seen through a porthole. Much as I'm sure you do. Would you like to see them again?" She asked the question tentatively.

His expression turned dark. "That's right. I forgot you're from a galaxy beyond the Pleiades." His voice smacked of contempt.

"I am," she whispered, unable to stop the hurt from crowding into her voice.

Buzz moved away from her. Anger vibrated from his body. "Knock it off! You know I can't go back into space and no amount of pointing at the sky is going to get me there. So stop asking stupid questions you already know the answers to. Your little act isn't fooling anyone."

"Act?" She frowned, attempting to digest his words.

His hands curled into fists at his sides. "I bet the other astronauts bought into your wide-eyed innocence hook, line, and sinker. But you made a mistake when you made a play for this washed up flyboy."

"What other astronauts?"

He threw his arms up in the air in frustration. "Oh come on, drop the act already, babe. I'm onto you. You're a flyboy groupie." He shrugged. "You may be foreign but you're like all the others."

Anger surged through Cassandra. How dare he speak to her this way! She'd done nothing wrong. She backed away from him as fury gathered around her. Her eyes stung as tears welled and she forced the drops away. "You listen to me, Buzz Rittner. I know not of other astronauts. I did nothing to you other than offer you my body, my heart. If you're too pigheaded to understand that, well…then that's your problem." Cassandra gathered the blanket around her and swept back into the room like a queen dismissing her subjects.

She'd had enough of his arrogance, his mean-spirited words and his male stubbornness. If he would only listen to his heart he'd know she was telling the truth. She plopped down on the bed and bundled under the covers. Cassandra purposely turned away from the shadowed figure standing on the balcony. Right now, she was too angry to look at him.

* * * * *

Buzz gripped the railing of the balcony, his muscles tense from the surge of anger still simmering just below the surface. He didn't even know this woman. She shouldn't be getting to him like this. What in the hell had he been thinking? He knew better than to hook up with a groupie. They'd fucked a couple of times, so what! The act didn't exactly constitute a commitment.

Keep it together, buddy. His gut clenched, telling him it was too late for that.

He didn't know why he'd snapped at Cassandra. Had he thought she was rubbing in the fact he'd never be able to experience space travel again? His radiation poisoning wasn't exactly common knowledge outside of NASA.

He released the breath he hadn't known he'd been holding. All that was certain was he'd taken out all the frustration and pain he'd been feeling over the past few years and directed it right at Cassandra and she hadn't done anything wrong.

A curse slipped from his lips as he leaned over the balcony and inhaled the fresh sea air. He ran a shaky hand over his face and through his short hair. He was in trouble—big trouble. Three days of fabulous sex had managed to turn him inside out and upside down. He didn't know whether he was coming or going and it was all Cassandra's fault.

She'd opened herself up to him body and soul, wrapping those long legs of hers around his waist, taking his cock repeatedly into her channel. Just thinking about it had him growing hard.

But it was more than that. There was more to the woman. Somewhere in the midst of their tumbles they'd gone from having sex to making love. During that time she'd managed to wedge the door to his heart open and he had no idea how to get it closed.

Chapter Four

ဆ

Cassandra awoke with her body on fire. Where was she? What was happening? Her lids fluttered open as she glanced down at the source of her pleasurable discomfort. Buzz's head lay buried between her thighs, his tongue fucking her slowly, in and out. Her legs trembled and threatened to close. As if anticipating the move he grasped her thighs and held them open. Cassandra groaned as her head dropped back onto the pillows.

Mad one minute, a lover the next. She had no idea what to make of this man. She wanted to scream at him, rail against his stubbornness but she couldn't. He held her in thrall, his fist firmly wrapped around her heart, as he attacked her cunt with a vengeance.

Hungry little noises emanated from Buzz's throat telling her without words he enjoyed his task. Her gaze narrowed in on his face, holding his gray-green eyes. The pressure inside her built as he gently tugged at her clit, flicking it with the tip of his tongue. Cassandra shattered, her breath breaking in short gasps as pleasure exploded, traveling to the far reaches of her body and back again.

He gave her pussy one last lick before looking up. "I take it you like that." It wasn't a question.

"So you are no longer mad at me?"

He stroked her pussy with his fingertips as he spoke. "I wasn't really mad at you, only myself."

"And?"

He shrugged. "You are who you are and I am a man looking for a second chance."

She smiled and arched a brow. "Then we are the same."

His expression clouded.

"I, too, am searching for a second chance."

He grinned then making him appear much younger than his actual Earth age. "Then I guess it's a good thing we found each other."

She nodded, crooking her finger to get him to come to her. Buzz moved without hesitation. His cock was hard and heavy against her abdomen as he rested his weight upon her body. Cassandra sighed, relishing the feel of his warm skin upon her own. The crinkly hair tickled her breasts and thighs, and his cock pulsed.

Buzz's gaze locked with hers. "I want you so bad. I want to feel you without anything separating us. I've been tested and I know I'm clean. How about you?"

Cassandra frowned, not sure what to say.

"Have you been tested for diseases?" he asked his expression serious.

Cassandra probed his mind for a second so she could understand his questions. Her eyes widened. "Of course I'm healthy. I do not get ill," she told him matter-of-factly.

"Good." He grinned wider. "But there's one other problem. If you're not on birth control you could get pregnant."

He was discussing babies. Cassandra's heart swelled. She was well aware of the dangers of one having sex with their true-mate. A birth was not only hoped for, it was welcome. She just wasn't sure if Buzz held the same beliefs. Yet she could sense no discomfort, no worry.

"I accept your offer."

He blinked then laughed. "All right, as long as we're both going into this with our eyes open."

Cassandra pulled his mouth down to hers, stopping just short of touching. "Shut up and fuck me, Buzz."

His eyebrows waggled. "Yes ma'am."

With that he positioned the head of his cock and surged inside her. Cassandra felt the ridge on his crown as he drew back only to thrust forward again. She squirmed as sensation shot through her inflaming the Atlantean's heat until she could no longer hold back the energy.

Gold floated in her breath as it built up inside her. Buzz's eyes remained closed and sweat beaded his brow.

"You feel better than anything I've ever experienced before—even space travel." He leaned down, searching for her lips by touch.

Energy spread through her body and into Buzz's mouth. Heat radiated between them so intense Cassandra was convinced the bed linens would ignite. She clutched his sides when the feelings became too extreme. Buzz's eyes flew open, his gaze locked to hers as gold energy swirled around them, between them, inside of them. His nostrils flared a second before he inhaled, taking as much of the energy his lungs could hold into his body.

* * * * *

Buzz's head was swimming. He blinked, trying to clear the gold from his vision but it didn't work. It wasn't a trick of the light, it was actually there, floating like a shimmering fog. Cassandra's hand scraped along his back following the ridge to his butt. Her nails dug into his ass a second later and he found himself exhaling the breath he'd been holding, until she'd filled her own greedy lungs.

His body burned as if he were going through a giant growth spurt times a million. His muscles ached as he thrust into her cunt, his cock stretching and filling her velvet walls. Cassandra cried out as her body rocked and pulsed with a tsunami-sized orgasm. The wave sent Buzz tumbling, his cock exploded like a loaded gun emptying round after round of his seed into her womb.

They lay together locked in a myriad of emotions. Buzz's cock remained hard, his body covered in sweat, as he gradually floated back to reality. The surreal events mixed with what he'd witnessed forming a volatile cocktail in his mind. Buzz stiffened then pulled out of Cassandra and sprang from the bed. His mind was traveling at light speed as he tried to understand what had just occurred.

She'd drugged him. There could be no other explanation. *Other than maybe she'd been telling the truth,* his traitorous mind whispered. Where in the hell had that thought come from? That would mean she'd actually been in space which wasn't possible, was it? *She did know all about the various galaxies.* Knowledge easily gained from a book or the internet. But what about the gold he'd seen? Had it really been there? And if so what was it?

It just didn't add up. Nothing about Cassandra added up, as if she was too good to be true. Anything too good to be true probably was. Nope, it had to be drugs. "What in the hell did you do to me?" He staggered. "Did you slip me something?" he asked, pulling on a pair of jeans and a T-shirt.

She frowned, drawing the covers around her body protectively. "I did nothing wrong."

Buzz stepped forward, anger and hurt surging through him. "I'm going to ask you again, what did you give me?"

Her lower lip trembled and tears filled her eyes. "I gave you nothing but love."

Buzz felt his chest constrict in a manner painfully similar to heartbreak. "I want you to get your things and get out." His mind protested the order.

Pain and disappointment slashed across her face. Cassandra rose from the bed like a goddess from the sea. Chin held high, she let the covers drop and walked naked across the room, grabbing her clothes and dressing quickly. Afterwards, she reached into her sack and withdrew a silver object which she brought to the side of her head.

"What are you doing?" he asked, his voice breaking with emotion as he slipped on his Reeboks.

"I'm leaving like you asked."

"The door is over there." He pointed, his fingers trembling from the effort.

She snorted. "I don't need the door where I'm going."

Buzz frowned. The hair on the back of his neck stood on end as all the conversations they'd had played through his mind. "Cassandra?"

She held her hand out to stop his words. "I've told you the truth. It is up to you to choose whether to believe me or not."

Buzz's gut clenched. He knew she was completely insane and obviously her insanity was rubbing off onto him.

Energy crackled in the room. The air around Cassandra thickened and began to swirl. Buzz's eyes bugged. *Had she been telling the truth? Was she really from space? It wasn't possible, was it?* His muscles locked as her lower body became fuzzy.

Last chance, she whispered in his head.

He flinched. *Could he live without knowing, without her?* The latter thought sent pain rocketing to his heart in a resounding no! He didn't stop to think, he just leapt. There was a bright light and the room disappeared. When the spots stopped floating before his eyes Buzz realized they were standing on the bridge of a ship which appeared to be in the middle of a jungle.

"It's true," he murmured to himself, his tense muscles relaxing one by one.

Cassandra smiled. "Of course it's true."

"I'm sorry," his voice trailed off.

"Don't be. You're here now."

He glanced out the viewing window. "Where are we?"

"In the jungle I grew up in." Her gaze shifted to the instrument panel. "We're still on Earth."

Buzz nodded, trying to comprehend all that was happening around him. "Where are we going?"

"Planet Zaron."

Excitement swept through him. His dream of returning to space was about to be answered. Fear and anticipation filled his mind reminding him again that he'd been grounded from space travel for a reason. Buzz shrugged it off. He'd worry about the radiation poisoning later. "Never heard of Zaron."

She laughed. "You will." Cassandra motioned toward the instrument panel, then as if reading his mind she said, "You need not worry about the remnants of your illness. You've been healed."

Buzz stood in shocked silence as he digested her words.

"Do you doubt me?" She arched a brow, daring him to question her statement.

He glanced around at the bridge, his gaze lingering on the controls. "Not anymore." He laughed then sobered. "I love you, you know." He paused. "Both of you." Buzz wrapped his arms around her stomach and tenderly kissed her neck.

Cassandra's eyes filled with fresh tears. "You know about the baby?"

He nodded. "I had a gut feeling after we'd made love."

"And you don't mind?" She bit her lower lip.

He smiled and kissed her again. "Mind? Are you kidding? I'm over the moon."

"Not yet but you will be soon." She laughed. "I love you too."

"I know." He grinned. "I just wish my sister Carrie knew about all this."

Cassandra smiled. "That can be arranged."

Buzz stilled. "Seriously?"

She nodded. "Absolutely. I'll arrange for someone from Zaron to notify her. Perhaps I'll have Orion send a Phantom Warrior. They can easily slip on and off the planet without being detected."

He frowned. "I don't know if I like the sound of that."

"They aren't too bad once you get past their intimidating appearance." She laughed. "They will do her no harm. You have my word."

"As long as you're sure..." He shoved his hands in his pockets. "I don't want her to worry about me."

Cassandra's grin widened. "Then it is done."

Buzz's lips quirked, everything had turned out better than his dreams. "Let's go home."

*   *   *   *   *

Cassandra listened to the message Orion had left her and then followed his instructions to the letter. She gathered the stones which made up the transport outside, permanently disabling the device. The Atlantean people would now be safe from humans.

Back inside the ship she pressed several buttons and flipped a few switches, firing up the engines. Buzz's face held pure joy as the craft lifted from the ground. He turned to her and smiled, love shining in his gray-green eyes. Cassandra's heart gave a little flip.

"Does this ship fly itself?" he asked, mischief twitching the corners of his mouth.

"Practically," she answered cautiously, her eyes narrowing in suspicion.

"Perhaps you'd like to give me a tour," he suggested, his eyes widening in innocence.

"If you wish," her voice purred.

The answering smile he gave her was feral. "Great, let's start with the sleep chamber."

Cassandra felt her eyes widen. Her channel flooded as his heated gaze swept over her body telling her without words how he planned to pass the time.

Buzz stalked forward, his outstretched arms telegraphing his intent. Cassandra giggled then spun around out of his reach. She raced for the ladder leading to the sleep chamber. Buzz caught her a second before she could climb down.

"You can't get away from me that easy." His arms closed around her shoulders, sliding down her arms and around to cup her full breasts.

She moaned as he pressed his thumbs against her nipples. "Who said I was trying to get away?" Cassandra smiled. She finally had her true-mate by her side. All was right in the galaxy.

The End

RETURN

Dedication

ଈ

This book is dedicated to all the readers. I'm sorry it's taken me so long to finish this final installment of the Atlantean's Quest Series. I appreciate all of the emails and encouragement you've sent my way. I hope you enjoy this book.

Author Note

To avoid confusion, I wanted to let you know that this story time line takes place at the same time as Atlantean's Quest Book Three: Redemption and Atlantean Heat.

In this work of fiction, unsafe sexual practices are depicted. In "real" life ALWAYS practice safe sex.

Happy Reading,

Jordan Summers

Atlantis...

Many myths surround the disappearance of this mysterious island continent and its advanced civilization. Some believe everyone perished in a cataclysmic event that caused the ocean to rise and open its gaping liquid mouth, swallowing all evidence of their existence. Others speculate that some of the people survived and fled, returning to their true home many galaxies away.

What if they were both right and the truth lay somewhere in between?

Atlantean's Quest is the tale of three women, Rachel Evans, Jaclyn Ward, and Brigit Taylor, whose ordinary lives become extraordinary upon encountering these mythical people. This cosmic interaction changes these friends' lives forever. In the quest for survival, lives are lost, but friendship and love remain.

This is Brigit's story.

Chapter One

 හ

"Warning! Warning! Warning! Planetary object approaching rapidly," the computer blared, followed by a quick burst of sirens.

Orion's ship broke through the atmosphere leaving a wispy vapor trail in its wake. The craft shuddered, his muscles strained to hold it steady as the outer alloy panels heated to a glowing red. Sweat broke out across his forehead. If it got any hotter in here, he'd roast like a *corgal tanger* on a spit. Orion pushed a button on the control panel above his head. The computer quieted. The ship cooled an instant later and then accelerated, throwing him back against his seat.

Hang on! The mental command went out to his passenger, Cassandra. He didn't bother to look at the Atlantean woman while he steered the ship. She would be of no assistance. Like his brother, Ares, Cassandra was born and reared in the jungle on this planet. For all intents and purposes, she was an Earthling, which was one of the many reasons she'd asked to come along on this mission.

The primitive radar system on this planet would only pick up a brief blip before he disappeared altogether. They'd consider it a momentary malfunction and not bother to check it out. A Zaronian warrior would not be so careless. Even the most innocent ping could turn into a major threat to planetary security.

He'd spent the past month studying everything there was to know about this tiny blue-green planet known as Earth. Queen Rachel and Jac were only too happy to fill in any missing gaps from his knowledge. He knew the foods, the topography and the weaponry. He'd even mastered the subtle nuances of communication. Their cultures might be different, but soon he'd acquire that knowledge too and be like every other Earthling, only better.

Orion was confident he'd be able to blend in with the primitive natives long enough to convince Brigit that her friends were safe, unharmed and now resided on planet Zaron. It would be a "walk in the cake" as Jac liked to say.

He sensed Cassandra's interested gaze before seeing it. She caressed his muscled form, focusing on the male bulge between his thighs. He tensed as his cock responded. *Be careful, little one,* he communicated telepathically, the preferred way of the Atlantean people. *I can read your lustful thoughts.* He looked at her from beneath hooded eyes.

Cassandra shifted under his regard. As an Atlantean woman in her sexual prime, she was not shy about conveying her thoughts or acting upon her natural urges. Like Orion, she too searched for what could not be found on Zaron.

Don't worry. He shook his head and smiled. *I'm not interested in you either, and I believe I can contain my boredom for an hour or so longer.*

Don't flatter yourself, warrior. Cassandra laughed. *It was just a thought, not a proposition. I would think you of all people would know the difference.*

He grinned. *I do, hence the warning.*

Such conceit. She straightened in her seat. *Not that it isn't warranted, but I look for something…different. Less Atlantean.*

And you think you'll find it in an Earthling?

Perhaps…

You'll forgive me if I disagree.

'Tis your choice. She shrugged absently.

Orion flicked switches transferring fuel into their reserve tanks. He wouldn't argue his point. *Where is it you wish me to take you?*

I've longed to see the ocean again. Cassandra sighed, her expression turning dreamy and distant. *Queen Rachel told me I might enjoy a place called California.*

Orion frowned and punched another button, bringing up a holographic map of planet Earth. *Where did she say this place is located?*

The same piece of land you need to be on to find Brigit.

He glanced at her, not liking the reminder about his current assignment. Cassandra stared at the swirling map. Her eyes widened as her gaze alighted on a spot that glowed like a jewel under the sun.

What do the glowing lights represent on the map?

Colonies. He pointed to a spot on the east coast of the North American continent. *The brighter the light, the more populated the area. This is where I must go.*

Cassandra reached out and touched a spot on the opposite coast. *I want you to take me here.*

Orion glanced, then pressed a button to zoom into the area she'd indicated. *The place you wish to visit is called Los Angeles.*

Cassandra smiled. "Los Angeles," she murmured aloud, testing the name on her tongue. *That's in California, right?*

He nodded.

Good, then it's settled. I will go to Los Angeles, California to begin my search.

Queen Rachel said you will need something called money. I've researched this item. It is what the humans use to barter with in exchange for goods, lodging and food.

Do we have any of this…money?

Yes. The replicator managed to produce a travel sack full of the stuff. You should have more than enough for what you need. I've also taken the liberty of placing a deciphering unit in your bag. You'll be able to find any meaning or item by thinking about the object. It should help when it comes to communicating with the humans.

Orion slid his hand across a panel at his side. It opened silently. He pulled out a rectangular metal device.

What is that?

A communication device.

Like the deciphering unit?

No. He flipped a switch on the side of the object and a tiny screen appeared. *If you need assistance or come to your senses and want to return home, flick this switch and hold the device next to your head. It will pick up your thoughts, in the same way we're having this conversation, and transport you to the ship. Make sure you allow yourself plenty of space when you activate it, because the device is powerful enough to transport objects around you.*

Cassandra nodded and reached for the communication device.

Orion pulled it out of reach. *Are you sure you want to do this? 'Tis not too late to change your mind.*

She forced a smile and faced him unflinchingly. *I've never been so sure of anything in my life.*

He stared at her for a few moments, assessing her sincerity, deliberating her fate. Finally, he nodded. *California it is.*

Reluctantly, he dropped Cassandra off in Los Angeles, California. She waved goodbye as his ship rose, a contented smile planted on her face. He still didn't like the fact he'd left an Atlantean woman alone and unguarded on a beach, but Orion understood her need to carve out her own destiny. For he held the same desire. With her departure, his ship's weight and readings adjusted to accommodate his lone presence.

Over the last few moons, Orion had grown restless like the other unattached males and females on his home planet. Zaron did not hold the same appeal to him as it once had. He itched to stretch the boundaries set in place for centuries. Maybe, while here on Earth, he'd take some time to do just that, between babysitting the Queen's friend, finding the Seer and making sure Cassandra was doing well. He frowned as his latest assignment intruded on his thoughts.

He'd earned the title of warrior long ago, due to his birthright and his proven abilities. Later, he'd reached First in Command. His thoughts trailed off. He could no longer claim the position of First in Command with Ares' return. Orion squelched the bitterness threatening to rise. He was happy to have family again. Truly. It was far more important than any position, but... It would take some adjusting to get used to his new role.

That was the main reason he'd stepped forward for this menial job. He wanted the chance to leave the planet and clear his head, even if it were only for a few days. He needed to make decisions about his future. Mingling with the Earthlings, with their primitive minds and underdeveloped bodies, just happened to be an unpleasant byproduct of the trip.

Perhaps not so unpleasant, Orion thought, as he considered Queen Rachel and Jac's appearance.

They were attractive enough, in an *exotic* sort of way, but far inferior to Atlantean women in strength, beauty and agility. Although he'd never expressed his private thoughts, Orion still could not understand how his brother, Ares, and King Eros settled beneath their stature. And he wasn't the only one. Whispers caressed the winds of Zaron, leaving emerging doubts in the minds of the people that their energy binds held. Still, no one dared to step forward and challenge the King...yet.

Perhaps their choices came from being marooned on Earth for so many years. Isolation did strange things to one's thought processes. Coupled with the fact that this was a primitive planet, it would make the time here nearly unbearable.

Despite his brother and the King's reassurances that their energy binds were intact, Orion held doubts. It wasn't possible to bind with a human, *was it*?

He shook his head at the absurdity of the question. Earth women were good for one thing, and one thing only — sex. Anything more would make him as foolish as his brother — and Orion was far from foolish.

But, he was *curious.*

He recalled Jac's parting words, "Curiosity killed the kangaroo". Orion wasn't sure exactly what type of creature a kangaroo was but it mustn't be too fierce if a mere thought could slay it. He mentally brushed her warning aside. He wouldn't allow the words of an Earth woman to deter him, even if said woman was his brother's alleged true-mate.

Once he encountered Brigit and found the Seer, he'd take several days and explore the planet. Perhaps, experience a few of the female delights available. Orion shifted as he imagined sinking his silver-ringed cock past a woman's petal-soft folds into her wet quim. It should only take ten to twenty females before he was suitably spent. Afterward, he'd head back to Zaron where he would pick out an Atlantean woman, perform an energy bind and settle down.

Should be easy enough.

It mattered little to Orion that he hadn't been unable to find anyone thus far who'd kept his attention for more than a few physical joinings. He was sure upon his return he'd succeed…or leave Zaron for good. Love would not be part of the equation. It was a useless emotion that could only get a warrior killed — or worse, weakened to the babbling state his brother, Ares, and the King existed in.

At least that was the plan…

* * * * *

Brigit adjusted the fabric in front of her. The wasabi-green galactic dragon costume turned out even better than she anticipated. The fabric horns protruding from the headdress were perfect in their burnt-orange splendor. The matching claws on her feet were equally as impressive. No one would beat her out of first place in this year's most original costume contest, not even her ex, Rocket Man Rick, and his new girlfriend, Dorothy, the galactic slut puppy.

She giggled. He'd be sorry once he caught sight of her costume. Brigit continued to check the satiny material for any remaining straight pins she might have accidentally left behind. The last thing she needed was to get stabbed in the middle of her stroll down the catwalk.

The turnout for Conlunar this year was the biggest yet. The packed Marquis Hiltonia Hotel drew sci-fi and fantasy lovers from all over the world. Brigit came every year to take part in the costume contest and to be close to people who shared her dream of space travel. It was one of the few places she could talk about visiting the stars without hearing snickers of laughter.

Even her best friends, Jaclyn Ward and Rachel Evans hadn't been able to keep a straight face when she'd discussed space travel. One day, when it became accessible to everyone, Brigit would have the last laugh. She only hoped she lived long enough to see that day.

Located on forty-five lushly wooded acres, the hotel facility offered every amenity. It boasted an indoor and outdoor pool, large work desks in all the rooms, two phone lines, robes and a fitness center.

Not that Brigit ever looked inside the latter. Blech, sweating wasn't her thing. Nor were bugs, with their beady little eyes and clingy little legs and gnashing little mandibles. She didn't do woods, mountains or the ocean either—too many creepy, crawly, bitey things in those places. Basically, anywhere without a department store and sidewalk was strictly off-limits in her mind. That's what made outer space so perfect...no bugs.

If God meant for Brigit to explore deeply wooded areas, She would have put in sidewalks and made skin bug repellent.

Brigit gazed out the window at the scenic dusk-draped landscaping and shuddered. She could appreciate the beauty of life and the lush panoramic garden views with its wall-sized hedges as long as she remained safely on this side of the windowpane. Green, growing, creeping, alive things were fine for the planet, but not her. Brigit rubbed her skin to dispel the sensation of tiny spiders crawling over the fine hairs on her arms.

She took a calming you're-not-outside-so-you're-safe breath, then glanced back at her latest design. Tingles raced along Brigit's spine as she imagined the crowd's reaction to her galactic dragon costume. In her mind, she could almost hear the applause.

Would it be mere applause?

She smiled inwardly. Nope, they would roar. She might even receive a standing ovation. She could almost see the people now. Brigit took a couple of practice bows, then waved and blew kisses to the invisible crowd like she'd just been crowned universal prom queen.

The only thing that would make her moment in the spotlight better was if Rachel and Jac arrived in time to cheer from the front row. But that wasn't going to happen.

A momentary rush of worry swept through Brigit and she faltered mid-bow. Ever since Rachel had gone missing while on a research assignment with her boss, Professor Donald Rumsinger in the jungle, Brigit had known something wasn't right. The professor had returned without Rachel, but quickly left when rumbles of a lost tribe surfaced briefly in the media. Jac went looking for Rachel a week later and Brigit's sense of foreboding worsened. Now they were both missing. There was no doubt that something had gone wrong. Very wrong. She tucked the anxiety away, refusing to traverse that mental path. Worrying never helped anything.

If anyone could find Rachel, it was Jac. She may not be a commando, but she was the next best thing to it. Her ex-Navy

SEAL father had made sure of it before he passed away. Brigit reminded herself again that her friends hadn't been gone *that* long.

Despite Jac's flippant *be back by the weekend* remark, Brigit knew it would take longer to find Rachel than that, especially with Rachel's boss blocking Jac's way at every turn. Heck, flying down to the jungle and back would eat up at least two days each way. She may be a bit on the flaky side, but Brigit prided herself on her ability to think clearly under pressure. Well, her version of clear anyway.

"It's only been a little over two weeks," she said aloud as if to reassure herself.

But deep down Brigit knew there was more going on than just Professor Rumsinger deceiving Rachel. Her best friends' horoscopes read like the who's who of planetary alignments. She'd never seen anything like it. Greater forces were at work, but for what purpose, she did not know. She only wished that Rachel and Jac had believed her when she tried to warn them.

Subconsciously, her hand moved to the talisman around her neck. She fingered the medallion to ward off the ominous feelings coursing through her. The urge to flee was great. But from what? Brigit's gaze darted around the empty room, before landing once more on her costume.

"Screw with the planets and they'll screw you back," she muttered, while ignoring the moths fluttering in her stomach. Wasn't she doing the same thing with her own astrological chart? Shouldn't she have stayed home after reading the travel caveats? And what about the warning of a stranger changing her life forever?

Brigit brushed the disturbing thought aside. She wouldn't be meeting any stranger from a faraway land. How could she at a time like this? It was best to focus on what was happening today, right this moment, no matter how frivolous. That being the case, she needed to get ready to kick Rocket Man Rick's ass in the costume contest. Yes, that was what she should concentrate on. The future would take care of itself, with or without her assistance.

That's what I'm afraid of. The thought came unbidden in her mind. She dropped the talisman and proceeded to dress.

* * * * *

Seven o'clock finally arrived. Brigit padded out of her room and down hall toward the lavishly decorated banquet room. She strolled past the front desk, hearing the employees' muffled *oohs* and *ahs* through the thick material surrounding her ears. The muted sound reminded her how she'd miscalculated one little teensy weensy thing on the costume — earholes.

How was she supposed to hear the roar of applause through what was effectively earmuffs?

She continued ambling forward, taking care to pick up her enormous feet, so she didn't trip over her orange dragon claws. No sign of Rick so far. Brigit knew he'd planned to dress like Apollo from the original Battlesun Gattica series. Begrudgingly, she admitted he did sort of resemble the actor who used to play that part. That had probably been why she'd fallen for him in the first place. She'd always had a childhood crush on the men from that television show.

Brigit passed several people who smiled, their eyes briefly alighting on her costume, before looking beyond her in horror. She glanced over her padded shoulder, but didn't see anything unusual. She shrugged and continued on.

A six-foot hard plastic tail, attached by thick string to the rest of her costume, swung from side to side like a scythe as she walked. From a distance, Brigit heard muffled grunts and a few groans, which she assumed were fellow contestants expressing their imminent defeat. She giggled, ignoring the drag of her tail.

They know a winner when they see one.

Brigit turned to smile and acknowledge that defeat, only to see two people lying on the ground gripping their stomachs. She frowned. What in the world was wrong with them? They did a "desperate Montezuma's revenge" roll onto their sides, before staggering to their knees. Hmm...It looked like it was a good thing she'd skipped the catered buffet this afternoon. Brigit kept walking. The contest was in the bag.

* * * * *

Orion set his ship down in the middle of a grove of trees. The branches swayed dangerously to the side before settling back into place. With a flick of a switch, the craft disappeared, cloaked in the fading tendrils of sunlight. He glanced down at the time indicator. The number seven-fifteen blinked back.

He pressed another button at his wrist and a blip pulsed on the hidden sensor. The building where Brigit appeared to be, brimmed with human activity. No matter. He still must contact the woman before finding the Seer in the jungle and exploring the rest of the planet.

Orion passed his palm over a scanner and a panel on the far wall slid open, allowing him to exit the craft. He sent out a quick probe to ensure he was alone. It came back "humanoid life undetected". Using stealth, Orion made his way through the woods, heading toward the main building. The gathering darkness did not hinder his progress. He could see the trail in front of him clearly.

The blips on his wristband grew stronger, their red pulses resembling beating hearts. The trees thinned a little, giving him a good view of his intended target. He stopped, slipping behind one of the huge bark-covered trunks. Orion watched as ornately dressed couples entered a portal, which quickly closed behind them. They didn't appear to have to display papers, so perhaps he'd be allowed in.

He was about to step away from the tree when a scurrying noise caught his attention. He looked around, watchful for an oncoming attack. Bark rained down upon his head, bouncing off his shoulder. He spun, sword drawn, ready to face the unseen threat. A gray creature with beady brown eyes and a bushy tail froze mid-motion. Orion relaxed, for it appeared harmless enough.

The animal stared at him a moment, then began to chatter and squeak. It hunched its little legs and launched itself off the tree and through the air straight at him. Orion's eyes widened in surprise and he jumped back unsure how to battle the unwarranted attack.

The creature hit the ground a few feet from him, then stood on its hind legs, his chatter rising in volume. Orion hit several buttons on his wrist, but nothing seemed able to translate its angry words.

"I know not what you want," he bellowed, as the creature picked up something small with its front paws and lobbed it in his direction.

Orion ran his hands through his hair and then sheathed his sword. He backed away slowly, his gaze never leaving the animal. Jac hadn't warned him about hostile beasts. Given her sense of mirth, she probably hadn't done so on purpose. He groaned inwardly and made a mental note to speak with his brother.

Now that he realized an attack could come from any direction, the next creature Orion encountered would not fare as well as this one.

He took stock of his weapons and equipment, then strode toward the door cautiously, alert to any further threats. Several of the people entering the structure ahead of him appeared armed. Orion patted the Zaronian sword strapped to his thigh. If a battle broke out, he was prepared.

As he approached the portal, it slid open silently. Orion glanced around, but no guard waited on the other side of the threshold. He took a deep breath and consciously relaxed his tense muscles, before stepping inside. A rush of cool air greeted his skin. He held his breath and immediately pressed a button on his wristband. The pressure within the structure registered as normal, oxygen levels steady, no poisonous gases detected. Orion released the air from his lungs. So far he'd been fortunate to have gone undiscovered this long. He refused to acknowledge the bushy-tailed, bucktoothed beast in the woods.

Several men and women stood behind a waist-high structure, their gazes locked to him. Dressed in similar blue uniforms, their curious whispers rose as he approached their location. Orion struggled with the urge to greet the women in the traditional Atlantean manner. Jac and Queen Rachel warned him not to do so. He thought it wrong, but followed their instructions.

A couple of the people before him pointed to the mark he bore on his cheek. Regardless of their primitive nature, they obviously recognized his position. The Zaronian burn identified him as a warrior of courage and honor. They bared their teeth when he stopped in front of them, but none bowed in respect.

Orion pushed another button on his wristband. The showing of one's teeth appeared to be some form of greeting called a smile. Without thought, he mirrored their behavior.

A couple of the women, one fair of hair like Atlantean women and the other onyx skinned, stepped forward, their gazes raking his black synthetic uniform in hungry appreciation. Orion didn't need to consult his translator device to know what that meant.

Despite their unique appearance, women didn't change much from species to species—except on planet Radon, where the females' quims were located where their faces should be. That slight *alteration* had initially given Orion pause, but hadn't kept him from fucking a few dozen of them in the end. His smile deepened as he made a mental note to return to the two women and take them up on their *offer*, after he located Brigit.

This Earth visit may not be so bad after all.

The roar of a crowd snapped Orion's attention away from the two women. He bowed slightly to the females and then strode down the long hall toward the growing sound. When he reached the great hall he saw the source of the uproar.

A platform of sorts stood in the middle of a pulsing throng made up of men and women. The warm fragrant air reminded him of the spice and bloom fields on Zaron. Orion glanced around in an attempt to ascertain the source of the merriment.

Several people stood on the platform dressed in fineries, facing the crowd. A couple strolled down to the end of the walk, hands clasped and smiling at one another. They were handsome for Earthlings with their brown hair and matching clothing. Perhaps they ruled these people.

Caught up in the festive atmosphere, Orion almost missed the deadly slithering creature stalking the group from the side. His hand sought his sword. He curled his fingers around the hilt in preparation for battle. The creature stood not much higher than his waist, but looked threatening nonetheless. Size did not necessarily indicate fighting ability. He'd learned that the hard way in his youth and only moments ago with the furry beast outside.

The creature's green skin sparkled under the bright focused beams of light shining down from above, while the orange thorny spikes protruding from its head looked as if they could rip a man asunder. His gaze traveled down to its unsheathed claws. Orion shuddered at the thought of having one of those sticking out of his abdomen. He must act swiftly.

The people on the platform walked out one by one toward the middle of the masses. The crowd erupted as each person stopped and waved, drawing more appreciation from the adoring multitude. Orion pushed his way forward, shoving people out of the way, his gaze locked on the hideous creature as it crept toward the unsuspecting group. With the

Goddess's blessing, he'd be able to slay the beast before it harmed anyone.

* * * * *

Brigit ambled over the steps, her plastic-clawed feet clacking as she reached the top of the platform. Her ex, Rocket Man Rick and his slut, Dorothy were returning from their stroll down the catwalk. They smiled until they caught a glimpse of her costume, then frowned in unison. Brigit giggled.

Prepare to be trounced, you mutant turds.

The announcer introduced Brigit and she stepped out onto center stage, dragon tail swinging from side to side. The crowd applauded. With each step she took, the roar grew louder.

This was exactly what she'd hoped for. Better than she'd imagined. Rick and Dorothy probably quaked in their boots right about now. The contest win was a sure thing. As she reached the end of the platform, Brigit took a bow, then turned her head to make sure the crowd received the full effect of her costume.

It was at that moment that she realized the people in the front row appeared to be staring at something behind her. Brigit swung around, sending her tail slashing through the air. People gasped and ducked. That's when she saw him.

A man well over six-six strode toward her with a wicked looking sword in his hand and a dangerous glint in his two-tone eyes. His hair, a turbulent shade of black with light blond stripes, flowed freely over his wide shoulders and down his back. He swept the runway like a storm, his silver hoop earrings giving off lightning-like flashes under the spotlight. He wasn't so much a man as a force of nature. And that microburst was coming right for her.

Brigit squinted through her costume's eyeholes and strained to hear around the fabric muffling her ears. Had the announcer introduced him? So drunk on adulation, she hadn't bothered to listen. She knew she was the last contestant, so who was he?

Her gaze strayed back to the man's face of its own volition. His features could make angels weep, choirs sing and sinners repent. He was sensually beautiful, while retaining a fierce savagery. And there was no doubt that he was truculent, if not downright hostile. A wild palm-sized Celtic knot tattoo encircled his left cheek. Instead of deterring from his appearance, it only added to his devastating presence. If a genie mated with an alien, this would be their love child.

The skin-tight material of his costume left little to the imagination. Brigit saw the outline of another set of rings through his nipples. Her stomach tightened and gooseflesh rose on her arms. Something primal roared to life inside of her and moisture pooled between her quivering thighs. Brigit's heart paused, then begin to thrum madly. She felt the beat all the way to her clit. So this is what instantaneous attraction felt like. Her attention moved back to his nipples. How many piercings did this guy have? The thought of finding out the answer to that question sent a wave of dizziness through her, threatening to buckle her knees.

Her gaze swept him like tornado over Kansas, dropping of its own accord to the area below where his belt should have been. The bulge there made Brigit's breath stutter in her lungs. She blinked. That wasn't humanly possible, was it? The bulge grew under her perusal.

Heck, a second ago she thought the sword was impressive. Goodness!

Transfixed, Brigit almost missed the glint of silver as he raised his weapon, preparing to attack. And there was no doubt in her mind he was going to strike her. She screamed and took a step back. Her clawed foot caught the edge of the stage, knocking her off balance. Brigit flailed helplessly, trying to keep from falling into the crowd. The movement sent her headpiece cascading onto the front row. She heard groans and grunts coming from the people behind her. She looked around a second before her tail slammed down into the groin of one of the men trying to help her back onto the stage. His eyes crossed and he keeled over.

"Sorry," she said, wincing before turning back to the immediate threat. Tall, dark and deadly's gaze locked on her face. Sudden confusion marred his flawless features, but it was too late he'd already swung the weapon. The hiss of the blade stung the air.

Brigit screeched and tried to flinch away, but her bulky costume slowed her movements, while the hands behind her pushed her forward into the oncoming blow. She watched in fascinated horror as the blade came crashing toward her. This was it. She was going to die at Conlunar.

The burly announcer caught the man's arm mid-swing, nearly toppling him, but it prevented the deadly blade from reaching its destination. The weapon stopped inches from Brigit's face. The breeze from the motion fluffed her hair. Even this close, the sword looked real…and incredibly sharp. With a microphone in one hand and the man's arm in the other, the announcer addressed the crowd. "I don't think we need a judge's score sheet for this one, do you folks? But to keep everything fair, let's see the scores." The score sheets were gathered and handed to the announcer. "I believe we've found our winner. Let's hear it for the dragon slayer."

The audience roared, coming to their feet in a standing ovation—*her ovation*. Brigit could see Rick and Dorothy hooting and hollering in the background. This couldn't be happening.

Someone pushed Brigit from behind, taking an extra minute to allow their hands to linger on her dragon-tailed butt. She glanced around and glared, but couldn't ascertain the guilty party. It didn't matter. She had bigger fish to boil. Mr. Tall, Gorgeous and Sneaky had just walked away with *her* trophy.

Well he wasn't going to get away with it. She planned to protest the results.

Brigit turned on the sword-carrying, Chippendoll-looking warrior, who'd just snatched victory out of her grasp. She planted her hands on her green material-covered hips. The man continued to stare at her as if one of her orange horns protruded out of her forehead.

There was something about the way he looked at her that made Brigit decidedly uncomfortable and it had nothing to do with the fact that one of his eyes was aqua blue and the other was jade green. Any other time she'd consider that particular trait unusual, but at that moment she was too mad to think.

His gaze traveled over her costume-covered body, raking her length, as if by doing so he could see beneath the wasabi-colored material. Brigit's nipples swelled, puckering painfully beneath her lace bra. Sweat beaded her lower lip, when only moments ago she hadn't been hot. Her panties dampened to a puddle.

Poor ventilation, that's all. He wasn't causing it.

Confused and angered by her body's response, Brigit squared her shoulders and pinned him with narrowed eyes. *Uh-huh! You're not getting out of this that easy, buddy.* He didn't even blink.

Her fingers curled into fists as she fought the urge to pummel him where he stood. It might take a ladder and a baseball bat, but she could do it. They had to have those items somewhere in the hotel. She continued to seethe. And what did he do? He actually had the nerve to look amused.

That's it, you dragon slaying perv! You're about to encounter my wrath. Duck down here so I can reach you. You won't be smiling in a minute.

His lips quirked as if he'd heard her thoughts.

Brigit stepped forward to tell him exactly what she thought of him or to box his ears, she wasn't sure which. His nostrils flared, along with his multicolored eyes. He straightened to his full height as if readying for her approach. No, readying wasn't the right word. He practically *dared* her to come forward.

Well she wasn't going to do it. Not if it would play into his plans and make him happy. *No way! Uh-huh!*

Brigit shifted, trying to regroup. She battled the impulse to step back. From his appearance, the big gorgeous bully was probably used to intimidating people. Luckily, she wasn't *most* people. Brigit knew she was scowling, but she couldn't help herself. He'd stolen her win, humiliated her in front of her ex-boyfriend and his slutty new girlfriend and the bastard didn't even have the decency to look guilty about it. Hell, she threw her arms up into the air, he actually looked pleased.

Had Rocket Man Rick put him up to this? She met her ex's gaze. He smiled and had the temerity to wink. Furious, Brigit longed to smack that smug look right off his face, but first, she'd take care of the dragon slayer, who continued to look at her like he'd never seen a woman dressed in a wasabi-green dragon costume before. What planet was he from? Didn't he know it was impolite to stare?

The man's gaze skittered across her face to settle on the front of her zippered costume. He paused there, lingering on the exposed vee of her skin. He moistened his full bottom lip with the tip of his tongue. Heat radiated from him, penetrating wherever he looked.

What was he, a human blast furnace?

Brigit resisted the urge to zip her collar. The last thing he needed to know was that his goo-goo eyes affected her. Had she learned nothing from her last encounter with a splashy space guy? Obviously, not. What was she saying? The dragon slayer's smooth moves weren't working on her. But even as the insidious thought crossed her mind, Brigit's heart pounded madly, nearly deafening her while her throat went Sahara dry. She sucked on her tongue hard, trying to garner enough to spit in her mouth to yell at him.

The announcer quieted the crowd, before she could speak. "Let's find out the winner's name." He smiled as he swung the microphone in front of the dragon slayer's sensuous mouth. And it was sensuous, the way his full lips curled slightly, covering perfect white teeth and a tongue made for laving the most sensitive skin on a woman's body.

The warrior said nothing.

"What's your name, dragon slayer?" he asked again.

"Orion." The man's smoky voice echoed throughout the ballroom, sending ominous shivers down Brigit's spine.

"All hail Orion from the planet..." The announcer paused.

"Zaron," the warrior said, his gaze never leaving her as he took a bow.

She squeezed her legs together, ignoring the throb coming from her clit. No way. No how.

Brigit's horoscope slammed in her head. It wasn't possible. It had to be some kind of cosmic joke. First Apollo, now Orion.

Not happening.

Chapter Two

Orion stared at the woman before him with something akin to terror surging through his body. Yet, he feared nothing. His heart pounded painfully against his rib cage as he considered how close he'd come to killing her. He didn't want to think about it. Couldn't think about it. Had she not staggered back at the same time the man grabbed his arm, she would be dead. His blood froze in his veins as the implications of his actions sunk into his mind.

He would have failed his mission for the first time in his life if he had killed an innocent. A good rationale for feeling the way he did at this moment, but that wasn't the only reason. Orion refused to look too closely at what the other might be. He didn't understand these feelings and he didn't understand this world. Why would a woman cover herself in such hideousness? Especially one as lovely as the vision before him. His gaze locked on her glowing red hair. He'd never seen anything like it. He longed to touch the flame to see if it was a hot as it appeared.

The man straining to hold Orion's forearm released him and shoved a cup of some sort into his palm. He stared at the alloy, turning it from side to side. What was he supposed to do with this? He examined it, but other than holding a fair amount of Zaronian ale, he saw no use for it.

Orion gave the man a curt nod, then stepped toward the flame-haired woman. She was unlike anyone he'd ever encountered. Remarkable. Her green eyes spat fire every time she glanced his way. He understood her anger. He'd been close to death on several occasions while in battle.

But there was more than simply anger in her gaze. There was hurt, envy and something else. Something he recognized instantly...*awareness*. His eyes widened at the realization. Despite her anger this woman wanted him, almost as much as he wanted her. That thought sent a surge of urgency through Orion's body, one he hadn't felt in a very long time—if ever.

He flashed her a look that normally brought women flocking to his quarters on Zaron. Her gaze flared a fraction, then narrowed dangerously. Orion watched her tiny hands curl into fists. Did she think to harm him? The thought was ridiculous, but he admired the courage it took coming from one so small and it intrigued him. Perhaps all the small creatures on this planet were fierce.

Crimson color swept her neck and over her face. He debated whether to probe her mind, but decided against it. Her species was far too primitive to accept such a prolonged invasion without a true-mate energy bond in place. But he was tempted, especially after accidentally catching a few of her racier thoughts.

He stroked her with his gaze and heard her bite back a growl. Orion's lips twitched as he fought the urge to laugh. He loved a good fight, on and off the battlefield. This woman would not come easily to his bed, but she would *come* many times once she got there. The thought provoked, aroused and surprised him. He wasn't at all certain when he'd made the decision to have her. He only knew it to be so, as if the Goddess herself had leaned forward and whispered *take her, she's yours* in his ear. Never one to "look a prized zebra in its teeth" he accepted the Goddess' gift without question.

"The first prize goes to Orion, dragon slayer from Zaron," the man announced to the masses, motioning to the cup in Orion's hand.

Dragon slayer? Why did the man keep calling him that? He wanted to check his wristband to see what kind of creature that was but he didn't want to draw any more attention than necessary.

The crowd exploded. Loud whoops filled the air as he followed the announcer's lead and tentatively raised the cup above his head. Orion was deep into his fantasies about the woman when the announcer's next words dowsed his ardor as effectively as if he'd ripped the Katronian rings from his cock.

"Second prize goes to crowd favorite, Brigit Taylor for her celestial dragon." The man held out a document to the spirited woman. She hesitated a second before snatching the paper out of his fingers. Her gaze swept past the announcer going straight to the cup in Orion's hand, before she turned to the crowd and waved. Brigit smiled sweetly at the people, until she glanced back at him. Her happiness faded, replaced by a massive ball of rage. Without touching him, she slayed him repeatedly with her eyes.

This was the woman he sought? This was Brigit? Impossible! The man had made a mistake. Yet, even as Orion considered the probability, he knew there'd been no error. He could almost hear the tinkling sounds of the Goddess' laughter over the crowd's din. She hadn't blessed him with this woman, she'd cursed him.

Orion's gaze swept Brigit once more, taking in the hidden curves, imagining the feel of her skin beneath his fingertips, the taste of her nipples in his mouth. He swallowed hard. What would she look like without the hideous covering? His palms itched and his body tightened. So this was Brigit Taylor, friend to Queen Rachel and Jac.

This changed noth—everything.

There had to be a compromise somewhere. He knew his orders, but conveying his message and then leaving no longer seemed like a viable option. Besides, his orders mentioned nothing about refraining from touching, although perhaps they'd implied as much. King Eros and Ares should've been more specific. They'd left seduction floating in the realm of possibility. Orion's smile deepened as he considered the prospects. There was "more than one way to skin a weasel".

He sheathed his sword and laughed under his breath at the fates that brought him to this tiny blue-green planet. The Goddess certainly worked in mysterious ways. Suddenly the thought of babysitting didn't sound quite so unappealing.

* * * * *

Brigit seethed in anger as she rounded on him. "Who are you? Did Rick hire you? Damn, that's desperate even for him."

"No, I—"

"Then where in the hell did you come from?" she asked as she steamrolled past Orion, not waiting for an answer. "And don't you dare tell me Zaron," Brigit shot back over her shoulder as she unhooked her six-foot plastic tail and shoved it under her arm. What kind of name was Orion anyway? He might as well call himself Spock. Talk about unoriginal.

Like Brigit expected, the man followed her as she exited the stage. Rick and Dorothy laughed and pointed at her as she passed, but quickly stifled their mirth when the dragon slayer shot them an admonishing look. She fumed. She didn't need this…this…man sticking up for her. She could take care of herself. Brigit still couldn't believe she'd lost to a guy wearing what appeared to be spray-on clothes. It didn't matter that he looked like some kind of fabled god in them.

She glanced at him. He stalked behind her. There could be no other way to describe his movements or his grim expression. Brigit took a moment to examine his costume. It reminded her of something you'd get if Fred E. Rick's of Hollywood designed a spacesuit for men. Sexy even without a splash of color beyond a couple of jade accents. Were the judges blind? The crowd had decided the winner. The judges score sheets were simply a formality. She huffed. There was no accounting for taste.

Brigit turned forward in time to avoid colliding into a structural beam. He would've loved that, having her so distracted that she walked into something. Bastard! Grr…why did he have to look so good in that outfit anyway? The contest should have been based on talent, yet it had turned into a beauty contest. And there was no way in hell she could beat him in that arena. Heck, the chick who played Lara in Tomb Ryder would have a hard time and she was beyond gorgeous.

It wasn't fair. Brigit slapped the second place certificate against her padded thigh and glared over her shoulder once more. She groaned aloud. Just what she needed, a male version of an actress who embodied perfection following her around. As if things didn't suck enough at the moment.

Sweat from the crowd permeated the air. Brigit pinched her nose and fought to keep from gagging. Would it kill some of these people to use deodorant?

When they reached the relative quiet of the hallway, Brigit spun, dropping her plastic tail at her feet. The man almost slammed into her. She hadn't realized he'd closed the distance between them. She craned her neck and tried to ignore the heat coming off his body. Brigit straightened her spine before she did something stupid like sway into him. The fact that she found him attractive only angered her more. "I don't know who you think you are, coming in here and snatching victory from my hands, but I want you to know that I think it stinks. If I were bigger, you'd be sorry."

He frowned, his expression going to one of utter confusion. "I'm not sure what I have done to offend you, but…" He hit a button on his wrist. Something crackled, then buzzed. "I apologize."

Brigit glanced at his wrist and back to his face. "Don't you think you're taking this sci-fi convention a little too seriously? The spotlight isn't on you now. By the way, what's your real name? Bob? Fred? Tom? Percy?"

"I know not what you speak of. My name is as I told the people. I am Orion."

Brigit planted her hands on her costume-covered hips and gave him her best withering stare. He didn't crack a smile or even blink. Maybe he was telling the truth. She relaxed a fraction. "Hippie parents, eh? I understand. I came this close," she raised her hand and pinched her fingers together, "to being named Moonbeam."

Orion shook his head as if to clear it. "What do we do now?"

"What do you mean what do *we* do? I'm going back to my room to change into my next costume and you...you..." She poked him in the chest to punctuate each word. Touching him was a mistake. Her fingers quivered, hovering an inch away from his flesh, before balling into a fist. "I don't care what you do. It's your business, but I better not see your perfect ass on stage in twenty minutes."

He grinned. "You think my ass is perfect."

Brigit snorted. "Oh, please. You know you're gorgeous. If your head swelled any bigger, you wouldn't fit down this hallway." She waved her hands around to encompass the area.

A look of horror crossed Orion's face as he reached for his head. He examined it carefully with his fingertips for a few seconds, then dropped his hands away. A moment later, he seemed to relax. "My head is fine."

She rolled her eyes. Was this guy for real?

"I should come with you. We need to speak."

"What do you think we're doing right now?" She taunted. "Besides, we're finished talking. You've done all the damage you could possibly do to me in one night." *Unless you decided to fuck me blind.*

"I have not injured you."

She blinked, terrified that he'd read her wayward thoughts. His expression remained impassive.

"Oh, forget it." She swatted the air in front of her face in frustration. "I'll see you around."

Brigit turned to leave. Orion's hand swept out before she could take a single step and grasped her elbow. Heat zinged along her arm, going straight to her clit. Her body came to life under his touch, colors brightened and sounds intensified. One minute she'd simply existed and the next, she became an active participant. She fought an outward tremor as her gaze narrowed to him. The power he held in that simple touch frightened and intrigued her. Yet, the last thing she needed was for this guy to know how much he affected her. Brigit glanced down at his fingers, which curled possessively around her arm, and then to his face. The message she intended must have gotten through because he immediately dropped his hand.

"That's more like it," she said, wanting more than anything for him to touch her again, but lower.

"Please allow me to accompany you to your quarters," he requested, yet his eyes flashed with what appeared to be...desperation. But that couldn't be right, what would this guy have to be desperate about? Apprehension colored his features.

If he'd been arrogant she would have told him to go stuff himself. Instead, Brigit felt herself soften. "Okay, but just to my door and no further. I have to warn you that I know karate." She whipped her hands in front of her, frantically chopping the air. "You try to pull anything funny and you're toast, got it?"

Orion stepped back, watching her with something akin to amusement filtering across his face. His lips quirked, but he did not smile. "Rest assured I will pull nothing, unless you wish it."

Brigit refused to read anything into his strange statement. She looked away unable to maintain contact with his jade and aqua eyes. The intensity burning in them was too fierce. At a distance, the man was gorgeous, but up close he was deadly. What she'd thought was a Celtic tattoo on his cheek looked more like a tribal brand of some sort. But that couldn't be right. He didn't strike her as the face branding type. What was she saying? She didn't even know him. He could be one hotdog short of a bun and with a name like Orion, he probably was.

That realization didn't stop her from making more covert observations. His smooth skin held a strangely clean odor, not soapy or freshly scrubbed, but clean. Almost as if he'd been sanitized. The silver hoops in his ears sparkled as they caught flashes of the muted light from the fluorescent bulbs above. Brigit found herself mesmerized by the sight, longing to swirl her tongue around the circle until she encountered his sweet fleshy lobe. No! No! No! This was definitely not good. Orion grinned like he'd read her mind. Brigit sniffed and then picked up her tail to continue on.

This man could charm a Rabbi out of his long winter gatkes.

She made a mental note to hide her underwear.

* * * * *

Orion wasn't sure what exactly he had done to garner the fiery-haired woman's rage, other than almost killing her, but he knew what he could do to assuage it. Mirroring the behavior of the people at the front desk, his smile widened. Brigit glowered. Her expression did little to deter the rings on his body from quivering in excitement and anticipation.

What was he thinking? No matter what he'd considered only moments ago, he couldn't in good conscience bed Jac and Queen Rachel's friend. His orders were to deliver a royal message and then leave. That did not require removing his body armor flight suit and exercising his cock.

He watched the sway of Brigit's hips from beneath her padded covering, hypnotized by the gentle swish from side to side. He longed to see her without the bulky material. She was a small-boned woman, the top of her head barely reaching the piercings dangling from his nipples. Yet, it would matter not, for they would still fit together nicely.

No! The word echoed in his head, even as the rings around his shaft vibrated, hardening him instantly beneath his clothing.

Orion shook his head, sending his hair cascading into his face. He brushed it back in annoyance. He needed to stop thinking about this woman lying beneath him, writhing, his ringed cock sunk deep within her, her nipples feathering his lips, her soft moans filling his ears, feeding his voracious sexual appetite. He blinked to disperse the unsolicited image.

He could get that need taken care of by the two women standing sentry at the portal of this facility. But even as he thought it, Orion knew his interest in them already waned. Something far more tantalizing teased his eager senses...and she had red hair, luminescent skin and a temper hot enough to make a Zaronian *slithera* cringe.

They reached Brigit's quarters a short time later. She slipped the entry card into the lock and the door opened with a soft click. She took a step inside, tossed her tail onto the floor then turned, holding her hand out to prevent him from following.

The warmth of her palm resting against his chest burned through the thin material of his spacesuit straight into Orion's soul. His breath caught in his lungs. The touch wasn't meant to be sexual, yet it was as effective as stroking his cock. Her innocent caress scalded his insides, igniting a fierce primal need deep within him.

He wanted to possess this woman. That knowledge shook Orion to his antigravity boots. He curled his fingers into fists to keep from touching her and did something he never thought he'd do in front of a woman; he took a defensive step back. Her hand fell away and the instantaneous loss he felt crushed his insides. Something was wrong. There was something unnatural about this moment, this woman. The need was too great, almost overpowering. This was more than a simple urge to join.

"I said you could walk me to my door, but you aren't coming in. I don't know you and I certainly don't make a habit of inviting strange men into my room."

The thrill he felt over her admission shocked Orion. He shouldn't be so pleased that she didn't freely welcome men into her body, but he was. He fought to clear his head. He must stop these foolish thoughts. He was on a mission. "I am Orion from Zaron," he repeated like a battle mantra more for himself than for her.

"Yeah, yeah, so you've said, but that doesn't make us friends." She leaned closer, beckoning him with her finger. "I'll let you in on a little secret," she spoke in a low voice. "I've never heard of Zaron and neither has anyone else. You may want to try making the name more realistic sounding next time."

Just because this primitive planet never heard of Zaron, did not mean it didn't exist. He struggled with his anger. A muscle ticked in his cheek as he spoke through clenched teeth. "We must talk."

"We can talk like this." Her hands went to a silver clip on the front of her covering. It slid down with a hiss. The material surrounding her small frame fell open, exposing a black outfit that hugged her curves like a second skin and caressed her abundant thighs. A citrus scent filled the air. He realized the delicate fragrance emanated from Brigit.

Orion's mouth went dry as she stepped out of the material and stood before him with her hands resting at her sides. For a full second he couldn't think, his mind spun, he couldn't even breathe as his gaze swept her body. It was as if the Goddess herself struck him about the head. Perhaps he'd developed space sickness during his journey. Could that explain his symptoms? Finally Orion found his voice, "I bear messages from Jac and Queen Rachel."

Brigit's mouth dropped open. For a moment she remained speechless. "Why didn't you say so in the first place?

Come inside." She reached for the front of his spacesuit, sank her finger into the lightweight material and pulled him through the doorway.

Orion didn't argue. He took the opportunity offered and stepped into her quarters. The room seemed to shrink with the soft click of the door closing behind him. The beige walls pressed in from all sides. He battled the urge to wrench the door open and take a deep breath. His nostrils flared as he inhaled her sweet scent, the aroma intoxicating, reminiscent of ripe Zaronian fruit.

He watched Brigit bend over and pick up her dragon outfit to lay it on the gold-covered sleep paddock located in the center of the room. Jac and Rachel called it a bed. Pillows fell in disarray, some lying on the richly carpeted floor, while others teetered on the paddock's ledge. Part of the gold material had been peeled back, exposing twisted white sheets. Had she lain there with another? No! She'd told him none were welcome. Perhaps he'd be the exception. He grinned.

Orion's gaze slid from the bed to Brigit's tempting backside. She swung around in time to catch him looking, but only arched a brow. It mattered not, he wasn't trying to hide his interest.

"You said you've heard from Jac and Rachel. How? I didn't think there were phones where they're at."

He hit a button on his wrist translator to double-check her meaning. "No phones," he answered, clearing his throat.

"Then how?" her voice pitched higher.

Orion stepped closer. He couldn't stop himself. He needed to feel her warmth again, the gentle touch of her fingertips. "They are safe," he said, not answering her question.

Brigit's green eyes narrowed. "What do you mean safe? And how do you know?"

"Because they sent me here to tell you."

"Sent you here to tell me what? That doesn't make sense. They could've just come themselves." She shook her head, reaching for colorful material that glowed against her skin.

"The Queen and Jac are in no condition to travel."

"Queen who? I don't have time for puzzles, Orion. This is the second to the last day of the conference and the next contest is in fifteen minutes give or take. I have to get my costume together. So what's really going on here?"

He paused, unsure of where to begin.

"Listen, if you're looking for an excuse to hit on me, just say so. I'd be flattered. Really."

"Atlantean men never strike women. It would be dishonorable."

"Ugh!"

This wasn't as easy as he'd first imagined. Being near Brigit left him feeling ale-headed. Yet strangely, Orion found himself wanting to remain in her company. It made no sense. Instead of explaining why he was here, Orion decided to stall. He needed time to discover what was happening and Brigit had inadvertently given him the way to garner it. He smiled. "I shall assist you with the contest."

Brigit stopped shaking out the material, her attention riveted to his face. "You'd really help me?" Surprise colored her voice.

"'Tis the least I can do." He stepped closer and her pulse jumped in her throat. That small telltale sign of awareness pleased Orion beyond words.

She recovered quickly, hiding her discomfort by becoming bolder. "You're right about that." Brigit nodded. "It is the least you can do." She stared at him for a few seconds, her gaze taking in every inch of his body.

Orion tensed, when he realized she'd "turned the chairs" on him. He fought the urge to reach for her and give her a closer look. If she didn't stop looking at him like that, he would.

* * * * *

Brigit stared into Orion's eyes, the blue and green so strikingly cool, yet heating beyond inferno at the same time. There was no mistaking the need she witnessed. The walls practically expanded with each breath he took. It was like being trapped in a human pheromone factory. She shouldn't be in a room alone with this man. He did strange things to her. Made her wish for stuff she shouldn't want. Couldn't have.

Okay, maybe shouldn't have.

There was nothing really stopping her from reaching out and taking what he so obviously offered, except the fact that the last time she'd done something so impulsive she'd ended up with Rocket Man Rick, who'd fancied himself a lothario and cheated on her the first chance he got. Orion didn't really seem *anything* like Rick. There was true honor in him. She sensed a depth in him that her ex would never achieve and even though he banked his emotions behind a carefully crafted façade, she'd glimpsed kindness glowing in Orion's fierce eyes.

She was probably reading too much into Orion's offer anyway. She never could tell when someone was flirting with her. It was like someone scrambled the signals in her brain and left meant right, right meant wrong. In truth, the only thing Orion offered was to help with the costume contest, nothing more. Anything else was wishful thinking on her part.

Crap! Talk about the wrong weekend to forget her vibrator.

Brigit reached into her sewing basket and removed spools of thread along with a measuring tape. It was best if she got this part of her job out of the way first. The less touching the better. She stepped forward and his eyes narrowed.

"What is that?" he reared back.

Her voice rasped. "I need to measure you, so that the cape I'm about to alter fits correctly." Who was that talking? It couldn't be her voice. It was too...too...sexy. And she didn't do sexy. Quirky, yes. Sexy, no.

He glanced to the tape in her hands and back to her face, before punching a button on his wrist. A second later, he smiled. A wholly male, feral grin that had the hair at the nape of Brigit's neck rising on end. What was he up to? She hesitated.

What had that little thingy on his wrist just told him? And for the first time, Brigit had no doubt he'd received information from it. Was it a computer? She'd give him one thing, Orion certainly took his space captain-cum-dragon slayer part seriously, props and all. She made a mental note to ask him where he bought his accessories. Maybe she could pick up something for herself.

"Could you hold your arms out to the side?" she asked, willing her fingers to stop trembling. She'd measured men before, but Brigit had never fitted a man who looked like Orion. She'd also never had anyone stare at her the way that he did.

What was up with that?

She wasn't exactly in his league, not that he appeared to notice. She wasn't even his type. Didn't he realize that? Maybe she should drag him in front of the mirror and remind him. The man practically oozed sex. It would take a gallon of perfume to produce the same effect from her. Not that Brigit considered herself chopped liver, but she was a realist. The twenty-five extra pounds she carried firmly resided on her ass and thighs. This man didn't have an ounce of fat on him.

Aahh! Why was she worrying about this crap? It wasn't like he was going to see her naked.

She took a deep breath and stepped forward, holding out the numbered tape in front of her. Brigit's shaking hands barely reached the distance between his fingertips and shoulder. She ignored his impressive biceps. It was like measuring a basketball player, if they had layers upon layers of muscle covering their lean frames.

Brigit inhaled. Big mistake! She'd thought his skin held no odor, but heaven help her, she'd been wrong. He smelled fresh, like ocean air on a sunny day with a subtle hint of underlying...what was that? Whatever the fragrance was it had to be uniquely Orion. Brigit inhaled again to be sure, then bit her lip to keep from groaning aloud.

Her legs shook as she moved to Orion's chest next. It was like every naughty fantasy come true. She had to be on Today's Funniest Videos or whatever that other program was that played pranks on unsuspecting people. There was no way Orion was for real.

She struggled to reach around him, which brought her breasts snug against the rough slab of his abdomen. It was like smashing herself onto hot marble dipped in wax. Her nipples pebbled instantly and her clit twitched. Was he this hard *everywhere*?

Twitch. Twitch. Twitch. Her damn clit was sending out "fuck me" in Morse code.

Brigit's cheeks flamed at the thought. She took a step back, but forgot about the measuring tape wrapped around him and the close proximity to the bed. Her knees hit the frame and the tape tangled in her grip as she tried to prevent herself from falling. But it was too late, she'd already lost her footing. Brigit fell a second later, pulling Orion down on top of her. She closed her eyes and braced, waiting to feel the crush of his weight, but it never happened.

Her eyes flew open. She glanced into a face she'd hoped not to see this close. Ever. Brigit's heart sped. Orion watched her, his expression pained and beyond desire-filled. He'd managed to catch most of his weight with his hands. They lay tangled in the measuring tape, chest to breast, sex to sex. The urge to kiss him rode her hard. Brigit's body softened as she felt his shaft grow and thicken against her belly. She gasped in surprise. He'd inadvertently answered the question she'd pondered earlier about the piercings without even opening his mouth.

How big was that thing? She toyed with the plastic tape in her hand, debating whether to measure it and find out.

Her gaze flicked to his lusciously cruel lips. Brigit had no doubt he could torture a woman for hours with those lethal weapons. Her tongue flicked out, wetting her suddenly dry mouth. Orion's nostrils flared. Instead of swooping in and taking what they both were curious to experience, he slowly lowered his head, giving her time to pull away. As if! Brigit thought she'd explode by the time his lips finally pressed against hers. Soft, yet firm, he waited for her to relax. The second she did, he started kissing her, not with just his mouth, but with his whole body — and soul.

* * * * *

Orion hadn't planned to touch her, but the second his body made contact with her lush curves his willpower snapped, abandoning him to his baser instincts. Her tongue darted out tentatively meeting his. She tasted pure, sweet and addictive. Her fingers slipped into his hair, threading through the length, caressing his scalp until he thought he'd burst. Having his senses overloaded was a completely foreign concept. He knew women well. Or at least he thought he had until encountering this one. How had he lived all these years without Brigit's touch?

Her mons gently cradled his ringed cock as if it were made for his body, and his body alone. He rocked his hips, grinding his shaft over her clit, drawing a whimper from her delicate throat. The sound caused excitement to rise inside of him. And still he kept kissing her, feeding from her mouth, ravenous for more. He demanded she be as needy as he was. Heat spread from their lips through his chest, scoring his skin like unsheathed talons, searing his flesh until he was convinced flame had somehow fused them into one.

Goddess help him, he wanted this woman. No, want wasn't strong enough to describe his desire. He *craved* her.

Without thought, Orion moved his hand to cover her small breast. His palm dwarfed the quivering mound as he kneaded her flesh. Her kernelled nipple poked through the material of her clothing into his hand, reaching eagerly for his touch. Orion groaned, deepening the kiss, devouring her lips. Hunger fed his movements as he released her breast and sought the corners of the material covering the front of her body from his greedy eyes.

He gathered the clothing into his fists, ready to rip it from her. The words that would bind them played at the corners of his mind.

Brigit pulled back from the embrace and gasped, scattering his befuddled thoughts to the four winds. Her small hands rose, stilling his actions. "We can't do this," she said through kiss-swollen lips. "Not right now." Her body trembled beneath him. "The contest starts in a few minutes."

Quarg! Pained, Orion nodded in agreement, since he didn't feel capable of speech. He forced himself to release her, his hand instantly feeling the loss of her womanly warmth. He'd given her his word he would assist her. And assist her, he would.

"We'd better hurry or we won't make it in time."

Resigned, Orion rose from the bed. His cock protested as he adjusted it to a more comfortable position in his flight suit. Nothing helped. His body quaked from pent-up desire—an emotion he had no right feeling with this particular woman. He chastised himself. That had been close, too close. If Brigit hadn't come to her senses when she had, he would've taken her without a second thought.

A wave of unease swept through him at how close he'd come to binding himself to a...to a...human. He needed to share the information the King ordered him to deliver and depart at the soonest. Remaining in Brigit's presence only complicated the situation he found himself in. Orion turned to divulge the message only to see purple material flying toward his face. He caught it automatically. "What?" He glanced at the cloth.

"Put that on. I'd planned to make myself a cape with a long train, but I hadn't gotten around to finishing it. My guess is it won't fit since I didn't hem it, but it'll have to do," she said pulling more things out of the container. Her arms strained and her butt wiggled enticingly. "You're not exactly Grabba the Hun, but you'll make a good master to my Princess Lena slave girl costume." She waggled her eyebrows. "We're lucky that I always bring extra costume pieces."

"I do not know these people," he said through clenched teeth, trying to ignore her ass and his erection. At least the latter was beginning to diminish somewhat.

Brigit stopped her movements for a second and turned to look at him. "You've never heard of Grabba the Hun and Princess Lena?"

Orion shook his head, trying to concentrate on the coldest regions of Zaron. Perhaps if he sat on ice that would help.

"That's weird." She frowned, but went back to the task of sorting clothing. "I didn't think there was a human left on the planet who hadn't heard of those Star Battle characters. You're at Conlunar for cripes sake. We live for this shit."

She pulled a baggy shirt over her head and began to slip out of her old clothes, while struggling into new ones. Fascinated, Orion watched each article drop to the floor, unable to tear his eyes away from her feminine shimmy. A flash of thigh here, an elbow there, his imagination filled in the rest.

Brigit turned a few minutes later. She whipped her shirt off and spread her arms wide, revealing the tiny scraps of material barely covering her womanly form. "What do you think?" she asked, smiling brightly.

Orion gaped for a moment. He couldn't stop himself. His barely softening cock rose to attention in less than a Zaronian second. She was a vision of desire, achingly lush and tempting as sin itself. He coughed to clear his throat.

His gaze traveled from her feet up her legs to her thighs, which peeked out in strategic locations. Brigit's wide hips left him salivating. He stared at the flat expanse of her bare stomach, imagining licking every inch. He continued upward on his visual journey over the soft swell of her... Orion's mind screeched to a halt. He pointed to the swirls of material cupping her breasts and pushing them up until they spilled over the top. "Are you going to wear that?"

* * * * *

"What do you mean?" Brigit glanced down at her outfit. There may not be much to it, but she thought it looked pretty good. "I'm supposed to be Princess Lena, while she's enslaved by Grabba the Hun."

"I understand," he said looking thoroughly confused. "But where is the covering for your flesh?"

Brigit matched his expression. "This is it." She waved a hand down her body.

Orion frowned.

"You didn't seem to care a minute ago about how I was dressed."

He spread his fingers, working his hand open and closed as if trying to relieve tension or get the feeling back. "That was before we joined mouths."

"Oh brother, give me a break. It was just a kiss." That was the understatement of the century, but she rolled her eyes anyway. The last thing Orion needed to know was that he kissed better than most of her ex-boyfriends fucked. "You aren't getting all possessive on me, are you?" As she spoke the words, Brigit realized a part of her actually hoped he was. Would that be so wrong? Of course it would. One good toe-curling kiss and she was ready to beg this guy to father her children.

"Will there be a gathering like the last time?" Orion asked, his voice dangerously low.

"A gathering?" What in the world was he talking about now? Soon she'd need a sci-fi decoder ring to decipher his phrases. It was almost as if his first language wasn't English, yet she could discern no accent. "Oh, you mean a crowd. Yes, I sure hope so." She began shoving items back into her suitcase. Brigit closed the lid, then sat on top of the bag, bouncing a couple times in order to lock it. The damn thing had to have shrunk after check-in.

Orion's eyes widened and his sensuous face turned down in scowl. "There were males at that last gathering."

Brigit glanced around the room to make sure she hadn't forgotten anything and to once again check for film equipment. There had to be a camera crew somewhere. No way was this for real. Men like Orion did not exist on this planet.

"Will there be males?" He tried to hide the annoyance, but didn't succeed.

His question startled her out of her packing. Why did he sound so grumpy? "Yep, there will be guys in the audience."

"Then I forbid it." His voice boomed and he slashed a powerful arm through the air.

Brigit giggled. She couldn't help it. That was the last thing she expected him to say. He forbade it. Orion's hands clenched. She glanced at his face once more and the giggles turned to peals of laughter. He looked so serious, but she knew he had to be kidding. No guy got serious after one kiss.

"That's a good one, Orion. In fact, it's perfect." Her shoulders shook. "I forbid it," she said, lowering her voice to impersonate him as she wiped tears from her eyes. "Save it for the stage, the audience will eat it up, especially once you put on that cape. Oh, I almost forgot." Brigit unsnapped the suitcase and dug to the bottom of the bag. She felt satin beneath her fingertips and pulled. The material slid through the other items like water off sex lube. "Put this on." She handed him the mask.

Orion stood there, turning the item over and over in his hands like he'd never seen one before and wasn't sure what to do with it. She thought it was odd, but didn't have time to delve into the subject or they'd be late.

"It goes on your face." Brigit grabbed the mask and then stepped behind him. She stood on her tiptoes and strained upward, missing the mark by five inches. "Duck down. I can't reach you."

He did as she asked.

Brigit slipped the mask in place, securing it against his head, and then spun Orion around. Her gaze locked onto his face. She'd been going for a bit of mystery and hadn't anticipated the impact a simple mask would make. Good God, he looked like an intergalactic bandit. All that was missing was for him to pull the sword from his side sheath and carve his initials into the wall.

"Um...um...that's good," she choked out and patted him on the arm before stepping back. The need inside her flamed, refusing to be doused.

"We need to talk," he repeated, his voice gruff.

"Later." Before he could say another word, Brigit grabbed him by the forearm and dragged him out of the room. It was either that, or do something insane like blow off the contest so she could throw him on the bed and fuck him senseless.

Chapter Three

ഇ

The crowd was even larger than at the last costume event. Wonderful! With Orion at her side, they should win easily. Brigit gathered the material of her split skirt and pushed forward. Her right arm muscles strained as she tried to pull Orion behind her. Was he purposely digging in his heels? She glanced at his boots, then back to his face. Orion's expression remained steely as he took in the crowd.

Wolf-whistles came from all sides as she snaked her way through the whirling masses. She couldn't wait to see the look on Rocket Man Rick's face. He'd left her to be with a winner. Well there was no way she could lose now. Brigit smiled inwardly. Her costume was a hit. Her partner was beyond perfect. She looked at him once more. He didn't look happy. Every catcall made Orion stiffen and his frown deepen. If he got any tenser, she'd be able to wax his ass and surf him to the Bahamas.

"Are you okay?" she asked, shouting over the din of the crowd.

He glared at the people nearby, but nodded in her direction.

She leaned in close to his ear, her lips *accidentally* scraping his lobe. "Are you ready to go up on stage?"

Orion's breath hissed out of his lungs and he straightened, putting some distance between them. He grabbed the cape she'd thrown over his head, twisting the clasp until it rested against his shoulder. "I am prepared for this event, but perhaps you are not." He studied her.

"What do you mean?" Brigit scowled, tugging at her outfit. "Am I crooked?"

"No." Orion reached up to the ear she'd touched and removed the silver hoop. His fingers singed her cheek as he slid his hand over her face to brush her hair back. He removed her simple gold post and clasped the earring, pressing it through her lobe, then caressed her again as he reluctantly released her. "Now you are ready," he said, presenting her with a smile that caused her panties to shrink. He put her gold post through his ear, creating a mirror image. The look of possession excited Brigit more than it should. Her heart flip-flopped and warmth spread to her belly.

Brigit didn't realize she held her breath, until she started to see stars. She gulped air and shook her head at her own foolishness. It was time to be honest with this man. He deserved the truth. "I should probably warn you that my ex is also in this competition."

His brow crinkled. "Explain."

She tugged Orion to the side, getting them out of the flow of traffic. "My ex-boyfriend has entered this contest with his new slut girlfriend, Dorothy."

Orion slipped his hand away from hers and hit the button on his wrist. The color in his cheeks rose, giving him an angry glow.

"I'm sorry. I should have told you earlier. The only reason I didn't is because I thought you might be working with him."

The muscle ticked in his jaw. "Your mate is here and you allowed me to enter your dwelling, to touch you. I was very near to entering your body." Disgusted, he pulled away.

"He's not my mate. Well, at least not anymore." She protested, suddenly as panic over his imminent departure set in. What was wrong with her? It had only been a kiss, not a promise of forever. So why did Brigit feel as if she'd somehow betrayed Orion? She reached for him, desperate to convince him to stay. "I said he's my *ex*-boyfriend. There's a difference. I wouldn't have let you in my room if we were still together and I damn well wouldn't have kissed you." She coughed. "I mean allowed you to kiss me."

Orion's expression grew murderous. "Where is he?"

Brigit swung around and scanned the crowd. No sign of Rick or Dorothy. Good! That gave her time to calm Orion. "I haven't seen him yet, but you don't have anything to worry about. It's over between us. And Rick, well, he's more a lover than a fighter." As soon as the words left her mouth, Brigit knew they'd been a mistake.

Orion's gaze narrowed and he grit his teeth. "Has he claimed you?"

"Claimed? Uh, er, I don't think you understand and you're definitely missing the point. Rick won't give us any trouble in this contest. We should win easily." She assured, ignoring the fact that she'd thought the same thing in the earlier contest and look what occurred. This time would be different. This time she had a secret weapon and he stood right beside her, looking like a sexy, albeit angry, galactic bandit.

The women were going to faint at the sight of him. She smiled a moment before her expression faded. Jealousy gripped her. Brigit wasn't at all sure she liked the thought of women fawning over him. In fact, the more she considered it, the less she wanted Orion standing in front of the crowd.

Orion reached for Brigit, cupping her chin in order to tilt her face so she could meet his eyes. "'Tis you who do not understand. I care not about winning. I plan to punish him for his treatment of you and challenge his claim." He looked as shocked after saying the words as she felt.

Challenge? Claim? Brigit gaped and pulled from his grasp. Fear grappled with excitement. "Whoa there buddy." She put her hand on Orion's chest and tried to ignore the luscious feel of the muscles beneath his costume. "I appreciate the whole macho bit as much as the next girl, but it's not cool to get into a physical fight at Conlunar. They'd kick me out and never allow me back in."

"But this Rocket Man dishonored you by displaying his whore for all to see." He shook his head, clearly confused. "I'm honor bound to challenge him."

Brigit wanted to laugh, but couldn't. Looking in Orion's eyes, she realized he meant every word. Her heart tripped in her chest. "That is so sweet, but I don't need you to kick anyone's ass for me. Winning this contest would be reward enough." Brigit cupped his cheek, much like he'd done to her. She smoothed her thumb over his brand loving the feel of his skin beneath her touch. "Rick hasn't dishonored me. I mean, he acted like a schmuck. No doubt. I was hurt for a while, but now I'm over it, over him." She had someone far more appealing to consider, but she didn't tell him that. "I should've known better than to fall for his smooth lines and handsome face..." Brigit stopped speaking the second she realized she could be describing her and Orion. She cringed inwardly. *Way to go, genius. Why don't you smack the guy next time?* "I didn't mean anything by that. I'm not saying you're the same," she tried to explain.

"You believe me to have dishonored you." Something akin to hurt flashed in his wild eyes.

"No! I didn't say that."

He looked around them and then back at her. "You didn't have to." His gaze penetrated, making her feel ashamed. And she was. Talking to Orion was the equivalent of dancing freeform before someone turned on the stereo. Every time Brigit thought she made the right moves, the music changed and she faltered. For some reason it was important to her that he understood.

Brigit reached for his arm. "Please Orion...I don't want to fight. Let's just enjoy the contest. Afterward, we can go our separate ways if you want. Okay?" she offered, even though the thought sickened her. She didn't want him to leave and wouldn't rule out begging if it came down to it.

His breathing had deepened and his body looked brittle enough to break in a strong wind. Brigit knew she'd insulted him, even though that hadn't been her intention. If he walked now, she was screwed. What was she saying? Panic enveloped her as she thought about Orion striding out of her life. Suddenly, the contest didn't seem that important.

"I'm sorry. Truly. I know you're nothing like Rocket Man Rick. It was stupid to suggest as much." Brigit fluffed her skirt absently. "You're more man than he'll ever be," she added, speaking more to herself than to Orion.

He seemed to weigh her words for a moment, before continuing through the crowd.

Why did Brigit get the feeling that she'd just screwed up the best thing that had ever happened to her?

* * * * *

Orion's mind was in turmoil. He'd never dishonor Brigit the way Rick had done. He'd never dishonor her, period. If she were his woman, she'd never have to worry about his faithfulness. He could be nothing but true to her. Honor and his people dictated as much. But would she do the same? He didn't know. Humans were not bound by Atlantean law or its customs. The thought left him feeling edgy.

Anger over this unfamiliar emotion began to surge through him. He wanted to pound this man out of existence. The fact that he'd claimed some part of Brigit only made the sensation worse. No man would touch her and live. That knowledge, along with the possessive feelings swirling inside of him, rocked Orion. He'd had no intention of claiming Brigit for himself or any other Earth woman for that matter. Yet, the thought of her lying beneath another man, spreading her legs, taking his cock, made reasoning impossible.

Why?

Why here? Why now? Why her?

The questions buzzed like angry *senties* in his mind. Still Orion felt no closer to the answers. They walked to the side of the stage and waited with several other couples. Orion didn't miss the secretive glances the women sent him and neither did Brigit, whose creamy skin now glowed fiery red, matching her hair. Her emerald-colored eyes shot Zaronian daggers, daring anyone to make a move. So his little ward cared more than she let on. Orion smiled, enjoying this costume competition for the first time.

His smile faded as a man made his way through the crowd toward Brigit. The man looked like an average Earthling with dark brown hair and tanned skin. He was above normal in height, but still much shorter than Orion. He held little muscle on his frame and would not fare well in a Zaronian battle.

The man stopped in front of her, his brown eyes devouring her lush curves in undisguised appreciation. He grinned, flashing white teeth, then stepped forward, pulling Brigit into a quick embrace before releasing her. The action was far too familiar for Orion's liking. Her mouth opened and closed a couple of times, then she appeared to gather her wits.

Orion heard his knuckles pop and realized he'd clenched his fists.

"I've missed you," the man said, his dulcet tones grated on Orion's nerves.

Brigit's flush deepened as she glanced over her shoulder at Orion and then back to the man in front of her.

Orion hadn't missed the sudden indecision on her face. Her emotions hit his gut like a blow from a *Taration* giant. Was she actually considering taking this human for a mate? Unease crept into his bones. He had the overwhelming urge to toss Brigit over his shoulder and carry her back to his ship where he'd hold her until she forget all about this human male.

"What are you doing?" she asked her voice low and brimming with confusion.

"I wanted to tell you how beautiful you look tonight. And to let you know that I miss you."

"Y-You m-miss me?" Brigit stuttered.

"I made a huge mistake." The man brushed a hand along her arm and she trembled.

Orion watched in disbelief, his every instinct telling him to kill the intruder, who dared touch his woman.

"Where's your girlfriend?" she asked, suddenly pulling away.

"It doesn't matter." The man's gaze shot over her shoulder to land on Orion. Smugness and a confidence that hadn't been there moments ago colored the man's expression. "I'm here now to wish you luck and to tell you that I want you back." He returned his attention to Brigit.

"I don't know, Rick," she said hesitantly.

Orion stood motionless, his entire body throbbing with churning fury. This was the man he'd sought. The same one who'd discarded Brigit for the company of a whore.

The man was a fool.

And now he stood here, attempting to win her back— attempting to take *his* woman away. If they were on Zaron, he'd already be dead.

Power surged through Orion. His hands began to glow, along with his skin. People glanced around, their voices rising in excited whispers at the scene unfolding before them. Orion pushed the power back, forcing it deep inside of his body. The last thing he needed was to alert the Earthlings to his *alien* origins. His vision dimmed and his ears rang. He could no longer hear what Brigit and Rick were saying, but their body language spoke volumes and he didn't like what it was saying.

They leaned into each other and laughed, the sexual tension thick, familiar. Rick smiled, a look of triumph on his marginally handsome face, as he glanced once more at Orion. A moment later, he placed a quick kiss on Brigit's cheek and departed.

Orion followed Rick's movements. He walked a few feet away, stopping beside a woman who could only be described as lush. She didn't look pleased. Rick's name was called and he stepped onto the stage, the raven-haired beauty followed closely behind. She smiled for the audience and they responded by whistling and screaming out her name.

So this was the temptress, Dorothy, who Rick had chosen over Brigit. Orion scowled. Like a Zaronian field flower, she was beautiful, but common.

The couple strolled to the end of the ramp where Rick twirled the woman before bending her back over his arm. He grazed on the white expanse of her throat, his weak lips reminding Orion of a *lemac* nibbling sugar.

Dorothy blushed, her face turning rapturous. Orion could not see what made this man or the woman in his arms exceptional. There was a falseness to their appearance, a shallowness in their chins. Their eyes while brightly colored showed fear and insecurity. Orion snorted. He'd seen enough. He turned to Brigit.

The crowed roared, snapping his attention back to the couple on center stage. Dorothy's dress dropped away, exposing one ample silver pastie-covered breast. Rick placed a kiss above the silver star, causing the men in the crowd to howl. Dorothy's mouth opened and she slid one finger between her teeth. Screams rang out, the sound deafening in the cavernous room.

"I swear that woman has no modesty. Talk about stooping low." Brigit spun, her green eyes flashing in the darkness. "Tell me you are not gawking."

Orion arched a disapproving brow. If he wasn't so angry, he'd be amused by Brigit's behavior. They had much to learn about each other.

"Just checking."

He saw her glance down at her own modest cleavage and frown. The couple exited the stage a minute later, passing Orion. Rick slowed as he neared Brigit. His smile brightened and he lowered one eyelid. Orion wasn't sure of the significance of the gesture, but he knew he didn't like it. Before he could stop himself, energy shot out from his hand, searing the man's backside.

Rick yelped, his fingers curving protectively around his rump. He glared at Orion, who shrugged in response. By the time Brigit swung around to see what occurred, Orion made sure he'd already looked away, an expression of placid boredom firmly in place.

Dorothy sashayed by a moment later. "Good luck, sugar," she drawled, her attention leaving her nemesis to rest upon Orion. "When you get tired of playing with sloppy seconds, let me know." She trailed her fingertips over his corded forearm.

Orion punched a button on his wrist, then coolly assessed the woman and found her lacking in substance. In another time, in another galaxy, he might have taken her up on her offer, but only if he was bored or had had too much Zaronian ale. She was disposable and interchangeable with any of his previous bedmates.

Brigit's gaze turned from hot to icy. Her face flushed as Dorothy's words reached her ears. "You bitch!" She moved to reach for the woman's hair, but Orion stopped her. "Let me go!" She struggled to free herself from his grasp. "I'm going to snatch that bitch bald. She practically threw herself at you and you just stood there, ready to catch. I can't believe what just happened. Can you?" she asked, vehemence behind her words.

"No, I cannot," he growled. "I thought you said this man shamed you in front of your people." He pointed to Rick in the crowd as if there were any doubt who he spoke of. "Even now he flaunts his new bed partner in front of you. Yet, you do not act like a woman shamed. Only moments ago, you lapped up his attention like a feline in heat. You practically rubbed yourself against him. A beast with no nose could've scented your lust."

"I'm not the one who's in the wrong here. He... She... A feline in heat!" She sputtered, her gaze narrowing. "What do you mean by that?"

"I mean do not welcome me in your bed, if your heart lies with another."

* * * * *

Brigit's jaw dropped. She wasn't sure what shocked her more, Rick trying to worm his way back into her life or Orion's jealousy and gargantuan ego in presuming that she'd planned to fuck him. *Okay, maybe she had, but still...he didn't know that.*

Men! Can't live with them and can't drag them behind a truck by their testicles.

Did Orion actually believe she'd fall back in her ex's arms, when this god of a man was standing in front of her? Obviously, he did, since he'd said so in so many words. Was he nuts? Or did Orion have that low of an opinion of her character?

Brigit shuffled her feet, as the truth slapped her face like an airbag during a collision. She didn't want him to think badly of her. So maybe she'd been a tad zealous to beat Rick in these competitions and in turn capture his attention. She was a natural flirt, but it didn't mean anything. So maybe she'd felt like she had something to prove. It wasn't that she wanted Rick back, but she did want him to realize what he'd given up.

Was that so wrong?

No, darn it!

However, Brigit didn't want her point verified at the expense of everything else, and she certainly didn't like the look Orion gave her. He thought less of her. She could see it in his two-toned eyes. It was as if someone dimmed the lights, leaving nothing but shadows behind. So she'd been a little shallow. And maybe she took frivolous contests too seriously. She knew she wasn't perfect. Why did she feel the need to be that way around him?

Up until now, Brigit had never cared what anyone but Jac and Rachel thought. Why did she care what Orion thought? It bothered her that a guy she barely knew could get under her skin so fast, especially since after tomorrow she probably wouldn't ever see him again.

Was this some kind of rebound? She considered the possibility. Rick broke up with her a few months back. She'd been heartbroken for a while or so she'd thought at the time. She might even have wanted a little revenge in the beginning. Not mature, but the ugly truth. She was over that now. Brigit had moved on and Rick had too. End of story.

She needed to convince Orion that since the moment she'd laid eyes on him no one else had existed. But how? What could she do? And why was it so bloody important?

Damn him! She should send him packing. She didn't need this crap right now. Brigit wished Jac and Rachel were here. They'd know what to do. Her gaze went of its own volition to the front row of seats. They were packed with people she didn't know. Sadness swamped her. She looked back at Orion. He watched her, weighing her worth as the seconds ticked by. She felt lower than a dust bunny.

Well she'd show him.

Brigit considered multiple possibilities, discarding one only to pick the next. Hmm…but where to begin? She glanced at the spotlighted stage and licked her lips. She decided to give the audience one hell of a show, one that would make Rick and Dorothy's performance look as if they'd auditioned for a children's flick and convince Orion that she wanted him only. He wouldn't know what hit him, by the time they finished their stroll down the catwalk. She almost purred in delight.

* * * * *

Orion didn't like the look Brigit gave him. Like a *farcat* eyeing a fat *esuom* meal, her gaze raked him from head to boot. The skin at his nape prickled, warning him trouble lay ahead. He straightened, not allowing her to see how off balance she left him. Never had a woman churned such emotion in him. One minute he felt like shaking her senseless and spanking her luscious ass, the next, he longed to bury his cock inside her warmth for at least thirty moonrises.

He had no idea where he stood with the firebrand. She wanted him. That much was clear. He felt fairly devoured in her presence. Yet she also seemed to want the mere Earthman.

Shocked, and more than a little disappointed, Orion found her lack of discernment and taste only reinforced his opinion that Earth women were only good for sex. He hated the fact that he'd wanted Brigit to be the exception. But, she wasn't. He'd created an illusion out of wishful thinking and must now accept that fact.

Everything beyond a physical coupling with her was mired due to her indecisive behavior. Earlier, that would've matter naught. Why now? What had changed? For the first time in Orion's life, joining wasn't enough. It pained him to acknowledge such, but he needed more, wanted more from this woman.

Was she capable of giving him what he sought? He knew not, for the search had yet to reveal any answers.

The announcer called out their names. Brigit smiled, but it did not reach her eyes. A second later, she stepped onto the stage. She stuck her hand into a hidden flap in her skirt that Orion hadn't noticed before and pulled out a gold chain with a gem-encrusted hoop at one end. She latched the collar around her neck and then held out the leash for him to take. The action seemed meaningless, but he knew better.

Heat flared, sending a surge of power, along with an onslaught of sexual awareness through Orion. She was offering herself to him, giving freely what he could so easily take. Her gift was simple yet primal, more powerful than had she spread her legs and bent forward, offering her ass and honey-laced quim for his immediate consumption. Orion shuddered. His gaze locked onto the chain a second before grasping the cool links in his hand. It felt satiny to the touch, yet scalded like flame.

The gold sparkled in the spotlight, spilling droplets of light over their skin and onto the floor. He longed to tongue every twinkle that caressed her soft feminine body. He watched the rays dance for a moment, then turned his attention back to his *gift*.

He gave the leash a gentle tug, drawing in the slack until it pulled taut. Brigit's eyes flashed, then melted into an emerald pool of desire. Orion saw promises in their depths, along with something else. Something that if he were in his right mind should worry him, but didn't.

Her body subtly moistened. He could smell her heat in the air. He inhaled, drunk with need.

Orion's cock hardened, demanding release from the confines of his spacesuit. The fragile chain stretched between them, frail in its substance, but substantial in significance. He was going to like this new game. A lot. And from the expression on Brigit's face, he wasn't the only one.

Are you certain you want me to have this little one? Be sure, for once I accept your offer I will not release you from this unspoken bargain. The question filtered wordlessly between them. Her gaze widened, then her brow wrinkled in confusion. Had she heard him? If so, how? There was no link in place, only this delicate chain. Orion ignored his own question. He would discover the answer later. It was time to reel in his pet.

Chapter Four

ഇ

Brigit pretended to struggle against the leash, her hands clawing at the collar, causing Orion's muscles to flex under the light. She watched his breathing deepen and his pupils dilate. Seeing his response sent a thrill of triumph coursing through her blood. Color bloomed in his cheeks. He liked this game.

She continued to lead them down the catwalk. Halfway to the end she dropped to her knees and slinked toward him on all fours. For a second, Orion looked as if he'd take a step back, then he stilled, his gaze zeroing in on her. The intensity she saw there sent delicious shivers rippling over her body, hardening her nipples, wetting her sex until she feared the audience would see her drip onto the stage.

Brigit rubbed her body against Orion's calf, arching her back like a cat in need of attention. Then she sat back onto her knees and raked her nails down the length of his thigh. She saw the material of his spacesuit costume to bulge below his waist. Brigit flicked her gaze up, capturing his eyes. His fists bunched. Suddenly, she couldn't resist. She reached out and clasped his hand. Her tongue flicked out a second later, tasting the salty desire covering his skin.

She knew she played a dangerous game, but for the life of her she couldn't stop. Something urged her on. Something feminine and needy demanded Brigit stake her claim on this man in front of Conlunar and the world, even if it was only for a day.

Brigit dropped his hand, after taking a teasing nip and then started to crawl away. A quick yank on the chain brought her up short. The look in Orion's eyes arrested her. Brigit felt the proverbial chain of control slip from her grasp. She'd pulled the tiger's tail one too many times and she loved every second of it.

Her clit throbbed, pulsing beneath the material of her dress like a deep-sea beacon. God, she wanted this man. Screams and hollers rang out from around them. Brigit could barely hear them over the sound of her blood roaring in her ears. She wished the room full of strangers would disappear. If they did, Brigit knew she'd shamelessly fuck him right here on stage. The skin on her body pulled tight as if her nerves attempted to bore to the surface.

The chain grew slack. She decided to move, it was either that or stand and rip Orion's clothes off. Bad idea. It would probably cause the women in the room to stampede. And right now, Brigit wasn't about to share. She tried to slink down the stage, but it was hard to do with her arms and legs shaking beneath her.

She glanced over her shoulder. Orion's glazed eyes remained locked on her ass, following its movement like an angry bull obsessed with a matador's red cape. She added an extra wiggle to her hips, watching his nostrils flare and his lungs labor.

This was fun.

Suddenly, the game came to an end. Orion pulled on the chain, drawing her nearer. Brigit knew she should be worried, but really, what could he do onstage surrounded by a room full of people? His thick fingers reached under the collar to pull her to her feet. He stuck his nose against the side of her head and inhaled. She trembled and the crowd let out a collective whoop. Orion seemed unconcerned with their presence. He drew one of her hands away from her body and started nibbling her fingertips, slowly making his way up her arm. His tongue swirled over each bite, caressing and inflaming.

Brigit tried to pull away, but he held her steady. Then he stuck out his tongue completely and licked her like an ice cream cone. Her eyes bugged. Orion could shame that bass player from that famous makeup-wearing rock band with that thing.

Where was her measuring tape when she needed it?

Orion didn't give her much time to dwell on his tongue's impressive length. Brigit realized the flaw in her thinking, when he wrapped her in his arms, draping the cape vampire-style around their bodies for privacy. He swept her mouth into a searing kiss while his fingers played ring-around-the-rosey with her clit beneath the cape.

Brigit gasped in shock, but couldn't stop him as heat surged through her and she came hard. Orion's lips devoured her cries of release. She bucked in his grip, but he held her against him, protectively. The crowd only saw a couple exchanging a passionate embrace. Stars swirled behind her eyelids. When he finally pulled back, Brigit heaved air into her lungs. The cape fell away, but he kept his hand resting casually at her waist. Only she and Orion knew he was the only thing preventing her from collapsing to the floor.

The announcer climbed onto the stage and walked toward them with microphone in hand. "Wow! What a kiss! I think it's hot in here, don't you folks?"

The crowd screamed.

"Brigit and Orion are one hot couple. Let's hear it for them."

The audience applauded.

"The judges are tallying the votes now. While we're waiting, I'd like the other couples and solo entrants to come out on stage."

Rick and Dorothy pushed their way to the front. Both wore scowls. Brigit couldn't care less. She blinked, trying to bring reality back. She'd never orgasmed so quickly or quite so hard. Orion's hands definitely had a magic touch that would be far too easy to get used to.

Someone walked onto the stage and handed the announcer an envelope. He ripped it open and glanced at the names. A second later he smiled at the audience. "The third place winners are Ryan and April with their alien huntress and prey costumes. Give them a hand."

Brigit clapped, her hands clumsily coming together on the off beat.

"The second place winners are…Rick and Dorothy."

Rick and Dorothy's lips thinned over their teeth in sneers. They stepped forward and accepted the trophy. Dorothy's eyes spit venom, while Rick looked at Brigit sheepishly, not bothering to hide the longing in his brown depths.

Orion squeezed Brigit's side and she jumped.

"The first prize goes to, yep, you guessed it. Brigit and Orion come over here."

Orion released her and Brigit instantly felt the loss of warmth. They stepped forward in sync. He reached for the trophy, then passed it over to Brigit, who beamed. She couldn't help it.

"We did it!"

Orion grinned. "Is this piece of metal all you remember about our *performance*?"

"Hardly." She blushed. "I can't believe you did that."

"Did what?" he asked, his face the picture of innocence.

"You know."

"No one knows what happened, but you and I."

Brigit glanced around at the people and realized Orion was right. "You were terrific with the chain and all. Thanks for holding me up so I didn't fall."

"I'd never let you down," he stated with such sincerity that her heart clenched in response.

They strolled off the stage, accepting congratulations as they made their way through the milling crowd. Brigit didn't even mind that Orion seemed to be dragging her along. She chuckled. Someone was obviously in a hurry to get back to the room.

When they entered the relative quiet of the hall, he stopped. "We must speak. I have much to tell you." Orion met her eyes before continuing on.

Wow! He'd gotten serious all of a sudden. Brigit hoped she wasn't about to receive a "Dear Brigit" speech from him. She didn't think she could handle that after what they'd shared on stage. Her mind scrambled to recall what he'd said earlier. Jac and Rachel's face swam before her eyes. She was such a schmuck. She'd forgotten about her friends and everything else but her orgasm and winning this stupid contest. She glanced down at the gold trophy in her hands.

It didn't seem nearly as impressive or shiny as it had only moments ago. What was wrong with her? She'd never been *this* flaky.

They reached her room a short time later. Orion opened the door without asking for a key. She frowned, wondering how he'd done it, but stepped in the room behind him. The lights were off because she'd forgotten to leave them on. She heard him somewhere on the other side of the room. A second later the lamp came on, bathing the room in buttery light.

He watched her like a hungry lion ready to take down a gazelle.

She cleared her throat. "Y-You said you wanted to talk."

"I've changed my mind. We'll talk later," he growled, pulling off his boots.

All Brigit's senses went on alert, yet she stood frozen just inside the door. Blindly, she reached behind her to snick the latch, locking them inside.

"Come here." Orion's voice sounded raw like his throat was sore from gargling pebbles. He raised his arm and beckoned her with a lone finger, which was as effective as placing her on a conveyor belt.

Brigit registered his words and the meaning behind them, her body moistened and her nipples perked. Eager and more than ready, it still took her a moment to get her wobbly legs to cooperate. *Move, damn you.* She sauntered across the room, which only took a few steps, but felt like a zillion miles in her current condition. Heat pooled in her limbs, leaving them leaden. Her skin bristled against her nerves, causing a thousand tiny explosions to detonate at once.

Orion didn't grab her immediately. Instead, he caressed her with his gaze, drinking in her shape like a dehydrated hitchhiker guzzling water in Death Valley. A moment later he reached for her.

* * * * *

The clothing ripped easily as he tugged the covering away from her glistening white skin. She glowed like the moon that orbited this planet. Brigit whimpered as his mouth descended to her pert nipples. The second his lips made contact with her skin she gasped. Orion growled. The taste of her flesh was intoxicating and he hadn't even delved into her woman's center.

How many years had he spent searching for this sensation? This taste? This touch? This type of connection?

Too many.

Orion peeled the rest of the barely there costume away from her body, then reared back to look his fill. She was small, but perfectly shaped. Enough for him to feast upon. He'd tease her into pleasure she'd never even known existed, taking her body to heights she'd be unable to return from. He fought to keep from throwing her on the bed and plunging his cock inside her quim.

He glanced at the trophy on the container holding her clothes, happy that he'd been able to help her obtain it. But it was nothing compared to the lush prize in front of him. Now that he'd managed to get her away from the Earthman, he'd make sure she stayed away.

Orion plowed his hands into her red tresses, luxuriating in the feel of the silky hair as it glided through his fingertips. He'd never seen anything quite so beautiful. It reminded him of Zaronian sunsets over the *Tazda* Sea, as the last rays of the sun bled into the water.

In the back of his mind he heard the tremor of a warning that he could no longer heed. He was too far gone to stop touching her now. He skimmed her dusky nipples with the back of his knuckles, grazing her flesh until they puckered even tighter, bringing a whimper from Brigit's throat. He catalogued the sound in his mind, planning to replay it later after he'd delivered his message and departed.

Brigit quivered as he teased her lush peaks. Sweat beaded his brow as he exerted viselike control over his growing need. He expected to hear fabric ripping any moment as his cock expanded, tenting his flight suit.

Orion skimmed his rough hands over Brigit's bare shoulders, her skin flushed and fevered beneath his touch. Gooseflesh rose in his wake. The citrus scent of her skin blended seamlessly with her natural juices. He couldn't seem to get enough of touching her. He wanted her this second, but held back. He had to make sure her body was prepared for his invasion. Orion knew he wasn't a small man and Brigit seemed diminutive by comparison. He wouldn't rush and take the chance of injuring her, when it was unnecessary.

* * * * *

Brigit's head was spinning. Her nipples were so engorged they hurt. Every rasp of Orion's fingertips brought her closer to completion. Never in all of her years of dating had she ever brought a guy back to her room and allowed him to rip her clothes off. None of the guys she'd gone out with were the clothes-ripping type.

She had to admit that Orion didn't exactly fit into the "typical" guy category, but still...

She followed his large hands as they moved to the front of his costume. It didn't exactly unzip when he touched the material, it simply separated without a sound. Brigit had never seen anything like it. Later, she'd ask him where he got the material, but for now she wanted to feast her eyes on what the outfit revealed.

She watched as Orion pulled the cloth away from his chest. His blue and green eyes glittered with intensity. Brigit licked her suddenly dry lips as the rings piercing his nipples appeared. She'd never dated a guy with piercings before. She had a whole new appreciation for body jewelry. Brigit moved, lifting the tattered material from her arms, not once looking away from Orion's chest—until he dropped his pants.

Good God, what in the hell was that? And why was it silver?

She blinked. Then did so again, but it remained unchanged. Well that wasn't exactly true. It was growing, rising like a leviathan out of the dark nest of curls surrounding it.

Brigit felt her eyes bug out of her head. Where did he think he was going to put that monster? She reached over and grabbed the measuring tape from the bedside table.

"What are you doing?" he asked stepping out of reach.

"Humor me, I have to know. What is your length?"

Warily, he watched her hands move toward his shaft. "Length? I know not what you mean."

She rolled her eyes. "Oh, come on. You mean to tell me you've never measured that thing?" she asked pointing at his cock, incredulity filling her voice. "I don't believe it."

"Why would I? I've never had complaints." He crossed his arms over his massive chest. "Quite the contrary."

Brigit snorted. "I bet not. That would be like spitting on Santa for bringing you a new sports car on Christmas morning."

Orion blinked. "You speak in riddles. Who is this Santa? Translate."

"You really are a trip." She shook her head, ignoring the strange sensation in her gut that told her something wasn't right. "You have to know that you're hung like...like... Well let's just say I'm going to start calling you Godzilla."

His face reddened and his nostrils flared. White lines bracketed his thinning lips. "I know not what creature you're comparing me to but you should know I do not appreciate your harsh words."

Brigit laughed then, she couldn't help it. Since when did a guy get pissed over his anatomy being compared to a gigantic lizard? "You are a very strange man, Orion. Gorgeous, but strange."

"I assure you I am quite acceptable where I come from. Women all over the galaxy seek me out."

"I have no doubt. You want to tell me where you got those rings?" Brigit pointed casually, but she could feel her face heating under his perusal and her hand shook. Crap! She locked her fingers behind her.

"They were applied on *Katron*. I was young and foolish at the time, but they've since served me well." His lips quirked upward.

Brigit arched a brow and then inched closer. "Do you know the rings are beginning to glow?"

"Yes," he purred like a Bengal tiger nursing a bucket of milk. "I can feel them." The smile that spread across his face was positively illegal.

Brigit stepped back instantly, her body on alert. "What?"

"Would you like to see what else they can do?" He removed the mask she'd given him and strode forward, leaving his uniform pooling at his feet.

She grunted and scooted back. There had to be a battery pack somewhere. "I-I don't think so, hotshot. I believe I've seen enough." But she hadn't, not really. If she were brutally honest with herself, Brigit would admit that she could stare at him forever. Her heart somersaulted at the thought. It would be so easy to fall for this man. Part of her already had.

"You may have seen enough, but you have yet to experience my *Katronian* rings. They say the rings can transport a woman to another galaxy." He licked his bottom lip and inched forward, stalking her.

Her body thrummed at the prospect of him catching her, but her mind had other ideas. Brigit glanced around, looking for a quick escape. Orion was bigger than she was and probably a lot faster, which wouldn't take much since she never ran anywhere, for anything, not even to catch a cab. She'd make an exception now.

Could she make it to the door before him? As if he'd read her mind, Orion pounced, knocking her to the bed. He landed on top of her, keeping the bulk of his weight balanced on his elbows, pinning Brigit to the mattress from the waist down.

She squeaked. Not a very ladylike sound, but it was the best she could muster given the circumstances. She inhaled. Her breasts made contact with his bare chest and her mind ceased to function. The silver rings piercing his flat disk-like nipples scraped over her skin. Instead of being cold, the metal seemed to heat on contact. Her body bowed. God, he felt good. More than good. Decadent. And a damn sight better than any Belgian chocolate she'd ever consumed. He even beat Squishy Bears candy.

He shifted and the rings of his cock slid between her legs, resting on the soft, moist nest of curls between her thighs. Brigit tried to move, squirm away, to escape. The rings pulsed.

At least that's what it felt like, but that was impossible, wasn't it?

She'd seen his cock, it wasn't a dildo. The strange vibration occurred again, sending delicious tremors through her clit. Brigit whimpered in need and decided to search for the hidden battery pack later. Heat spread from between her legs, surging through her body like a flash fire. She slipped his nipple ring into her mouth and gently tugged, eliciting a hiss from his lips. She pulled away.

"Kiss me," she begged, air sawing in and out of her lungs.

He smiled. A second later, his mouth descended, but instead of fiercely taking her lips, he grazed her. The butterfly-wing touch sent shivers dancing over her skin, hardening her already flushed nipples and stiffening her clit until Brigit thought she might scream if she didn't get relief.

She wanted him to fuck her already.

"Is that what you want, little one?" he murmured, nuzzling her neck and nibbling on her ear, before swirling his tongue at the hollow of her throat. He trailed wet kisses over her collarbone until he reached her nipple. He seemed fascinated by her breasts.

He'd probably never seen a pair so small before. Brigit groused inwardly for a second until he curled his tongue around one nipple and sucked it into his warm depths. He drew on her flesh, his teeth scraping her skin while he laved and worshipped her. He squeezed her breast in his massive hand so he could bring it closer and deeper into his hot seeking mouth. He released her long enough to blow hot air across her puckered skin.

"You are perfect," he murmured, his eyes glowing with adoration.

Brigit went up in flames. If it were possible to spontaneously combust, she would be a flash burn on the sheet already. His molten lips fed from her, drawing her need like fire to air, while his ringed cock twitched and lengthened as she writhed beneath him. If it got much bigger there wasn't a chance in hell it could fit anywhere in her body, not that she wouldn't love to die trying.

He returned to her mouth, his kisses drugging her as he slid his large hand between them, memorizing each curve, each dip. His expert fingers sought out and found her lower lips, parting her tender flesh while his tongue danced with hers. Brigit moaned as he slipped one digit into her drenched passage. Her body sucked him inside, gripping rhythmically to match the searing kiss.

Another finger quickly followed the first as he stretched her channel, preparing it for an even larger invasion. His thumb circled her clit, careful to avoid touching it. Brigit shimmied, chasing his elusive finger like it were a scrap of paper caught in a windstorm. Her hips rose, bucking in order to urge him closer.

He chuckled against her mouth, before pulling back. "Stay still or I'll stop." Orion brushed her cheek with the back of his knuckles.

She could smell her juices on his fingertips. Brigit went rigid, her body aching as she prevented movement. If he stopped right now, she'd scream, then kill him. Her nerves stretched taut, leaving her skin sensitive to his touch, his breath, his need.

"Please," she sobbed, not above begging at this point. She'd never wanted a man's cock so bad in her life. Later, she might actually get pissed off about this scenario, but right now she wasn't about to play the hypocrite.

He nipped her lip, drawing her attention back to him. "Tell me you need me, then tell me what you want, little one."

"I-I…" she cleared her throat. "I want you."

He grinned. The unholy smile spread across his face and should have had her running for the hills. "Then you shall have me," he said, returning one hand to her quim, while his free hand held her head in place. He teased her a second, then pressed on her clit until she saw rainbows. Yet somehow he prevented her from reaching orgasm. What the fu—

His mouth descended upon hers, cutting short her scream of frustration. For a second before their lips met, Brigit thought she saw Orion's hand glow, but it had to be a trick of the light. His tongue probed her mouth, tasting and dipping. He pulled back a fraction, his gaze unfocused and began chanting low under his breath. His lips stroked across hers like a brush over canvas.

Brigit couldn't make out the words, but they sounded serious—and ancient. Her body surged with energy and soaring heat. The air practically sparkled with it. She actually felt better than she had in years. She longed to stretch her muscles.

He flicked his wrist and suddenly Brigit didn't care what was being said or done for she was coming...and coming...and coming. Her body trembled and shook like a 9.8 quake on the Richter scale as rolling orgasms ripped through her one after the other.

"I'm sorry. I'm sorry. I'm so sorry about the pain." His face twisted in unfettered concern.

What was he talking about? Was he sorry for giving her the best sex she'd ever had? Brigit forced herself to focus on his face, which was hard to do with the world spinning around her. She could actually see remorse in his eyes, but for what she had no idea.

"You haven't hurt me," she sputtered trying to get her tongue to work so she could reassure him. Yet, Orion seemed unable to hear her as he repeated his apology again and again. His eyes remained distant as if his spirit no longer occupied his body.

"You must relax," he whispered against her skin soothingly, before stroking the hair at the side of her head, then he mumbled a few more foreign-sounding words.

This felt incredible, but it was getting weird.

Brigit had just managed to calm her frantic breathing when he entered her. She gasped in shock as something, which felt suspiciously like her deceased hymen, ripped. Impossible! Her eyes bulged. The mixture of pain and pleasure surged through her violently and she came again on a keening cry. God, he was big enough to make her feel like a virgin and he hadn't even started to move.

Talk about rocking her world.

Orion waited, his cock buried deep, his breathing matching hers. The muscles in his arms trembled as he stroked her mouth with his fingertips. "I'm sorry. It was unavoidable on the first time."

"What? Why? H— Ow!"

He thrust without answering her incoherent questions and for a second Brigit wasn't sure she'd survive the ride.

Even as the thought crossed her mind, something strange began to occur. The rings on Orion's cock started to vibrate in earnest as he slowly pulled his length out of her, then glided sensuously back inside. Her world narrowed to the point at which their bodies joined.

"Oh my God!" she shouted, unable to stop the desire from building once again. Her back arched, scraping her nipples across his chest. The vibrating rings encircling his cock, brushed her clit with each downward stroke. "This isn't p-possible," she stuttered as she attempted to gulp air into her straining lungs. Her vision dimmed. Her body trembled as she bucked her hips against Orion to keep him from slipping away.

His smile widened. "I assure you little one, 'tis quite possible." He dropped a quick kiss on her nose.

"But your penis is vibrating," she gasped, her mouth opening and closing like a fish out of water.

He shook his head, sending his silky two-toned hair into his face and across her shoulders. The featherlike strands tickled her bare skin. "'Tis not my shaft that vibrates, 'tis the rings that surround it. I've been told they can make a woman sing, although I've yet to hear anything other than their screams of ecstasy." He grinned. "Will you sing for me?"

Brigit didn't want to hear about the other women in his life. The subject made her decidedly uncomfortable. She opened her mouth to tell him as much, but the rings took that moment to vibrate again and she nearly swallowed her tongue. Her eyes had crossed twice already, yet Brigit could still see the smug male expression on his face as he hovered above her, stroking steadily in and out of her well-lubed channel.

She had only two questions for him. Did he want an aria or an opera? Not that she could hold a tune in a bucket. Secondly, was it possible to die from an orgasm?

Brigit thought that might be the case as her body gave new meaning to the words "multiple orgasms". Veins bulged in Orion's neck and sweat covered his brow as his hips thrust harder. He came seconds later, a bellow ripping from his chest. Brigit felt like a washrag left on the spin cycle too long. She remembered screaming and then she'd lost consciousness for a second or two as his cock shuddered and the rings vibrated at a fever pitch.

When she came to, Brigit could feel her body twitching almost as if an electrical current ran laps beneath her skin. Her hair was matted against her head and Orion lay beside her, staring blindly at the ceiling, his breathing labored. She glanced at the digital clock on the nightstand, two hours had evaporated.

Something inside her melted. Brigit wanted this man for more than a night. A lifetime with Orion wouldn't be enough. Normally that thought would send her packing, but not this time. This time was different.

She felt it inside, a shifting in her heart to make room for Orion. Brigit couldn't wait until she saw Jac and Rachel again.

She wanted them to meet him. She knew beyond a doubt that they would approve.

"I must tell you the message I was sent here to deliver." His voice held an edge she hadn't heard before.

She frowned. That wasn't exactly normal after-nookie chitchat, but so be it. She closed her eyes and braced herself. "Shoot."

Silence.

"Shoot," she repeated.

"Do you wish me to proceed?"

Brigit opened one eye and looked at him. He was dead serious. Her stomach flip-flopped. She got the feeling she wasn't going to like this conversation. "Yes." She took a deep breath and released it slowly, waiting.

Orion didn't speak.

The feeling in her gut got worse. "Tell me already."

He gave her a curt nod. The movement reminded her of historical palaces, charming royals and courtly gestures. Funny, that she'd never made the connection before. She brushed the thought aside.

"Jac and Queen Rachel now reside on the planet Zaron."

Uh-oh, here we go with the Queen Rachel thing again. Brigit smirked, then mustered enough energy to laugh. "Sure they do," she humored, expecting him to tell her he was kidding, but he didn't.

"I speak the truth."

"Yeah, right. My friends are on another planet. As much as I wish that were the case, we both know it's not. Jac and Rachel are stuck in some godforsaken jungle a few thousand miles away."

"I tell you I speak the truth."

Brigit opened both eyes and stared at Orion. He appeared sated but serious. His strong jaw set and unyielding. *Oh geez, why her?* She had the worst taste in men. Somehow she'd gone from cheater to loony in one fell swoop. Did she have "loonies welcome here" tattooed on her ass?

"I speak the truth," he repeated.

She groaned, struggling to her feet. Her legs shook as they supported her weight. Why her? This truly couldn't be happening. He seemed like such a—well normal wasn't exactly the word she was searching for—decent guy. Just her luck that the first guy she could see herself falling for since Rocket Man Rick would turn out to be insane. Something inside of her died a tiny death over the loss.

Brigit wobbled toward the shower using the wall to prop her, unable to stop the mini-quakes from reverberating through her. She kept her attention focused on Orion. None of this made a lick of sense. How did he know about Rachel and Jac? She talked about her friends a lot to other attendees, but hadn't mentioned them to Orion. Brigit's stomach clenched.

"Did you have something to do with my friends' disappearance?"

He hesitated, then slowly released a breath. "No."

Well that was good at least.

Moisture trickled between her legs, momentarily drawing her attention away from their conversation. She glanced down. Her mind refused to acknowledge what she saw. Holy crap, was that blood? Had Orion's amazingly talented ringed-cock ripped her in two? *Calm down. Let's think about this logically.*

"Did your rings do this?" she blurted, knowing instinctively that wasn't the case.

"No." Orion shook his head vehemently.

Brigit knew what she'd felt wasn't that kind of ripping pain. If it had been, they would've stopped before they got started. Funny thing was, it did remind her of something. The memory niggled at the back of her mind. She reached for it, but damned if it wasn't too much effort to recall.

She watched him, but he seemed content to lie on the bed. A myriad unanswered questions pummeled her thoughts. Why would he make up these terrible lies about her friends? Why didn't he say something before he stole her heart? What did he have to gain from all of this?

The word *nothing* hovered in her mind. It just didn't make sense. Brigit vowed to discover the truth.

She glanced once more at the small trickle of blood. She'd seen that before, but where? Her gaze flew to Orion.

He stared at her intently, his eyes fixed on the same spot. He looked as unhappy as she felt.

Torn hymens, loss of virginity, Bobbie Huntsicker's basement her senior year of high school, all very real pictures that flashed consecutively in her mind. No way! She searched Orion's handsome face for answers, yet found none other than the impossible.

"Who are you really? And what in the hell just happened?" She wasn't a virgin. So what the fu—

We linked. His answer popped into her mind like a waffle out of toaster, just like it had on stage earlier.

"Stop that!" She hissed through clenched teeth. "Stop that right now! What are you a mesmerist? Or are you some kind of psychic?"

Orion's eyes widened, then his expression turned to one of resolve. *No, I'm not psychic. I know not what the future holds any more than you do.* Or I would've avoided this situation was left unsaid. Yet he might as well have shouted that thought through a megaphone.

Her heart clenched. "Did you slip me something?"

His expression hardened. *I would never do that.*

Brigit's hands automatically flew to her head to cover her ears. "I don't know how you're doing that, but just knock it off." She inched closer to the door, this was insane. She knew it and he knew it. Her mind returned to dwell on his choice of words. Eventually, curiosity got the better of her and she had to ask, needed to know. Brigit braced herself. "Linked? You said linked. What does that mean exactly?"

Orion looked away, unable to or unwilling to meet her eyes.

This was bad. Very bad.

"We are joined mentally and can never be separated completely."

Fear gripped her. She wasn't about to be "joined" to a crazy man. Brigit prided herself on her independence. "Linked" meant acting...she shuddered...responsible. This had to be some kind of joke, a very cruel and decidedly vicious cosmic joke. Obviously, Orion was a one galactic starship short of a fleet. Brigit did not want to believe it, but the truth stared her in the face with his aqua and jade eyes. Her heart jumped for joy a second before her mind tackled and hogtied it.

Star travel, other planets, alien worlds, yeah they were her dream and why she was here at this conference, but they weren't real. And no amount of wishing it were so would make it a reality. Yet, she wanted too much to believe.

She focused on Orion. "Okey-dokey, then." The flippancy of her tone left Brigit cringing, but she didn't care. She needed to get as far away from him as possible. If she hung around Orion any longer then that would make her just as crazy as he was. Who cared if she'd just had the best sex of her life?

Heat flared in her face as she reached the bathroom. She slipped inside, shutting the door behind her and locking it. Brigit pressed her back against the wood a second before sliding to the floor. What was wrong with her? She knew better than to bring a stranger back to her room. It didn't matter that she felt a connection with Orion that ran deeper than anything she'd experienced in her life. Orion was obviously nutso. She needed to remember that. This was what she got for going against her good judgment.

Good judgment? Ha!

Her fingers trembled as she ran her hands through her hair and thought about the man lying on the bed in the next room. She didn't think she could face him after his admission. Hell, after what they'd done. She snorted. Since when had she become a coward?

She pressed her ear to the door to see if she could hear him moving about the room and frowned. Brigit heard a woman's crackly voice. Had someone come into the room? No…the woman sounded like she was speaking though a bad phone connection or walkie-talkie. That was weird. She reached for a glass next to the sink and put it against the door, pressing her ear onto the end to amplify the sound.

"Have you found the Seer in the jungle yet?" the woman asked.

Brigit gasped, clasping a hand over her mouth to muffle the sound. Was she talking about the jungle where Jac and Rachel disappeared? What were the chances she meant somewhere else?

Slim to none.

"No, I've encountered a complication," he answered. "I'll be on my way tonight once I get things settled here. Have you found that for which you'd sought?"

"Yes, and I couldn't be happier."

"Be well. I will contact you soon."

"Be well." Static followed the last words.

Brigit pushed away from the door and crawled across the bathroom floor until she reached the shower. She definitely needed the water to clear her head. What did that conversation mean? Who was the Seer? Why was she in the jungle? And what did Orion have to do with these people?

Son of a bitch! And here she'd thought he was crazy. He was—crazy like a fox and she'd almost fallen for his act.

She pushed her hand under the tap until the temperature leveled off at just below scalding. She slid the handle to the right extinguishing the tap to allow the spray. Brigit used the toilet as leverage to stand, then stepped inside the tub, pulling the curtain closed behind her.

The hot water rained down upon her head, washing away her thoughts, if only momentarily. Her body ached in places she didn't even know she had muscles in. Brigit begrudgingly admitted it was a good ache. Anger surfaced. Too bad great sex didn't excuse lying.

She needed to find Rachel and Jac. Unfortunately, there was only one place they could be located. The jungle. Maybe Orion could lead her to their location. If he had anything to do with Jac and Rachel's disappearance, she'd hit him—hard.

Brigit shivered and picked up the lavender soap and began lathering her body. The more she thought about the situation, the more Brigit realized she needed to play it cool. Act casual. Her heart flipped in her chest at the thought.

"Get over it," she gritted out under her breath. *You just met him, you can't be in love with him.* Her chest ached in protest. She needed to push aside her feelings and focus. Jac and Rachel were depending on her.

She didn't want to tip Orion off or she'd never find her friends. They'd simply had a bit of fun. Nothing earth-shattering, even if it sort of felt that way. Time to cut her losses.

While she finished showering, Brigit constructed a plan. They'd get dressed and rush straight to one of the conference rooms for an after-party. She'd wait for him to leave. With any luck, he'd lead her straight to her friends. If not, she knew where she had to go.

Following Orion would require that Brigit leave the conference early. She was okay with that. She just prayed he didn't catch her.

Her conscience pricked her. Was it wrong to spy on him?

Under the circumstances, Brigit didn't think so. It was logical and levelheaded, so why was her heart threatening to burst?

* * * * *

Orion couldn't move or refute her claims of subterfuge. He could barely breathe as he spied the redness between Brigit's pale quivering thighs. He vaguely remembered saying the words of binding and feeling the link pop into place. Instantly, he felt himself stroking in and out of her.

A second later Brigit's emotions invaded his mind. He'd shared her hopes and dreams, experienced her fears and saw the boundless love she hid deep inside of her. He had no idea why he'd performed the ritual. It was as if the great Goddess herself forced the words past his numb lips. He'd had no choice but to say them, binding their hearts together for an eternity. Or that was what he would like to believe, but Orion knew better. Even now he could feel the bond between them growing in strength. Soon they wouldn't be able to stand to be apart for any length of time without suffering pain and discomfort from the separation. They'd both feel the loss.

The second he'd slipped his ringed cock inside Brigit's warm quim he'd felt as if he were home. After that, linking had simply been a formality. Her body was everything he'd imagined and more. Her soft cries still filled his ears while the delicate scent of their lovemaking permeated the room. Orion could still taste Brigit upon his lips. The sensation brought a groan from deep inside of his chest to the surface. He hardened, already wanting her again.

His insatiable need for her didn't change the fact that linking oneself to a human was tantamount to insanity. Look what it had done to his brother, Ares, and King Eros. They behaved like besotted fools, catering to their women's needs above their own. It went beyond embarrassing.

The Queen and her friend, Jac held the men's cocks firmly in their dainty hands. Orion shuddered at the thought. No woman would ever hold him in such a manner. He and Brigit could not be bound. He'd just have to explain to her that there had been a mistake. Yet, the damning evidence he'd seen, left little doubt that's what had occurred.

Cassandra's call interrupted his thoughts and reminded him that he was way off schedule with this mission.

What in the name of the Goddess had he done?

Before he could answer that question the bathroom door crashed open and Brigit stood in the frame with a white towel wrapped firmly around her body. His thoughts scattered from his mind like Zaronian leaves in the wind. His eyes feasted upon the sight of her exposed ivory-colored skin. Her red hair was damp and lay pressed against her forehead, feathering her delicate shoulders like the wings of a bird.

Orion cleared his throat to find his voice. "Are you well?"

Brigit stiffened, then gave him a half smile, before walking across the room to the container that held her clothing. "I'm fine. Why wouldn't I be? How are you? Ready to go?" The words fell out of her mouth in rapid-fire succession.

Orion had no idea what Brigit talked about, but he hadn't missed the change in her demeanor. She'd realized the mistake their joining had been too. He ignored the sudden discomfort in his chest. Sensible and beautiful, she was the perfect woman. What was he saying? There was no such thing as the perfect woman. He'd mated out of instinct and to continue his bloodline. It mattered not that linking couldn't occur without the existence of a true-mate.

She dropped the top half of the towel, but didn't turn to face him. The material pooled around her slender waist, exposing her delicately sloping back. Orion found himself wishing that he could get one more glimpse of her rose-colored nipples. Brigit shimmied, pulling clothing into place before allowing the towel to drop further.

"There is no need to hide yourself from me. I saw your form only moments ago."

She laughed. "Yeah, well, that was then, this is now. I need to get dressed."

Orion didn't say anything more. He refused to acknowledge how much her sudden coolness affected him. This was what he wanted after all, a quick joining to relieve tension, nothing more. He'd delivered the message. It was her choice whether to believe it.

Now he could move on to other women and Brigit could seek other men. The second the thought formed, rage engulfed Orion. His hands curled into fists. *How dare she hide herself from him? How dare she seek other men to assuage her need? Did she not understand she was his?*

He stopped, his heart hammering in his chest as the words reverberated in his mind. His entire body shook with unremitting anger. It took him a few seconds before he could focus. He released an unsteady breath. Orion's lip curled in disgust at his own weakness.

He needed to get back to his ship and file a report on his progress thus far. He paused, deciding it may be necessary to censor part of his entry. Perhaps, he'd even send a message to his brother, Ares, while he was there. Not that he needed his older brother's advice. He simply wanted confirmation of what he knew was the truth.

Brigit was not his true-mate, even though he'd said the binding words. The ceremony was incomplete without his people's blessing and would remain so. She was a mere Earthling. She had no control over him and he didn't control her. He wanted it that way. He girded his loins against the unpleasant knee-jerk response in his gut.

Orion gave her back one last look of longing. He could already feel his cock roaring to life and the link between them growing. He refused to accept what fate dealt him.

And this was how it would remain...for all eternity.

Chapter Five

෩

Orion rose from the bed and dressed without another word to Brigit. They left her room and found a Star Battle party taking place in one of the nearby conference areas.

They'd been milling around with other conference attendees for the past hour. Brigit thought of a half a dozen strategies for sneaking out of the room so she could pack and be ready to follow him, but Orion thwarted her at every turn by keeping his attention locked on her—ass.

Brigit tried to ignore the tightening in her nipples and the moisture gathering between her thighs. She found it as easy as attempting to put contact lenses into a hippo's eyes.

Several minutes dragged by. She'd all but given up hope, when Orion suddenly pulled her aside. "I must go back to my ship for a while." Something akin to regret passed over his features, but was gone so quickly she didn't get a chance to analyze the emotion.

"Of course," Brigit said, realizing her chance had come. "I'll wait right here," she lied, praying he couldn't hear the excitement in her voice.

His brow drew down. He opened his mouth as if to say something, but then closed it.

"Well, you better get going. It was nice fuc—meeting you." She forced a smile.

"I will return as soon as I can."

"Yeah, sure. Great." Brigit shrugged. "Take your time," she added hastily. It wasn't like Jac and Rachel were nearby, but hopefully Orion would leave her a clue to their whereabouts.

Orion's jaw clenched for a second and Brigit thought she saw hurt in his eyes. But that wasn't possible, was it? He reached out and stroked her cheek with one finger. Her heart threatened to leap out of her chest and shatter. What was the matter with her? How could she feel so much for a man who in all likelihood was deceiving her?

The word "link" slammed into her mind. Brigit shook her head in denial and closed her eyes a second. They were not "linked". He was not from another planet called Zaron. And there was no spaceship.

"See you soon," she said a little too cheerfully.

Orion hesitated, then dropped his hand away and turned to stride across the room. People stepped aside to get out of his way, their gazes darting nervously in his wake. He paused in the doorway, his knuckles turning white as he clasped the frame. Brigit half expected it to break off in his hand.

He glanced back to look at her one last time. His eyes met hers. The longing in their depths nearly knocked Brigit to her knees. Something akin to panic struck her, but she refused to move. She had to wait until he was out of sight. She couldn't risk him catching her. Brigit inhaled and counted to ten. The next second he was gone. The wrenching sensation she felt in her heart was all too real. At that moment, Brigit wasn't at all certain she'd survive the separation.

* * * * *

Orion forced himself to leave the building when every instinct told him to stay. He'd delivered his message as ordered. That part of his mission was now complete. It was time to find the Seer and Coridan. He wasn't proud of his behavior with Brigit, but would be *Atlantean* enough to do what was right for them both. He'd leave this place and allow Brigit to get on with her life, find a human mate and settle down. They had no place in each other's worlds.

And he'd keep telling himself that until he believed it.

His jaw clenched as he reached the clearing and punched a button on his wrist. The woods were quiet and a warm gentle breeze stirred the air. The ship appeared before him a second later. Orion hit another switch and the portal opened with a slight swoosh, allowing him entrance.

Brigit accused him of lying. She didn't believe her friends resided on Zaron. She didn't even believe he had a ship. Orion stared at the control panel, knowing it would be so easy to prove his words if he brought her aboard. But he wouldn't. He didn't dare. For that would mean acknowledging their *link*. And Orion flat-out refused to be bound to an Earthling, no matter how beautiful, sensual and obstinate a creature she was.

Why had he said the ancient words? Orion still could not believe he'd done so. Never in all his years had he acted so foolishly. His behavior went beyond foolish and straight to reckless. No one uttered the words of binding without weighing the consequences first. It was as if he'd been unable to control himself. What for the love of the Goddess was he going to do now?

Orion hit several buttons on the control panel in order to display a map of the planet. The holographic image swirled before him as he searched for the jungle. He entered the coordinates his brother Ares gave him and found the location the Atlanteans lived in before their *exodus*.

It would only take a few minutes to reach the deserted village. He could retrieve the Seer and Coridan and return to Zaron before Brigit was any wiser. Prior to that, he'd contact Cassandra to see if she'd had enough of this planet. Goodness knows he had. Brigit's face fluttered before his eyes and his body tightened.

The thought of the redheaded spitfire brought an unexpected pain to his chest. He ignored it. He'd suffered far worse injuries on the battlefield. Like those, this would eventually heal. But even as the thoughts filtered through his mind, Orion wasn't convinced of their truth. He'd survived many wounds, but none quite as deep as those caused by the fear and disappointment he'd witnessed floating in Brigit's green eyes after he'd told her the truth.

He entered the coordinates into the onboard data system. The ship hummed to life and rose silently off the ground. He cloaked the craft from prying eyes. Perhaps once he had performed his duties Orion would return and bid Brigit a final farewell, since he had promised to do so. He shook his head. No, that wouldn't happen. 'Twas best this be the end for both their sakes. Orion wasn't at all sure if he saw her again he'd be able to let her go. That thought alone scared the Zaronian fires out of him.

The urge to reach out and touch her mind was strong. His body ached with need. Orion battled it as he strapped himself into the seat and flew the ship away from a woman more dangerous to his wellbeing than any beast he'd ever encountered.

* * * * *

Brigit rushed to her hotel room, packed and checked out in record time. She knew if she hurried she could catch Orion on the highway. He couldn't be that far ahead. She stilled as she realized she had no idea what he drove. Jeez, she forgot to ask even the most basic information all because the man could fuck like a god.

Pathetic!

If this was what mind-blowing sex did to a woman, Brigit wanted no part of it. This was her last chance to locate her friends and escape with her heart unscathed. Who was she kidding? She'd passed unscathed the moment Orion sank that ringed cock into her body. Even now she could almost feel the vibrations in her clit.

She groaned and threw her suitcase into the blue rental car, then jumped into the driver's seat. Orion told her he was going back to his ship. Ha! She truly must have "I'm a moron" tattooed on her forehead. As much as she'd love to believe he stood on the deck of some starship, Brigit knew that right now Orion sat behind the wheel of his car probably phoning the woman he'd spoken to earlier.

Her heart gave a little flip at the thought of him leaving without saying goodbye and going to this woman. Brigit growled. She could not be jealous. Not when he'd deceived her.

As far as she was concerned, they'd said hello, goodbye and have a nice life the second he'd slipped out of her body and told her that whopper story about her friends.

Yet, he'd appeared so sincere.

And that pissed Brigit off even more. How dare he make up stories about her best friends and then act innocent? Didn't he know how much she missed them? If he were a real man, he'd come right out and admit what he'd done and rectify it. Hell, he was probably on his way to the jungle right now. She slammed her fist onto the dashboard.

"Ow!" Brigit's hand throbbed as she shook it out, trying to ease the pain.

She thought about Orion's ability to speak into her mind, the wrist device that seemed to give him information, his ringed cock and the fact he wasn't familiar with basic knowledge. Nothing made sense.

Orion didn't seem like the type of guy who got off by hurting women. He'd been genuinely upset when he saw the blood between her thighs and was quick to assure her it hadn't come from his rings. There was no way he was telling the truth, was there? Brigit knew only one way to find out.

She dropped her head onto the steering wheel and banged her forehead, while repeating *stupid, stupid, stupid* in her mind. When Brigit finally straightened, she had a big red mark the size of a strawberry to show for her foolishness. Her hands shook as she fought to get the key into the ignition. Hopefully with a little distance things would get better or at least clearer. *Yeah? Tell that to your heart.* She ignored the insipid little voice. It didn't know everything.

She drove, looking for any sign of Orion. It was like trying to find a flea in a shag carpet. He'd disappeared, but at least she knew where he'd gone. She needed to get home. Maybe Jac and Rachel had returned while she was away and she could chalk this whole situation up to a huge clusterfuck. She'd check their apartments first. If she didn't find them there, Brigit knew she'd need to make a trip to the jungle.

The one place Jac and Rachel didn't reside was on planet Zaron. Brigit shuddered as she realized she was about to go on the long journey her horoscope warned her about. Was she up to taking a trip to the jungle?

Hell no!

Her fingers trembled as she drove back to Manhattan, breaking every speed limit along the way. She glanced in the rearview mirror, catching sight of the hoop earring Orion had placed in her ear before the contest. Her heart hurt and the sadness she felt seemed to be growing by the mile. Didn't he say something about not being able to separate? What was she saying? She didn't really believe that. Brigit stared a moment at her reflection in disgust. "You are so weak."

Brigit fingered the silver hoop while her eyes returned to the road. She scanned the cars around her, noting the drivers. Her heart swelled as she saw a dark head in the distance. Could it be? She held her breath and waited. As the driver drew closer, she realized he wasn't who she sought. Disappointment weighted her shoulders until they slumped.

The further away from the conference hotel she drove the more Brigit hurt. The pain reached viselike proportions at mile forty. If she hadn't felt fine earlier, she would've gone to the nearest hospital and demanded a doctor examine her. She thought about the men in the white lab coats poking and prodding her and came close to vomiting.

What in the hell was the matter with her?

The word *linked* popped into her mind. It wasn't possible, was it? *No! Definitely not.* He'd probably hypnotized her or something. Yeah, that was it. He made her believe her heart would break without him. Orion was damn good, she'd give him that. Almost too good, considering she really did feel heartbroken, which was impossible since she'd only known the man for a day.

No one could fall in love in a day.

Not even her.

She reached the rental car place an hour later. It only took a few minutes for the lot attendant to examine the car and then release her. She caught a cab afterward and headed to her apartment. With any luck, Brigit would have a message waiting from Rachel and Jac. They'd know what to do about Orion.

Please don't make me have to go down to the jungle. You guys know how much I hate bugs.

* * * * *

Orion resisted the urge to check on Brigit. Time and again his gaze shifted to the tracking panel on his control system. He knew it was wrong to place a tracking device on her, but he couldn't resist. He glanced one last time at the panel, then gave up the fight.

The second Orion flicked the switch he knew something was wrong. Instead of the blip remaining stationary, it was moving. He frowned and his body tensed. Orion hit the side of the readout, but it remained the same. Brigit headed away from the hotel, away from him. The pain he'd felt before suddenly became much worse.

She was running.

So, she'd decided to leave without bidding him a final farewell. Had he not told her he'd return on the soonest? She'd chosen not to wait. How strong could their link be if she could leave him without a second thought? Orion slammed his fist down onto the panel, making the instruments jump. He'd been a fool.

He knew he should be pleased. Her retreat only validated Orion's earlier decision to not return. This was the way things should be. They could not be joined like traditional Atlantean law dictated, so it was best they part company for good. Brigit had obviously come to the same conclusion he'd reached earlier. Yet, Orion was anything but pleased. How dare she leave him!

Orion's fingers hurt from gripping the guidance system. He would not turn back and seek her out. He would not allow foolish emotions to dictate his course. He was not joined to this red-haired menace. He might have tried to create a link, but it hadn't been successful. If he tried to reach out to her this second with his mind, it wouldn't work due to the distance. When the connection occurred earlier it had been a fluke. They'd shared their bodies and no more. And Orion would keep telling himself that until he believed it.

He pictured Brigit's quivering nipples and imagined the feel of his cock as it slid into her moist quim. He could almost hear her soft moans as she came hard beneath his burrowing thrusts. Orion's body responded instantly, demanding release. He ran a trembling hand through his hair and shuddered. Sweat broke out across his forehead.

Instead of trying to reach her, Orion concentrated on flying his ship. He'd arrive at the jungle in another minute or two. Once there he'd land and find the Seer and Coridan. They were probably still in the village Ares described. It should be easy enough to find. He wasn't being a coward by not seeking Brigit out. This had nothing to do with a lack of bravery. He was completing his mission as commanded.

So why didn't he believe it?

* * * * *

Brigit reached her apartment fairly quickly despite the typical New York City midtown rush. She rode the elevator to the seventh floor and the walked the short distance to her door. The key turned in the lock on the second try and Brigit entered her home to find five dead plants staring at her from the windowsill. Jac was going to kill her. She'd promised to water them while she was away.

Oops!

She dropped her suitcase next to the sixties-style dinette set and locked the door before heading to her answering machine. Brigit pressed a button on the machine. It beeped several times then came back with, "You have no new messages." Her heart sank.

Brigit grabbed her headset off the cradle and punched in Jac's number. The phone rang and rang before the machine picked up. She hit the disconnect button and then phoned Rachel, only to receive the same response. She knew they weren't going to be there. Brigit also knew that meant they were still somewhere in BFE, "bum-fuck Egypt".

If Orion had something to do with their disappearance, why was he at Conlunar? And why in the hell hadn't she asked herself that at the time? Brigit groaned and rushed to her bedroom. The white-washed wood stood out in stark contrast to the hot pink comforter. She moved to her matching dresser and rifled through the drawers. They had to be here somewhere. She needed answers.

Her hands closed around a silk pouch and Brigit released a sigh. She pulled her tarot cards out of the drawer and moved into the kitchen so she'd have room to lay out a Celtic Cross spread.

Two hours later she still wasn't happy with the results. The cards kept repeating the same thing. You'll take a trip and encounter a man of great power who will change your life. It wasn't clear whether he'd change it for the better or worse, but the cards left no room for interpretation when it came to it happening.

Brigit shuffled them again and threw down the Lovers card. "Crap!"

* * * * *

The next day Brigit was on a plane, sputtering its way like a playing card stick tied to a wheel spoke, to the jungle. She'd packed bug spray by the gallons, a fly swatter and had netting to wear around her head. With her roller bag tucked safely in the cargo hold and her designer jeweled sandals strapped to her newly pedicured feet, she felt prepared for anything.

Three aircraft and four fuel stops later, the plane came in for a landing. She couldn't believe it had taken two days to get down here. Wherever here was. Brigit pulled her gold wire-rimmed sunglasses down on her nose and stared out the tiny window in terror. Miles upon miles of endless trees surrounded the landing strip. There wasn't even a town built around the dirt airport. Heck, there wasn't even an airport. She gripped the arms of her seat and attempted to quell her rising panic. She couldn't do this. She could not do this.

The wheels slammed down, jarring her clenched teeth and grinding her palms into the armrest.

Where were the roads? Where were the trails? Good God! Where were the sidewalks? She knew there'd be some jungle to traipse through, Rachel had told her as much, but surely some of it was colonized. The plane's engine roared as the pilot hit the brakes, driving her seat belt into her waist. The aircraft bounced along the uneven terrain before coming to a stop in front of several tents.

Brigit choked on the dust that filled the non-pressurized cabin through a broken window that had been partially taped shut. She waved a useless hand in front of her face to clear the air. Heat Brigit didn't realize could exist this side of the sun, pressed in around her, melting her clothes into her body. She pinched her shirt with two fingers and pulled it away from her skin. The suction sound made her shudder.

Eww! Gross!

There better be a shower around here somewhere. She glanced out the window once more, squinting into the fading sunlight. Dirt and bug guts smeared the small pane. She swallowed the urge to gag. So this was where Jac and Rachel were located. She hoped. The immensity of the task before her deflated some of Brigit's optimism. How in the hell was she going to find them in this overgrown vine-tangled mess?

She released her seat belt with a soft click and rose. Her feet trembled inside her high-heeled sandals. She walked the short distance to the door and waited for the pilot to open it. He did a moment later, setting a stool on the ground for her to step on. He didn't offer to help her down. Instead, he turned and walked away, shouting orders to the men who'd been standing near the camp.

Brigit stepped onto the runway and the heels of her beautiful shoes sank two inches into the dirt. She screamed as something *crawly* scurried over her toe. High stepping, Brigit rushed toward the tents. One of the natives she'd hired brought her luggage over and set it inside one of the canvas structures. Brigit didn't ask if it was hers. She barreled in behind her bags and spun facing the open tent flap.

"Excuse me?" she asked, stopping the man before he could leave. She dug into her purse and pulled out a five dollar bill and slipped it into his palm. "Could you tell me if a man with a tattoo on his face, blond and black hair, piercings and two-toned eyes came through here in the last day or so?"

"Sorry, *Senorita*. I've seen no one like you described enter the jungle from here."

"Is it possible he entered from somewhere else?"

The native shook his head. "There is no other way to reach the interior without passing through this place."

"Thank you," Brigit said as relief spread through her. With any luck, she'd beat Orion here. "One final question."

"Yes."

"Could you tell me if there are any hotels nearby?"

He looked at the money and at her sparkly shoes, then shook his head, muttering something unintelligible under his breath, and left. Brigit's gaze darted to her shoes. The jewels sparkled in the fading sunlight. She sniffed as she followed the man's movements through the camp. He spoke rapid fire to several of the others, turning and pointing back toward her tent. A moment later laughter rang out as the men all looked in her direction.

Obviously, New York wasn't the only rude and unfriendly place on the planet. She glanced around at the menacing trees, suddenly missing the muggers of Central Park. Brigit wanted to go home. Now. But she wouldn't. She'd come all this way and she wasn't about to leave here without her friends.

A bird cried out somewhere in the trees, Brigit yelped and leapt on top of her cot, leaning forward until she could zip herself inside of her tent. She listened to the natives bustling around the fire, their singsong language blending in with the cacophony of sound emanating from the jungle. Brigit's heart raced and a thin sheen of sweat broke out over her body. She wouldn't be nearly as afraid if Orion were here. The thought brought a mixture of sadness and anger. Brigit refused to admit how much she missed him and how scared she was without him.

She stepped carefully onto the floor and then reached over to light the kerosene lamp that one of the natives left for her benefit. A quick strike of a match and sulfur filled the air. The flame rose behind the glass lantern, illuminating the shadows inside the tent. Something slithered along the seam of the canvas. Brigit whimpered and jumped back onto her cot.

Was that a spider or a lizard? Did it really matter? Either way this was going to be a long, long trip.

* * * * *

Orion searched the jungle again, making a wider sweep each time. He'd covered the area for two days and still found no sign of Ariel and Coridan in or near the deserted Atlantean village. Men crawled through the jungle, searching for what, he did not know. Orion avoided them easily, but didn't like what he'd seen. They were on the hunt and it wasn't for the animals, which were in abundance.

Anger surged through him when he overheard their intended targets. So they sought the Seer and Coridan. It was foolish for so few humans to pursue two Atlanteans in their prime. The Seer was powerful and he'd heard much of Coridan's abilities. The humans did not stand a chance, but that did not halt their pursuit.

Orion took care to set false trails. The men traveled in circles, closing in on nothing. Still, the more Orion searched, the less he found. Where were they? He'd sent out calls that only other Atlanteans could hear and received no response. *Quarg!* He needed to find them first and he needed to find them fast.

He returned to his cloaked ship as darkness fell upon the jungle. The night predators stirred, spreading out in search of prey. He could hear them slithering and stalking through the lush underbelly of the forest. The smaller creatures scurried seeking shelter from attack. Orion listened to the jungle fascinated by the many sights, sounds and smells.

For the first time since Ares' arrival on Zaron, Orion felt a closeness to his brother. One that came from shared experience. He hadn't understood Ares' love of this place until this moment. He took a deep breath, inhaling the fragrant flower-filled air deep into his lungs. It would be easy to make a home here, if you had the right mate at your side. His brother fought hard to win and keep his mate, Jac, risking death. Those last thoughts left a frown on Orion's face. He pressed a button at his wrist and the ship materialized in front of him. He entered quickly, then sent another command for it to return to stealth mode.

He walked past his personal chambers, which were sparse compared to his lush living quarters on Zaron, before striding to the piloting area. He slid into his seat, his gaze straying repeatedly to the tracking device on the panel. He hadn't felt Brigit in two days and the separation wore on him, frazzling his nerves and ratcheting his temper to near breaking point. His body needed her.

Before he could stop himself, Orion flipped on the device. A blip appeared on the scanner. That couldn't be correct. He wrinkled his brow and hit the side of the machine. It flickered once but the blip remained in place. That wasn't possible. Orion turned the machine on and off, but the location didn't change. She was here, in the jungle. Sweat broke out on his forehead as his blood roared through his veins straight to his ringed cock.

What in Goddess' name was she thinking?

Her parting words came back to haunt him. She'd accused him of having something to do with her friends' disappearance. He hadn't, but her accusation cut deep. That coupled with her soft moans of pleasure tortured his soul. She did not trust him. Why that should pain him so, Orion didn't know, but it did. He'd thought of little else since his departure.

He tried to imagine his red-haired wildcat trekking through the wilderness alone. Orion's heart slammed into his ribs. She wouldn't last a night in this place. The beasts that lived here would eat her up. Fear and panic raged within him. He couldn't let that happen. The only being allowed to eat her...*was him*. If he left this place, he'd be disobeying a direct order from the King, an infraction punishable by death on Zaron. Yet, if he didn't go and something happened to Brigit, he wouldn't be able to live with himself, so death would be an acceptable option.

Despite years of training and experience in multiple combat situations, Orion did the unthinkable. He sentenced himself to death by entering Brigit's coordinates into his data wristband and leaving his post to go in search of *his* woman.

Chapter Six

ଈ

Brigit woke to the sounds of banging pots and pans. She sprang out of her cot, her trusty fly swatter raised in defense. For a few seconds she didn't recognize her surroundings. Then her toe connected with the end of the cot and she let out a loud yelp and began hopping up and down on one foot. The zipper of her tent slid open and a brown-skinned man poked his head inside.

"I am Angel. Are you all right, *Senorita*?" he asked smiling.

She stared at the darkness behind his shoulders. What was everyone doing up in the middle of the night? Brigit stopped hopping and gripped the injured toe in her hand, before plopping butt first back onto her cot. "I'm fine thanks, Angel," she said, cursing jungles, trees, bugs, men and cots under her breath. "Everyone can go back to sleep now."

"Sleep?" he asked, confusion filling his voice. "But it's morning."

Brigit glanced over his shoulder again. Inky blackness shadowed the trees. The birds began to sing. "It's still dark outside," she pointed out as if he'd missed that fact.

His smile deepened. "Ah yes, the sun will be up in another hour."

"Then so will I," Brigit said lying back on her cot and covering her head with her pillow.

"Sorry, *Senorita*, but we must get started now. There is much ground to travel and we've heard word that there may be trouble ahead."

Brigit threw the pillow aside and cocked one eye open. "Trouble? What kind of trouble? You mean like headhunters?"

"No." He shook his head. "A loco man with hair like yours is rumored to have killed many." The smile faded from the Angel's face.

Rumsinger... Brigit's heart stampeded in her chest and she felt the blood drain from her face. Jac and Rachel had to be all right. Anything else was unacceptable. "You haven't heard about two women have you?" She choked on the question.

He squirreled his face and considered her question carefully.

Brigit took a deep breath and waited for what felt like an eternity. *Please God let them be alive.* She sent up the silent prayer.

"No, *Senorita.* I have heard nothing about their deaths, but I have heard they may have encountered a fabled ghostlike magical people, who have powerful magic in their hands."

She exhaled, hardly believing her ears. Her mind jumped to Orion and the glow in his fingers that she thought she'd imagined during sex. Could it be? "Do you believe they exist?" she asked, not sure what answer she hoped to hear.

He smiled again. "No, *Senorita.* That is only superstition talking."

"Of course, the thought is ridiculous," she said recalling Orion's far-out story about other planets and space travel.

Thirty minutes later the natives packed the entire camp and loaded it onto the shoulders of fifteen stout-looking men. Brigit offered to carry one of the backpacks, but they all looked at her as if she'd lost her mind. She really wished people would stop doing that. There was more to her than an amazing sense of fashion.

She wore a pair of khaki-colored pants and leopard-print shirt beneath her net covered hat. Brigit had a fly swatter in one hand and a can of bug spray in the other. Every few feet she stopped to swat and spray anything that flew in front of her face. The jungle heat took its toll, leaving every inch of her body covered in sweat. Her feet actually made squish noises inside her tennis shoes.

Brigit broke formation and strolled up to Angel. "Could we rest a minute?"

"*Sí Senorita.*"

She walked back to her position and found a nearby log to sit down upon. Brigit sagged then slipped her shoes off before asking the man carrying her suitcase to bring it to her. She spun the dial to align with seven, seven, seven. The lock slipped and her suitcase opened, spilling the contents onto the jungle floor.

Brigit dove for the ground, shoving items back into the bag before any bugs could crawl into them. Frazzled, she finally got everything into the suitcase. She found a dry pair of socks near the left side and pulled them out. Brigit closed her bag and spun the lock, then handed it back to the man given the task to carry it.

She sighed as she slipped the clean socks onto her feet and then rose, brushing her hands along the side of her legs. "Okay, we can go on now."

The men shot glances at each other, then continued on.

Several hours later the head guide, Angel called a halt to their sloth-like progress and ordered everyone to take a short rest. Brigit smashed a beetle, then brushed it aside with the end of her fly swatter. She'd run out of bug spray an hour ago. Obviously, she'd miscalculated the longevity of the two gallons she'd brought with her. Brigit found a fat leaf nearby and picked it so she could fan her net-covered face. At least she had one spot left on her body that the bugs hadn't tried to eat.

One of the natives reached into a pouch and pulled out a canteen. Brigit thanked him and accepted it, moving the netting away from her face in order to drink. She'd taken one sip when the hair on the nape of her neck stood on end. Brigit dropped the canteen into her lap and spun around.

The jungle remained silent, even the leaves refused to rustle. Several of the men in her party gazed warily, motioning toward the shadows that seemed to morph and grow with each passing second. Their hands tightened on the rifles they carried.

Something was near, lurking just out of sight. She hadn't had time to go over the flora and fauna of the area, but she knew there were predators down here. Predators big enough to eat her and a few of her guides for appetizers. Brigit swallowed the lump in her throat and rose slowly. "I think we'd better get out of here," her eyes met Angel's gaze and he nodded in agreement.

Brigit picked up the canteen and handed it back to the man who'd given it to her. She took her place in line, watching the jungle as she walked. Her skin prickled and her nipples tightened as whatever it was slid its gaze down the front of her. Her body's reaction seemed a little odd to Brigit, considering it was an animal. She dismissed the strange almost sexual sensation and urged the men on.

They had a long way to go before they'd be able to make camp. With any luck, whatever was out there would get tired and go after easier prey. At least that's what she hoped as they snaked their way along a nonexistent trail. Brigit kept a tight grip on her yellow fly swatter and continued to scan the treetops for movement. If anything attacked, she'd be ready.

* * * * *

Orion followed the small party through the jungle, his eyes drinking in every inch of Brigit's form. She had encased the lower half of her body in tan pants that cupped her bottom and surrounded her lush hips. A spotted shirt caressed her breasts, but appeared thin enough for him to catch a glimpse of her erect nipples beneath the fabric. Orion gripped the vine in his hand tighter. Her head lay beneath a mesh covering of some sort and she wielded a flimsy weapon that she waved in front of her face with regularity.

He longed to have her remove the headpiece so he could see the rich red of her hair shining in the twinkling sunlight. The little party continued on with Brigit complaining every forty feet. Orion smiled to himself. His little demon didn't like being out in the jungle. Perhaps, she hadn't been properly introduced to the pleasures to be had under the guidance of the right tutor.

Orion checked the area to ensure the group's safety and then journeyed ahead to prepare. He needed the right location to abduct his *ma – woman*. A river ran between this part of the jungle and the old Atlantean village. They would reach the area by nightfall, but would not be able to cross until the morning. It would be the perfect spot to detain Brigit.

His muscles tensed and his cock hardened as he imagined touching her once more. He could almost taste her lips and feel the stab of her nipples as they grew firm against his palms. The rings on his shaft vibrated, shooting a deep pleasure-pain along his spine. He'd gone without her body for only two days and yet it felt like a lifetime. The urge to join addled his thoughts, narrowing his focus to one thing, and one thing only – Brigit.

Orion would like to believe that he would've let her go if only she'd remained in New York, but he wasn't inclined to delude himself. The need surging through his body and the pain of separation was too great. He may have managed to get the ship out of the atmosphere, but he would have turned back shortly thereafter. He picked a tree that protected him from prying eyes and waited. It was excruciating to try to keep his mind from seeking contact. Seeing Brigit only made things worse. The sun retreated an hour before the small party finally arrived.

* * * * *

Brigit slumped on the first felled tree she found, her purse and swatter slipping from her grasp. She sighed as she watched the men gather wood and build a fire. She'd never seen a place this dark before. The tents went up within minutes and she decided if she crawled she could just make it to her cot before she fell asleep.

"*Senorita*, would you like some food?" Angel asked, scooping something onto a leaf.

Brigit smiled. "No thanks! I think I'm going to call it a night."

"You really should eat, *Senorita*." Angel grabbed another leaf and scooped some more of the stew-like substance onto the makeshift plate and handed it to her.

"Thanks." Brigit took it, staring at the glob of food while a bug crawled across the other end of the leaf. That was all she needed to see. She rushed the few remaining yards to her tent, so the men wouldn't witness her gagging. When her stomach finally calmed, she poked her head out the tent flap and checked to make sure no one watched. When Brigit was sure that no one would see her, she dumped the leaf and its contents into the thick brush.

Some of the men had settled into their tents, while others lay around the fire swapping stories in their native tongue. Brigit wished she could understand enough to join in. She listened to the sounds of the jungle around her, feeling alone for the first time in the world. Her friends were gone. She'd left Orion. A twinge of pain squeezed her heart at the thought of her intergalactic dragon slayer.

Was he down here somewhere? If not, where was he? Did he have something to do with Jac's and Rachel's disappearance? Did he miss her half as much as she missed him?

Orion wasn't a man she'd ever be able to control and Brigit didn't know if she could handle that or him. She was used to getting her way, from day-to-day business dealings in the design world to dating. She avoided men who threatened her comfort zone. And Orion not only threatened it, he exploded its very foundation.

She still didn't understand how he knew so much about Rachel and Jac or why he'd bothered to come up with that far-out story to begin with. And what about the woman she'd heard talking to him? How did she fit into this confusing picture? It was an awful lot of trouble to go through for no obvious return.

Brigit dropped her chin to her chest and closed her eyes as her body recalled the vibrating rings surrounding his cock. The way he felt when he first entered her. The drugging kisses Orion trailed over her nipples and the never-ending orgasms that left her a quivering pile of goo. She groaned and pressed her knees together to dampen the need in her throbbing clit. This line of thought was getting her nowhere. She slipped back inside her tent and zipped it shut. At least this time she'd remembered to bring her vibrator.

One hour and no orgasms later, Brigit lay on her cot covered in sweat. Her body throbbed in frustrated pain, demanding she get off. Yet, no matter how she approached her clit with her trusty vibrator it refused to cooperate.

"This is all *your* fault," she hissed between clenched teeth. "If you didn't have that damn vibrating cock that can make women sing my body would be floating back from 'Blissville' by now."

Brigit tossed the vibrator onto her suitcase and turned to hit her pillow a couple times with her fist. How in the hell was she going to get any sleep feeling like this?

* * * * *

Orion listened to the buzzing sound coming from Brigit's tent and her groans of frustration. The subtle musk from her skin permeated the area whetting his appetite and torturing his need. He wasn't sure what the first noise was from, but he knew what caused the second. Any man with ears recognized a woman in the throes of heat.

His gaze zeroed in on the men around the fire. Several glanced in the direction of Brigit's tent, but none made a move to go to her. Smart of them. Orion didn't want to kill any of her guides, but he would if they touched her. Her soft moans died down, eventually disappearing. The men settled back into an uneasy sleep.

Orion closed his eyes, going deep inside himself until he found the link that existed between him and Brigit. He hesitated as fear gripped him. What if he was right and the link didn't work? His chest clenched at the thought. He was no coward and couldn't live without knowing the truth, even if it were painful. Orion followed the blue mental rope back to its source and that's when he found her. He quaked as need devoured him. Brigit stood naked in the middle of a quiet pool of water, running her fingertips over its mirrored surface, sending out ripples to the far edges of the pond. She hummed something low under her breath. Whatever the tune, it brought a smile to her face.

For several minutes, he did not intrude. Orion watched Brigit move through her dream, reveling under the moonlit sky, her pearlescent skin glowing against the fire of her hair. Her pert breasts turned up at the ends showing off her berry-colored nipples. The vee, where her sex lay covered in a thin layer of red curls, widened and narrowed with every step she took. Multicolored flowers of all shapes and sizes surrounded the clearing, perfuming the air with placid perfection.

How could one woman be so infuriatingly beautiful?

His eyes refused to leave her. Orion stepped out of the shadows, his cock hard and curled against his abdomen. Brigit moved deeper into the water. She seemed unaware of his presence. Or so he'd thought until she glanced over her shoulder and smiled.

"I wondered if you'd come," she said, smiling. "I've missed you. The pain in my heart's been nearly unbearable."

The sentiment pleased him, even though he knew she'd never admit as much outside of this dream. "I couldn't stay away."

"Come." She held out her hand and waited for him to approach.

Orion forced his feet to slow. He would not allow her to see his need beyond the obvious. The rings around his cock glowed gold in the night as he walked the distance separating them. He reached for her. She weaved her fingers through his and pulled him into the water. The pond was unusually warm and obviously made for cleansing. Perhaps, in her dream, Brigit wished she could bathe.

He allowed her to lead him deeper into the water, enjoying the feel of the wetness lapping at his skin. They reached the middle and she stopped to face him. Orion tipped her chin and kissed her like he'd longed to do these past few days. She groaned and sunk into the kiss, releasing his hand so she could skewer his hair with her fingers. His scalp tingled in response.

Orion slipped his hands around her thighs and lifted Brigit until she could wrap her legs around his waist. He held her above his erection, feeling her feminine juices drip from her quim onto his cock. The rings vibrated so hard, they nearly buckled his knees.

"I need you so bad," he whispered against her lips, his hunger consuming him.

"Then take me," she urged with a roll of her hips.

"With pleasure." His lips claimed hers as he slowly lowered her onto his shaft, impaling her until the eye of his cock nudged her womb. The heat from the water formed a thin mist over their skin. Orion lifted Brigit by her ass, then allowed her to drop back down. She gasped, her lips parting enough for him to delve inside.

His tongue followed the rhythm their bodies set. He dipped in and out, rolling his hips, so he could take her deep with every thrust. Their lovemaking wasn't as hurried as it had been the first joining. This time they savored their connection, enjoying the musk floating in the air and the gentle glide of skin on skin.

His rings vibrated and she cried out, her back bowing until her hair touched the water. She locked her ankles around him, suctioning him deep into her body. The rings vibrated again, sending them both into an unexpected orgasm. Orion's muscles shook as he supported their bodies until their breathing slowed and Brigit was able to dismount from his cock and stand on her own. Reluctantly, he released her. She walked through the water, a contented smile on her face.

She turned as she stepped out of the pool. "Will I see you again?"

Orion stood in the center of the pond, shock waves reverberating throughout his body. "'Tis certain."

"Don't take too long," she said, then disappeared into the woods.

Orion's eyes sprang open and he grabbed a nearby branch to keep from tumbling out of the tree. His body continued to tremble from his recent release as his surroundings slowly came into focus. He sat perched above Brigit's tent. The animals of the day already started to rise. The sun would be up within the hour. The dream had lasted all night. Today, the party would start across the river after they took in nourishment. That's when he'd make his move.

* * * * *

Brigit awoke after having the most delicious wet dream about Orion. The kind that made the whole world look brighter and the birds sound cheerier. At least that's what she thought as she dressed and stepped out of her tent. Her body felt like she'd been pleasured thoroughly. Even now, her clit seemed overly sensitized. She figured it must be the jungle air. The men sat around the fire, eating their breakfast. She stretched her arms above her head and gave them a big smile.

They looked at each other with strange expression upon their faces, but said nothing.

"Come, *Senorita*. Have some breakfast." Angel encouraged. "Once we get across the river it won't take long to reach the village."

"Don't mind if I do." Brigit took the food he offered and devoured it. She felt like she could eat a water buffalo this morning. Her muscles twinged again in reminder. That was one hell of a dream. Course, Orion was one hell of a man.

They broke camp an hour later, tethering the bags and supplies with thick ropes, so that the river could sweep nothing away. Nervous chatter filtered throughout the men. Brigit approached Angel a minute later.

"What are they worried about?"

Angel swept the hat off his head and wiped a rag over his sweat-drenched face. "The river is swift and dangerous due to flooding upstream. There are anaconda and black caiman in these waters. The men are worried. Every year we lose a few from our village to these superior hunters."

Brigit gaped at the water, then swung her attention back to Angel. "There are giant snakes and what in the water?"

"Black caiman."

She frowned.

"They are like your American alligators."

"Oh my God!" She glanced up and down the shore. "Aren't there any boats or ferries that can take us across?"

Angel frowned in confusion.

"El boat-o, El Ferry-o," she said again, rowing in the air for emphasis, hoping that explained everything.

He shook his head.

Brigit shrieked in frustration and more than a little fear. "We can't get in the water with those things. We'll be eaten."

The men's voices rose. Their gazes darted from side to side.

"*Senorita*, please calm yourself. You're upsetting the men." Angel placed a reassuring hand on her shoulder.

Brigit brushed it off as panic set in. "I'm upsetting the men. There are animals in that water that have big teeth," she held her arms wide, "and long slithery bodies that can crush the life out of you." She squeezed herself for emphasis.

"*Sí*." Angel nodded and shoved his hat onto his head. "*Senorita*, if you want to find your friends, we have to cross the river. There is no other way."

Brigit stared at the churning water. "Jac and Rachel, screw you both. I can't believe you guys would do this to me," she muttered to herself, then stepped toward the water, brushing unexpected tears from her eyes.

"Load up," Angel commanded. "*Senorita*, you stay in the middle. It'll be safer that way." He grabbed her elbow and pulled her back.

Brigit nodded, cursing Rachel and Jac all the way to the middle of the line. If she lived through this, she was going to kick both their asses.

Angel took the lead, stepping into the swirling water up to his shin. He gave Brigit a nervous smile and proceeded deeper into the river. The rest of the men followed behind him. Brigit removed her mosquito netting from her head and hoped the water didn't get too deep or she'd have to swim for it.

* * * * *

Orion watched the group enter the river, then dove in with a splash.

"What was that?" Brigit called out, her head whipping around.

The lead guide shrugged and tightened his grip on his rifle.

Orion swam a few feet, fighting the current long enough to send out an energy pulse to scare away the larger predators. He then took a deep breath and dove below the surface, swimming hard toward the group. He only had one shot at grabbing her in this current. Orion wanted to avoid having to fight all the men, so he couldn't afford to miss.

The murky water clouded his vision to the point he reverted to searching by touch. He reached out a couple of times only to close his hands around a tree limb. One thing he clasped slithered away and almost cost him the air in his lungs. He finally found the small party. He gathered silt in his fist and then touched each person one by one until he'd counted seven in. He knew the next leg he grabbed would be Brigit's.

He leaned close and saw her tan pants. The next second he yanked. Even underwater Orion heard her scream. He dragged her kicking body away from the group and swam hard downstream toward the shore. His lungs burned, demanding oxygen.

He clamped a palm over Brigit's mouth to prevent her from inhaling water, only to have her bite him. He surfaced, filling his lungs with a huge gulp of air, then dove back down. Brigit was thrashing in a panic from not being able to breathe. Orion pressed his mouth to hers and exhaled, filling her lungs with much needed oxygen.

He moved them further down the river, until they were too far away for the guides to see them, then shot toward the surface with Brigit's limp body in his arms. She sputtered and gasped, choking on water while trying to breathe. Orion thumped her back to help.

"What the?" she asked blinking the wetness away. "How—what are you doing here? Come back to the scene of the crime, eh?" She coughed the last of the water out of her lungs, then smacked him on the arm. "You scared the shit out of me. I thought an anaconda or a caiman grabbed me and dragged me under."

Orion rubbed the spot she hit, but was otherwise pleased she was unharmed. "I came here to show you something I should have revealed at your gathering a few days ago."

Brigit frowned. "I should let the men know that I'm all right. They may be worried."

"'Tis better they believe you are dead."

She backed away fear swimming in her eyes.

Frustration boiled over in Orion. "I will not hurt you. I have told you thusly. Why do you insist on believing otherwise?"

"I heard you talking about the jungle back in the hotel room with a woman and now here you are. Not exactly a coincidence. You know things about Jac and Rachel—like the fact they're missing. Let's face it; you haven't exactly given me any reason to trust you."

He flinched at her words. "Then come with me and I'll give you *every* reason to believe what I say is the truth."

Wary, Brigit glanced at the swirling river as if debating her chances of escape.

"If what I say is not so, I shall return you to the men you hired and they can lead you out of the jungle and back to where you belong," he said, knowing full well she belonged by his side.

"Fine! But can you at least tell me where we're going?"

Orion smiled, running his hands along her arms. He didn't miss the quick intake of breath or the dilation in her pupils. "I am taking you to my spaceship."

* * * * *

Two hours later…

"I thought you said your ship was here." Brigit's hands rested on her wide hips as she slowly turned in a circle, searching the clearing.

Orion frowned. "It was right here." He pressed a button on his wrist.

"Is it invisible like Wonder Woman's plane?" She cocked a brow.

"You know I do not have any idea who that is."

"Yeah, yeah, that's right. You're not from around these parts." She shook her head. "You still didn't answer my question."

He glanced up from his wrist. "My ship has a camouflaging device built in to hide its presence from the primitive radar system on this planet."

Brigit snorted. "It works so good you can't even find it. Is there someone we can ask for directions? Oh, I forgot, men don't ask for directions. I guess some things are constant no matter what planet you're from."

Orion scowled. "We're in the right place."

"Yeah, I can see that," she said nodding to appease the crazy man.

He looked around. "It has to be here."

"We could try yelling "olly, olly, oxen free" and see if it comes out of hiding."

"A ship cannot hide."

She laughed. "Well yours is doing a pretty good job."

Orion's eyes narrowed. "You are not helping," he said before tapping the buttons on his wrist.

"Sorry, oh mighty warrior, what would you like me to do? Go beat the bushes with a stick."

He turned and leveled his gaze on her. "I know what has occurred."

"You finally realize there never was a ship." She ran her hands through her hair.

"No."

Brigit tilted her head. "Are you going to fill me in?"

Orion's lips twitched.

She didn't like the sudden change in his demeanor.

"Gladly, later," he said. Orion's gaze raked her, pausing at the vee of her legs, then moving slowly to her breasts. A second later, his mouth split into a lascivious grin.

Brigit's nipples pebbled and her clit throbbed. "Stop that!" Her voice came out as a breathy command. "We don't have time." She moved back as her fight or flight response kicked in.

"Actually..." Orion stepped forward. "Now that Cassandra has taken the ship into orbit around this planet, we have all the time in the world."

"Who the hell is Cassandra? You better not tell me she's your wife." Brigit threatened, intending to cause Orion bodily harm, if he gave her the wrong answer.

He laughed. "She is a fellow Atlantean, who came here to find her true-mate. I have not lain with her."

"Lain?" She frowned, then her expression cleared. "Oh, you mean fucked her."

"*Quarg*! Such a crude language you have." Orion shook his head.

"Yeah, yeah, whatever, tomato, *tomahto*! Is that the truth?"

His fingers moved to the front of his costume. He pulled it away, exposing the muscled planes of his chest, then slowly crossed his heart. "Cross my sternum and hope to drive."

"Okay." Brigit pressed her lips together to keep from laughing, or was it to keep from drooling? She doubted she'd ever tire of seeing this man sans clothes. She inhaled. The orchids growing nearby smelled intoxicating and left her feeling dizzy. Or maybe it was from standing so close to a half-naked Orion. She tore her gaze away from his flesh and glanced down at the ground. "We can't do it here." She pointed at the moss and ferns lining the jungle floor. "There are bugs and worms underneath there."

Orion threw his head back and laughed. When his gaze returned to her face, his smile faded. A look of concentration shadowed his expression. Sweat broke out across his brow and his hands began to glow. A golden beam shot out from his palm a moment later, creating a spot large enough to encompass two adult bodies. "It will be fine now. I have repelled the miniature crawling creatures," he said, reaching for her.

Brigit jumped, not realizing he'd covered the distance separating them. "I'm not even going to ask how you did that or what you just did. I don't think I want to know."

"Good, because the time for talk is over." He reached for her and ran a rough palm down her arm.

Brigit trembled. "We-we—"

Orion's mouth enveloped hers, cutting her words off. Brigit sank into the kiss as he worked his lips back and forth over hers. His teeth nipped her and she opened, allowing him to sink his tongue deep inside. She moaned as the wild taste of him exploded her senses. The man could kiss like a bandit.

His fingers slid to the front of her shirt and began popping buttons out of their holes. Orion's knuckles grazed her flesh inch by tantalizing inch until her shirt fell open, exposing her lace bra. He pulled back from the embrace to stare at the front of her. Emotions swam in the depths of his eyes. For an instant, the intensity scared Brigit. Before she could react to that fear, he recaptured her mouth, drugging her with his kisses. They were both naked in a matter of seconds.

Orion sank down onto the jungle floor, removing the rest of her clothes before pulling Brigit on top of him. "You should be safe enough here from the small creatures." His lips curled at the corners mischievously.

Brigit smiled back. "Safe? With you?" She laughed, but the sound cut short when Orion bucked his hips, sending his cock sliding through her already flowing juices. The rings around his shaft began to glow, and then vibrate. Brigit whimpered, grinding her pussy into him until her clit made contact with the rings. Her lids dropped as her eyes rolled back in her head.

She barely felt Orion's hands grip her hips and lift her. Her eyes flew open the second she sank down onto his fully erect cock. "I will never get over the feel of you entering me."

"You don't have to," he grit out between clenched teeth.

"You know that you've ruined me for other men."

"Good, because there shall be no other men welcome in your body. You are mine. This is mine." He pressed her clit for emphasis.

Their eyes met a second before he began to move. The ride was excruciatingly slow at first, the gentle glide rasping the inner muscles of her channel while steadily stroking her clit. The rings pulsed, sending waves of heat lashing through her body. Brigit's hands clamped down on top of Orion's arms.

"You're making me crazy," she gasped as her nails dug into his flesh.

Orion smiled. "I want you to know who possesses you."

"Possess? I don't think s—" He thrust hard. "Ohh."

"Think again," he said rolling Brigit beneath him. He began to fuck her in earnest.

All thoughts of possession scattered on the wind. Brigit wrapped her legs around his firm ass and hung on for dear life. Surge after surge of energy rolled through her sending her into an endless orgasm. Orion refused to stop, even after she started begging him to. Brigit didn't think she'd be able to take much more of this without her clit exploding, but she was wrong.

"Be still, little love. Our brief separation has left me famished and I'm not nearly sated." He stroked the side of her head, brushing her damp curls away from her face.

"I don't think I can do this," she ground out between gasps.

Orion kissed her. "Yes, you can." He pulled his cock from her body and rolled Brigit onto her stomach. He lifted her hips until she was kneeling, then pressed her face onto the soft mossy ground. "Ah, so beautiful," he murmured, brushing a finger though her swollen pussy lips.

Brigit quivered.

"You are like a flower in bloom for my eyes only." Orion brought the finger that dripped with her juices to his mouth and sucked hard. "Your feminine pollen is sweet. I think I need more."

Brigit moaned, the sight so erotic that she thought she might collapse under the weight of it. Her nipples stabbed toward the ground and her pussy ached with renewed fervor.

Orion lowered his head and stuck out his incredible tongue, until it was flattened from her anus to her clit. Brigit's body wept as she slowly curled it over her flesh. "Please Orion," she whimpered.

"Does this please you as much as it does me?"

Brigit rocked her hips in response unable to speak.

Orion chuckled, the vibration strong enough to reach her clit.

"Oh God," she cried out.

"The Goddess cannot help you now." He plunged his tongue into her greedy channel, filling her completely.

"Yes," Brigit screamed, trying to get closer, but Orion held her hips. Warmth spread through her, building in intensity. The sensation was strange, but wonderful.

Orion continued to tongue-fuck her.

"What's happening?" Brigit asked, gasping as her womb started to flutter.

He didn't answer. Orion's skin glowed one minute, then a wave of light burst from his body, washing her into oblivion.

Orion pulled his tongue out of her, then sank his cock in. He rode her hard, branding her with his body. Brigit mewed as her release reached a final crescendo, collapsing on the ground, taking Orion with her. A moment later, he grunted and emptied himself inside of her. His orgasm seemed to go on forever, bathing her womb in his seed.

He rolled off her and then pulled her into his arms. They lay panting on the moss covered ground, drenched in sweat and sated like two fat felines intoxicated by catnip. He stroked her hair, while placing tiny kisses on her shoulder. His touch was gentle and *loving*. Brigit closed her eyes against the well of emotion threatening to swamp her.

"What do we do now?" she asked softly, not wanting to break the fragile connection they'd just formed.

"We'll have to go through the portal."

Brigit sat up onto her elbows. "What do you mean we have to go through the portal?"

He glanced at her with a patience that hadn't been there before and then rose to get dressed. Brigit followed suit.

"Come and I shall show you."

He led her through a thick grove of trees into another clearing, much smaller than the last. An ancient-looking stone circle dotted with giant red crystals stood on end. Yellow flowers grew around the small field, their fragrance strangely arousing.

"What is that thing?" Her voice cracked.

"'Tis a portal or transport if you will."

Orion approached the stones and began rearranging them. When he slipped the last stone into place, the transport activated. Dark clouds began to swirl and form at its center, thickening before their eyes. The sound rose like a tornado dropping a car onto a tin roof.

Brigit gaped. "You're not getting me in that thing. It doesn't look stable." She scratched her thigh and then swatted another blood-hungry mosquito.

"It's perfectly safe," he said glancing uneasily at the swirling mass.

"Have you ever used one?"

"Yes."

She pointed. "Have you ever used that one?"

Orion shook his head. "No, but your friends did."

Her eyes widened. "Jac and Rachel went through that thing without coercion."

"Yes." He nodded.

Her brow knitted. "Are you sure? That doesn't sound like something Jac would do, unless someone was chasing her."

"Someone was," Orion's voice chilled.

Brigit glanced around at the jungle. "Are they still here?"

"Not that I can detect, but that does not mean we aren't in danger."

She hugged herself. "I don't know." She wasn't sure which was worse, dying by a spray of bullets or having that stone structure collapse and crush her to death.

"'Tis the only way to return. I would not ask this of you otherwise." Orion's face grew pained.

"Are you sure this thing leads to planet Zaron?" She walked behind the portal. "It looks like nothing but jungle to me."

"Yes, it leads to my planet."

Brigit began to pace. "Orion, I really want to believe you, but…"

His jaw firmed. "No 'buts'. Either you trust me or you don't."

She stopped and stared at the ominous entrance. "I trust you." She stepped toward him.

"But do you care for me?" His question brought Brigit to a halt.

She blinked in confusion. Where had that come from? Brigit searched her heart and realized she no longer felt the panic that rose every time she confronted her feelings. Shocked, she realized she did care about Orion. She might even love him.

"Yes, I do care for you," she admitted to him and herself.

"Enough to join with me?"

"I thought you said we were already *linked*."

Orion hesitated, uncertainty flashing in his jade and aqua eyes. "We are, but 'tis not complete without the blessing of the Atlantean people."

"Atlanteans? As in lost continent of Atlantis?"

"Yes."

"Whoa! This is too much to grasp, even for a New Age lover like me."

"'Tis your choice." He touched her gently, love shining clearly in his face.

Tears sprang into Brigit's eyes as the full import of his words hit her. "You are giving me a *choice*."

The silence stretched between them.

"You've always had a choice," he whispered so low she almost didn't hear him.

Brigit smiled, then let out a squeal before kissing Orion soundly on the mouth. Her fingers curled into his biceps, relishing the feel of his strength beneath her hands.

"Now I must contact Cassandra, so she can secure the portal behind us. I'll remove a crystal as I step through and she can disable the rest."

Brigit released him and then stepped toward the portal before she lost her nerve. "What are we waiting for?" she asked as she stuck her foot inside the tumultuous mass.

"Wait!" Orion shouted and tried reach for her. "You must lean back or you'll fall."

Brigit felt the tug the same second she heard Orion yell. She tried to turn, but it was too late. His hands swiped through the air missing her, while his words garbled in the roar of the machine. Had he said to lean forward? The dark air swirled around her, disorienting Brigit until she wasn't sure which direction was up. She screamed in terror, but the sound disappeared, swallowed by the churning gray mass. Oh God, she couldn't breathe. The air was too thick. The next second Brigit was falling. Instinctively, she held her hands out in front her.

She collided with something or someone hard, sending the object sailing a second before she fell to the ground. Her wire-rimmed sunglasses slipped to the floor. Brigit heard feet shuffling, but her eyes refused to focus. As the room slowly came into view she saw a man impaled on a sword, blood seeping out of his head. The other man holding the weapon tilted his sword and the body slid to the floor with a thump. Crimson pooled on the opaque tiles.

"I'm sorry. "I didn't mean to—" Brigit sputtered and frowned. She squinted and tried to make out the figure on the ground. "Who is that?" She pointed to the body lying twenty feet from her.

"Brigit!" Jac and Rachel's voices cried out in unison.

Brigit turned to see her "pregnant" best friends struggling to break the grips of the men holding them. She blinked, unable to believe what she was seeing. She picked up her frames and wiped the lenses on her shirt before slipping them back on. It was true. Everything Orion told her was true. Brigit didn't know whether to laugh or cry.

The transport once again whirled and darkened. The men who looked like guards raised their swords in preparation of attack. Orion appeared through the mist.

"Orion?" The men called out. Their voices held myriad questions.

"Honey, what have you done?" Orion asked, as his gaze went to the man lying on the floor. "I told you to lean back, transports always throw you forward."

Brigit glanced at the body and then over her shoulder and scowled. "Oh, shut up! I don't want to hear 'I told you so' from you, especially since I didn't catch all the instructions before that monstrosity sucked me through." She looked back at the body and began wringing her hands. "This is bad, very bad."

Rachel and Jac rushed forward. Rachel wore a long white diaphanous gown. Her rich brown hair was braided and woven with jewels the circumference of Brigit's thumb. Jac dressed in a short jade skirt that showed off her legs and complemented the single emerald and gold headband encircling her short blonde hair. Wow! Talk about a fashion statement. Suddenly Brigit felt woefully underdressed.

"Brigit, it is really you?" they asked at the same time.

She laughed. "Who were you expecting?"

"Only you." Rachel and Jac embraced her.

"Did you guys know you were pregnant? How?"

"How?" They giggled and looked back at the men who'd been holding them, before shooting a curious glance in Orion's direction.

Brigit followed their gazes. "Huh-uh, not me, sisters." Her gaze dropped to her flat stomach. The seed of doubt suddenly planted.

Jac and Rachel arched their brows as they stared at Orion.

"Don't ask," Brigit said, shaking her head. It didn't take a psychic to read her friends' minds. "It's a long story."

"We can't wait to hear *all* about it."

Brigit ignored their comment and stepped around them as the group converged to surround the body. "Is that Professor Rumsinger?" she asked, shock ricocheting through her.

Rachel nodded.

"Is he dead?" Brigit trembled as she leaned in to get a better look.

A blond-haired man crouched down, touching two fingers to the repulsive man's neck. The body twitched one final time and the professor's head cracked the rest of the way open, splitting down the middle like a melon from the sword blow.

The man touching the body turned to look at the group. Brigit felt the color drain out of her face and she swayed on her feet. Orion stepped behind her, resting his hands lightly upon her shoulders.

The man confirmed what everyone knew.

Brigit teetered again, her gaze beading on the professor's twisted pain-filled face. She leaned into Orion's body for support. She closed her eyes and took a couple of deep breaths. Brigit swallowed hard to keep from getting sick. This whole thing was surreal. She was on another planet, surrounded by an alien race and she'd just killed a man. How does anyone handle something like this?

Pull it together, Brig. A moment later, she nodded to herself and opened her eyes to stare at the group. She glanced back at the man who'd caused her friend so much pain and suffering. Killing someone wasn't right, but the bastard deserved it.

"It's about goddamned time," she declared, then glanced out the window at the green sky. "Did you guys notice that the sky is green?"

The unexpected statement exploded the tension filtering in the air as effectively as if she'd detonated a bomb. Nervous giggles came from Jac and Rachel while the men barked with laughter.

"Come. 'Tis over," the man holding Rachel said, then herded everyone away from the grisly scene toward a set of jewel-encrusted double doors, which appeared to be made out of crimson crystals. "I believe this and your friend's return is cause for celebration."

Orion's expression hardened. "Ares, I must speak to you before we feast."

"What is it, my brother?"

Orion dropped to his knees. "I have broken Atlantean law and accept punishment by death."

A hush fell over the small crowd, while the guards began to murmur in the background.

"Silence!" the blond man bellowed.

"Speak!" Ares demanded. "Tell us, what have you done? You know you shall be judged fairly."

Orion nodded. Brigit's stomach balled into a knot. *Broken laws, death sentence, what in the world had he done to warrant that happening?* They'd only been apart for two days, but she couldn't think of anything she'd witnessed that came close to what she'd just done to Professor Rumsinger.

"I left my post while in search of the Seer and Coridan to go find Brigit."

Ares' jade eyes narrowed. He shot a look at the blond man who'd been speaking only moments ago. "What were your exact orders?"

"To find Brigit and relay her friends' words then seek out the Seer and Coridan."

Brigit stepped forward, interrupting their conversation. "Hold it one minute. You mean to tell me that because he came to make sure I was okay you plan to kill him?"

The jade-eyed man Orion called brother stepped forward. "'Tis the law."

"I don't give two shits what it '*tis*. That's the biggest load of crap I've ever heard. I just killed a man. You all witnessed it. Where I'm from that can get you sentenced to death."

Silence, little one. The regal blond man stepped forward. Despite the fact his lips didn't move, Brigit knew he'd been the one who'd spoken to her.

"Don't you shush me, you big dumb Sasquatch. Who do you think you are? If anyone is being sentenced to death, it's going to be me." Brigit crossed her arms over her chest and faced him in challenge.

Orion snickered, followed by Ares, Jac and Rachel.

"What's so funny?" Brigit glanced at Orion, since on his knees they nearly looked eye to eye.

He shook his head.

"Who is that?" Brigit whispered out of the side of her mouth.

Orion smiled. "'Tis King Eros, Queen Rachel's true-mate."

"Queen? Rachel really is a Queen. I thought you were talking figuratively."

"I told you thusly."

She snorted. "Yeah, but I thought you were full of shit."

His gaze narrowed. "Watch your tongue woman or I'll have to capture it." Orion's eyes sparkled with mischief, despite the direness of the situation.

Eros faced Brigit. "Now that you know who I am, do you change your stance?"

Brigit craned her neck to stare him in his aqua eyes. Her knees quaked, but she refused to back down. "Hell no! Do you?"

Eros threw his head back and laughed. "I believe Orion's orders were to see to your welfare beyond all others. From what I can tell of your rapier tongue, he has done so." The King turned to Orion. "Rise, warrior. 'Tis time to celebrate." They followed the King down a long corridor as orders were given to prepare a feast.

* * * * *

The Atlantean people held a banquet in honor of Brigit's arrival and the defeat of Professor Rumsinger. Brigit felt a little like Dorothy after the house landed on the wicked witch. She stood in front of the massive crowd with Orion by her side. He announced that the evening would also mark their joining celebration, giving her no chance to back out of their earlier agreement.

Smartass, she thought, staring at the man who not only rocked her world, but silently held her heart.

I heard that, mate.

Brigit glared at him. "You know that's going to take a while for me to get used to. Every time you speak in my head, I think I'm becoming schizophrenic."

In time you will get used to it. In time, perhaps you'll prefer it. She could hear the smile in his voice, even though his expression hadn't changed.

The Seer stepped in front of them.

Last chance. Orion warned. *Once she performs the ritual there is no turning back.*

"You've said that before."

This time I mean it.

Goose bumps rose on Brigit's arms, but her gaze did not falter. "You're not getting rid of me that easy."

Orion did smile this time and it damn near took her breath away. *Why did the man have to be so gorgeous?*

You think I'm gorgeous?

"Oh shut up!"

The Seer said some ritual words then placed her hands on Brigit's head. A second later, Brigit heard a loud pop. "Yowza! What was that?"

Can you hear me?

"Stop shouting. I can hear you just fine." Brigit turned to the beautiful blonde woman who'd performed the ceremony and gaped as she realized the woman spoke into her mind like Orion.

The Seer smiled. *'Tis done.* She announced to the crowd.

Cheers rang out around them. Brigit didn't really understand what was happening, but went with the flow. She grinned and waved at Rachel and Jac, who beamed like the proud moms-to-be that they were.

Come. Orion grasped her hand and led her away.

Brigit followed him down a long hall that seemed to branch off in several directions.

Our quarters are this way, mate.

"Stop calling me that. I keep looking around for a naval battleship."

He snickered. *You are such a stubborn woman.*

"You knew that going into this whole thing." Brigit paused, feeling extremely vulnerable. "Do you regret saddling yourself to me?"

Orion turned and took Brigit's chin into his large hand. His thumb skittered across her lips as his gaze locked onto her face. "I regret nothing." He leaned forward as if to kiss her, then suddenly changed directions. He planted his mouth onto her forehead, lingering there, letting the heat from his lips permeate her skin. Slowly, he retreated.

Now come. He implored her to move.

The need shimmering in Orion's eyes glowed in the moonlight. He led her along a deserted corridor until they reached a pearl-encrusted door. There were shades of jade surrounding the massive frame. As they approached, the door opened noiselessly.

Orion stopped and turned to face Brigit before she could cross the threshold. He didn't say a word. Instead, he waited.

Brigit wasn't sure what she was supposed to do. She stood for a few seconds staring at him, hoping he'd give her some instructions. A hint would be nice. Yet, Orion's expression remained solemn. He gave nothing away.

"Okay, I'll bite," she said pushing past him so she could peek into the room. A massive bed of furs and silk, big enough to sleep twenty, took up center space. Off to one corner, Brigit spied a bath the size of a pond filled to the brim with steaming water. She practically groaned as she rushed inside, shedding her clothing as she went. She heard a heavy exhalation come from behind her, but didn't stop until she plunged into the gargantuan tub.

She surfaced in time to see Orion peeling off his costume. She paused, realizing it wasn't a costume after all. It was his uniform. Brigit dipped her head back and swept her hair away from her face. "What was that all about at the door?"

You had to enter of your own free will. I could not try to persuade you.

She laughed. "What do you call what you did to me back on Earth?"

He grinned. *That was Earth. This is Zaron.*

"So what you're telling me is that you roped me in on a technicality."

I was determined to get you at any cost, by any means necessary. His eyes glittered with promise.

"I see." Brigit sobered. "Even if you lost your life in the process?"

At any cost. He repeated softly.

Her eyes misted. "So what are you waiting for?"

Orion stepped into the water, taking his time to give her a full view of his gloriously naked body before the water swallowed it up. The liquid swooshed around his thick thighs, cupping his sac like she longed to do. Brigit wet her lips. She couldn't help it. The guy was candy and she wanted to lick him from top to bottom and front to back.

"Stop!"

He froze in place as Brigit swam the distance separating them. She ducked under the water and came up between his legs. Orion's nostrils flared as she reached out and grasped his erection, sliding her hand along his impressive length. The rings around his cock were hot to the touch or maybe it was her skin. Either way, Brigit relished the power she felt as she lowered her lips and took him into her mouth.

She licked his shaft, climbing the rings like a ladder with her tongue. Orion dropped his head forward onto his chest and groaned. He didn't reach for her, but she saw his hands open and close several times in an effort to remain at his sides. Brigit smiled inwardly, enjoying the thrill of having this mighty warrior wrapped around her fingers.

She sucked in her cheeks and slowly pulled him out of her mouth with a pop. Orion growled as she swirled her tongue over the weeping eye of his cock. His hips bucked of their own volition. Brigit took him deep again. This time his fingers curled into her shoulders, biting her skin as he tried to maintain control.

You are a witch, for your mouth casts a spell over me.

Brigit giggled, sending vibrations of her own through his shaft.

Enough! 'Tis time to fuck. He pulled her from his cock.

"I thought you didn't like that word."

Orion shrugged casually. *Your language is "clinging on me"*.

"You mean it's 'growing on you'?"

Enough talk!

Orion pulled her to the edge of the tub and sat her on the ledge. With one hand he pushed her back until she lay with her hips teetering and legs dangling in the water. His throbbing cock found her opening and plunged inside. Brigit gasped, then began to moan as he fucked her.

He nibbled on her lips between strokes until Brigit thought she'd lose her mind. Greedily, he devoured her, while milking her body for more. Brigit rocked her head from side to side and reached for something to hang onto, but came up with air. Her body undulated as Orion fed deep, driving her need along a razor's edge that threatened to slice her in two.

Brigit moaned, her orgasm ripping through her. She heard water slosh as Orion rose out of the tub to blanket her. She didn't have time to recover. He thrust deeper inside her aching pussy, driving sanity from her mind. The rings on his cock vibrated and his hands at the side of her head began to glow.

You are mine. He repeated with each thrust. *Say it,* he demanded as his hips pounded into her.

I'm yours.

Tell me again.

I'm yours.

And again. His voice dropped to nearly a whisper in her mind.

Brigit cupped his cheek. *I'm yours,* she said in his mind, meaning every word.

Orion smiled, his heart clearly showing in his eyes. He sent a burst of energy through their bodies, spiraling them into orbit and out of control. When they finally floated back to the planet, he lowered his mouth and kissed her tenderly. Brigit felt his love flow into her body. He drew back and stared in wonder at her face, before saying, *And I am yours.*

The End

Enjoy an excerpt from:

CHEER GIVERS & MISCHIEF MAKERS

When it was time for the women in the crowd to circulate, Isabelle unabashedly went straight to him. Had she been less fleet-footed, three or four other females would have gotten there ahead of her.

The man, still looking uncannily relaxed, had his elbows propped on the chair arms. He rested his chin on steepled forefingers and silently regarded Isabelle as she stood before him. The barest hint of his earlier smile lay both on his mouth and in his eyes. Very slowly, almost meticulously, his gaze slid down her body then up again. He didn't seem to care if this languid scan might be interpreted as rude.

Isabelle's nipples tingled into tightness.

He dropped his hands to his lap. "And you are…?" His eyes were fixed now on Isabelle's eyes.

"My name is Isabelle." She didn't offer her hand. "Do you mind if I sit here?"

"I don't have much choice, do I?"

Isabelle bristled. "Of course you have a choice. If you'd rather not waste your time on me, I'll go away."

The man's smile broadened for an instant. "I don't mind wasting my time on you." With a slight inclination of the head, he indicated the chair on the other side of the end table. "By all means, have a seat. I'm Daniel, by the way." He rested his head against the back of the chair and simply kept watching her.

Isabelle fidgeted, adjusting the bodice of her dress. Her nipples still plagued her, responsive as they were to Daniel's cool scrutiny. "Well," she asked, "don't you want to ask me anything?"

"Yes. Are you afraid of me seeing your breasts?"

Heat flared in Isabelle's cheeks. "No," she snapped. "What's the next thing you want to ask?"

Daniel lazily turned up his hands. "I believe it's your turn. I'm sure you have some trenchant questions."

Isabelle felt thoroughly flustered. What was his game? Why was he here? "What's your definition of the perfect way to spend Valentine's Day?" she murmured, then steeled herself for some saucy rejoinder.

But it never came. Instead, Daniel surprised her by pulling his chair around the end table so they were sitting almost knee to knee. He leaned forward. "Spending the evening, maybe the whole night, with a lovely woman who delights my senses and warms my heart." His voice, its sardonic edge gone, drizzled over Isabelle like warm maple syrup.

"Oh," she said, but no sound came out.

"I'm so sorry. It appears I've left you speechless." Daniel's fingers uncurled and drifted lightly over Isabelle's knees. She didn't even have time to react to this gesture before he straightened and moved his chair back into place.

By the gods, this man was diabolical! His direct gaze, his low voice, his casual masculinity had undeniably aroused Isabelle. Her nipples strained painfully against the tight fabric of her dress. Her pussy secreted more moisture. Oh, how she'd love to feel his silken tumult of black hair on her breasts, her stomach, the insides of her thighs. She suspected Daniel was well aware of the effect he was having on her...which strengthened that effect all the more.

"Do you think you'd enjoy my company?" she asked, her voice uncharacteristically meek.

He answered without hesitation. "I know I would—you've already met half my criteria—and I believe you'd enjoy my company, too."

Isabelle's heart was hammering. "What if I choose not to follow up on this meeting?" She wanted to find out if he would pursue her, persuade her.

Daniel shrugged. "There are bound to be other women who will. Besides, if I can't find someone here, although I'm certain I can, there are other options."

"Such as?" Isabelle asked. Her mind wasn't really on Daniel's "other options". More mystifying questions dogged her. *How can he be so passionate one moment and so lackadaisical the next? Why is he here if he doesn't really need to be?*

The man's behavior was inexplicable.

"Bars, parties..." Daniel turned up his hands and flashed a smile. "I'll have my Valentine. Even if it's just for the night."

Isabelle had to look away from him. She couldn't think straight while she looked *at* him.

She knew she was in quandary. Bryce needed a Cheer Giver much more than the confident Daniel, but this dark-haired enchanter strongly appealed to her. Way too strongly. She wanted to talk with him, learn about him, bare her body beneath his smoldering gaze and share it with him. And she wanted to enjoy *his* body. Daniel's physique wasn't as pumped up as Bryce's, but it was nevertheless beautifully tended.

Problem was, this mission had nothing whatsoever to do with Isabelle's desires. It was about bringing happiness to someone who needed it. She had to put her personal preferences aside.

Why an electronic book?

We live in the Information Age—an exciting time in the history of human civilization, in which technology rules supreme and continues to progress in leaps and bounds every minute of every day. For a multitude of reasons, more and more avid literary fans are opting to purchase e-books instead of paper books. The question from those not yet initiated into the world of electronic reading is simply: *Why?*

1. ***Price.*** An electronic title at Ellora's Cave Publishing and Cerridwen Press runs anywhere from 40% to 75% less than the cover price of the exact same title in paperback format. Why? Basic mathematics and cost. It is less expensive to publish an e-book (no paper and printing, no warehousing and shipping) than it is to publish a paperback, so the savings are passed along to the consumer.

2. ***Space.*** Running out of room in your house for your books? That is one worry you will never have with electronic books. For a low one-time cost, you can purchase a handheld device specifically designed for e-reading. Many e-readers have large, convenient screens for viewing. Better yet, hundreds of titles can be stored within your new library—on a single microchip. There a variety of e-readers from different manufacturers. You can also read e-books on your PC or laptop computer. (Please note that Ellora's Cave does not endorse any specific brands.

You can check our websites at www.ellorascave.com or www.cerridwenpress.com for information we make available to new consumers.)

3. *Mobility.* Because your new e-library consists of only a microchip within a small, easily transportable e-reader, your entire cache of books can be taken with you wherever you go.

4. *Personal Viewing Preferences.* Are the words you are currently reading too small? Too large? Too... ANNOYING? Paperback books cannot be modified according to personal preferences, but e-books can.

5. *Instant Gratification.* Is it the middle of the night and all the bookstores near you are closed? Are you tired of waiting days, sometimes weeks, for bookstores to ship the novels you bought? Ellora's Cave Publishing sells instantaneous downloads twenty-four hours a day, seven days a week, every day of the year. Our webstore is never closed. Our e-book delivery system is 100% automated, meaning your order is filled as soon as you pay for it.

Those are a few of the top reasons why electronic books are replacing paperbacks for many avid readers.

As always, Ellora's Cave and Cerridwen Press welcome your questions and comments. We invite you to email us at Comments@ellorascave.com or write to us directly at Ellora's Cave Publishing Inc., 1056 Home Avenue, Akron, OH 44310-3502.

Make each day more EXCITING with our

ELLORA'S CAVEMEN
CALENDAR

www.EllorasCave.com

erridwen, the Celtic Goddess of wisdom, was the muse who brought inspiration to storytellers and those in the creative arts. Cerridwen Press encompasses the best and most innovative stories in all genres of today's fiction. Visit our site and discover the newest titles by talented authors who still get inspired - much like the ancient storytellers did, once upon a time.

Cerridwen Press

www.cerridwenpress.com

Discover for yourself why readers can't get enough of the multiple award-winning publisher Ellora's Cave.

Whether you prefer e-books or paperbacks,

be sure to visit EC on the web at www.ellorascave.com

for an erotic reading experience that will leave you breathless.